ERA SINISTRA

BRAD MATHEWS

ISBN: 978-1-962577-00-7 (Softcover)

ISBM: 978-1-962577-01-4 (Ebook)

Re-release Second Edition 2023

ERA SINISTRA

THE SHADOW
BRAD MATHEWS

1
Victory

Cold numbed and tightened Art's muscles, yet the water smelled fresh and calm. Tangled with dust and dried sweat, his wiry hair scraped against his brow. He dipped his head into the water and withdrew it to scrub. Out here in the wild, Art enjoyed a certain liberty and tranquility one could not find in the city.

Freedom was enticing, yet the allure of danger wrought an irresistible thrill. Human civilization had soured his outlook beyond repair, which had its way of introducing a sensation of pure venom. Was it possible to defend oneself against the world or to disappear entirely? That was a question he asked himself years ago. He'd decided that in order to detach from society, certain precautions needed to be observed.

Planning the endeavor had proven the easy part. Initiating the plan defied reason by being onerous and costly. He knew the burden associated with removing himself from society and he accepted the risk. At times he had wondered whether a reward accompanied the danger, but understood that in a matter like this, one had to take the first step to realize the potential rewards and pitfalls. The plan: to become a shadow.

His fingers inadvertently grazed the rough patch of flesh at his left side. He dabbed at the visage of the gunshot wound he'd suffered ten years ago. The shot had grazed his side and the scar remained the only visible damage to his skin. The pain was still fresh in his mind. Though he prided himself on possessing a high threshold for pain, he couldn't deny that he was averse to enduring that sting again.

Art had to take action, but this endeavor could have been one of the pitfalls of going 'off the grid." Being shot eleven years ago hadn't been pleasant, and neither had running from those chasing him. The way he remembered it, St.Clair escaped without so much as a scratch. Art had defeated the deputies, but St Clair somehow managed to get off a lucky shot with one of their guns. If he hadn't he would be dead.

He slicked back his wild hair, narrowed his eyes, and growled. Vengeance would come. He knew exactly what to do.

Sunshine glinted on a dark green helmet to contrast azure beams darting through a cloudless sky. Sporting jersey Number 27, the blond girl scooted toward home plate, took a few heartless practice swings, and waited. Beneath the bill of her hat, golden bangs skirted her forehead. A pony tail with green highlights cascaded from beneath the helmet and ended in a curled point just above the number on her back.

The hum of chatter from the crowd didn't deter her. She entered her stance and stared down the pitcher, daring her to throw something she could belt over the fence. The pitcher wasn't intimidated. She wound up, took a giant step down the mound, and lobbed a perfect strike. Number 27 swung and missed, but she didn't hesitate.

Repeating her practice swings, this time with a modicum of vigor, she glared at the pitcher. A sly understanding crept over her. She dug her toes into the dirt, nonverbally communicating with the pitcher. *Ok, you got me on that one. Let's see what you can dish out next.*

The girl wearing the red number 16 jersey telegraphed her move and tossed the exact same pitch. Instead of shooting directly through the narrow strike zone, the pitch drifted wide. Ball One.

"You can do better than that, can't you?" she taunted.

The chatter from the crowd rose and peaked with increasing excitement. Her father, Reginald St. Clair hailed her with praise. "Smack this one over the fence, Taleah!" Her step mother whistled and Taleah waited.

Number 16 pitched a change-up that slid harmlessly into the dirt.

Taleah glanced to the scoreboard and eyed the one-two count, before narrowing her eyes at the score. It was 7-6 with Boise leading. The batter preceding Taleah had grounded into the gap between shortstop and second base. The shortstop mishandled it and bolted a wild throw to first base. The girl at first base jumped and caught it but came down too late to prevent the batter from making base safely.

The wait was longer this time. The pitcher in red seemed to be trying to ice Taleah. Taleah glanced to first base, intending to coax her teammate into stealing second. Number 16 caught on and nodded toward first, but didn't pull the trigger. Instead, she leaned toward home plate and pulled her dreaded fastball. Taleah saw it coming and nailed it. She dropped the bat and sprinted toward first base, but the ball drifted foul.

Instead of disappointment, her demeanor exuded confidence. Her teammate returned to first base and Taleah picked up her bat and resituated in her stance to await the next pitch. This time, she didn't take practice swings at all. All she needed to do now was to coerce Number 16 into delivering an off-speed changeup. In prior at bats, the girl's pitching cycle seemed to be a steady diet of curve, changeup, fastball, changeup, but not always in that order. Since she'd already seen the curve and the fastball, Taleah wagered a guess that the next pitch was indeed going to be a changeup. She dug her left foot into the dirt and tightened her stance.

The ball launched from the pitcher's hand and slowed as it approached home. Changeup. Teleah swung and crushed the ball deep into center field. The crowd roared. Taleah sprinted, waving at her teammate to round the bases toward home. The ball rolled to a stop near the center field fence as the Boise outfielder chased it down. With elation flowing through her veins, she watched Jessica round third base approaching home. The ball came to meet her as Taleah crossed second base, but the infielder missed it. She thought of sliding to third, but the ball was late. It was now or never. The crowd thundered in approval as she approached home plate. Just as the ball touched the catcher's glove, she leaned into her slide.

A swell of defeat raced through her, but before she could offer words for her thought, the umpire, Mr. Willis Ralston shouted "Safe!" The crowd went wild.

Her teammates poured from the benches to greet her in a fierce victory celebration as her parents serenaded her with chants.

Reggie turned to Rebekah and smiled. "What do you think? Pretty good for a seventeen-year-old."

She snorted. "Are you sure she's your daughter?"

"Never thought she'd grow up to play baseball." He shouted over the chanting crowd without trying to be overbearing. "Football, perhaps, maybe even golf, but baseball?"

She stood up and let the sun illuminate her beautiful face. With a smile, she landed a playful kiss on his lips. "I gotta hand it to you. She's turned out alright, considering."

Reggie looked offended. "Considering that punk she's dating?"

"Look, there's Tommy," Rebekah said, eyeing a young man with a blond mop-top and a skateboard, who was carefully surveying the perimeter fence waiting for his girlfriend. She respected Tommy more than Reggie did. After all, Taleah wasn't her daughter.

She clasped his hand and led him down the bleachers through the throng of celebrating family and friends. Taleah had removed her cap and was socializing with a trio of similarly-aged girls and one teammate. Taleah was cute and popular which had ways of making Reggie uncomfortable. If his observation was correct, she hadn't yet noticed Tommy prowling at the fence.

When Reggie stepped onto the field to the left of home plate, Willis greeted him, his mask still on.

Rebekah ran to high-five Taleah. "Great job!" she shouted. "You won it all by yourself."

Shrugging, Taleah joked, "We would have won by more, but our umpire sucked!" She emphasized the last part of her statement to be sure Willis and Reggie could hear her.

Willis Grinned. "You know we got to have young blood, but give me a break. This is the first time I've been in the sun."

"You couldn't ump a night game to save your life," Reggie sneered.

With his grin slightly drooping, Willis bared his teeth. "That's no way to talk to the undead."

Taleah gradually slinked away with the girls until she came face to face with Tommy. She smiled and flung her arms around him. Reggie watched.

With a flick of her hair, she turned toward her father. "I'll catch you at home, Dad. Thanks for coming!"

"I wouldn't miss it if an umpire was drinking my blood," Reggie said. Taleah grinned.

"They grow up too fast, don't they Reg?" By now Willis had removed the mask and was standing at Reggie's side like a long-enduring friend.

Hesitating, Reggie turned to him and frowned as Willis squinted in the sun and kicked a pile of dust. Reggie could swear Taleah surpassed twelve years old just the other day. Where, he wondered, had the last five years gone? Then again, the fault didn't entirely fall in his lap. The reason she'd seemed to grow up so fast could have been attributed to Art Rassine, the man who had kidnapped and murdered those innocent women. With Rassine still at large, the FBI had been dragging their feet for way too long. For Reggie, it was over. There remained nothing to worry about.

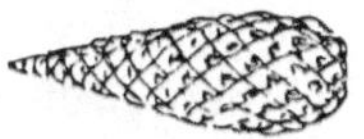

Tommy sat alone on a park bench, twirling locks of his shaggy hair in his fingers. He impatiently flipped his skateboard with his feet. He checked his cell phone for the time and then returned it to his back pocket. He had last checked the time just four minutes ago. Time always moved too slowly when waiting.

Tonight the wait was more difficult because, for the first time since he'd known Taleah, he had a plan. Although the evening didn't suggest the vibe of a'date night' due to Taleah celebrating with her friends and Tommy hanging with his buddies, he had a good idea of what he wanted to accomplish with his relationship with Taleah. Could he even call it a relationship yet? If not, tonight could change things.

He sighed and leaned back, letting his skateboard roll down a gentle slope and stop twelve feet away from the bench. For a moment, he eyed it as if he desired to practice his Ollie-ing and railing. Oh well. She *had* to be here soon, but he was beginning to wonder if she would show at all, considering that some thirty minutes had come and gone since their planned meeting time had passed.

Before that 9:30 hour came, he ran images through his mind on replay. He would invite her to sit with him on the bench. They'd talk and hold hands. He'd scoot closer to her. She would smile and lean her head on his shoulder. Together they would gaze at the stars, arguing about the names of the constellations and perhaps discuss more serious matters. He would look her in the eyes. Then he would drive her home, except that Taleah's father didn't trust him. Scratch that. They would sit together longer until she needed to go. Getting her to her father's house after curfew would prove to be a big mistake, so he had only a few minutes to work his magic. He imagined wrapping his arms around her. Then, at long last they'd kiss in the moonlight. Maybe her father didn't care much for him, but that was because Mr. St. Clair didn't know him. All the man seemed to know about him was that he had long hair and a skateboard. After all, it wasn't like he was going to try anything dangerous or force his will on Taleah. He had some standards—maybe not as many as Taleah, but some.

Ten more minutes passed, then twenty. He dug his phone from his back pocket and dialed Taleah's number. It rang, and continued to ring until her voicemail picked it up. He groaned and stood up. "Hi, I'm wondering where you are. Just trying to get you home by curfew. Call me back."

Trying to get her home by curfew? A forty minute wait and that was all he could come up with? No, that wouldn't do. He waited two minutes and dialed her again. Same result. "I was actually looking forward to spending some quality time with you tonight, alone. I understand if you couldn't make it because your friends took your whole night, but you can still call me right?"

I mean, please do, he thought. He paced to his skateboard and back, then to his skateboard again. He did a lap around the park and returned to the bench. Again he withdrew his phone and dialed Taleah's best friend Amy. She answered on the first ring, which he considered to be a bad sign.

"Hey Amy, this is Tommy." He paused. "You still hanging out with Taleah?"

She seemed annoyed. "She left almost an hour ago to talk to you."

"Well she wouldn't just go home would she?"

"You're kidding right? She's totally into you."

Tommy flipped his skateboard forcefully, intending to catch it with his free hand, but missed. He growled into the phone after the clatter of wood on pavement subsided. "Whatever. She didn't show."

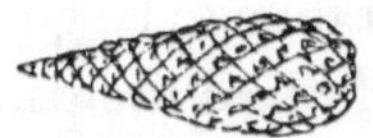

Reggie studied the clock on the living room wall and tried dialing Taleah's phone. There was no answer. He dropped the phone on the couch and pounded his fist in his hand. *If she's still with that punk kid...* He didn't get a chance to finish the thought, since his phone began ringing. He looked at the caller I.D. and rolled his eyes.

"Yeah, what's up?" he asked, trying not to sound angry.

Anna didn't hold anything back. "It's 10:30, Mister. Where the hell is my daughter?"

"*Our* daughter," Reggie started, bristling, "is out with her boyfriend, Tony or Terry, or whatever."

"Tommy."

"That's it. Tommy the Terror."

Anna laughed mockingly.

"Have you tried calling her?"

"Ten times." Reggie had instructed her to arrive at his house no later than 10:00 so that she could arrive home by 10:30, her curfew. More lenient than Anna, Reggie understood enough to allow Taleah to live her life. Rebekah had retired for the evening thirty minutes ago, but Reggie had decided to wait up for Taleah and talk with her over ice cream.

"It isn't like her to stay out late without calling," Reggie said. "Even I know that, and she doesn't spend a fraction of the time with me."

She sighed. "You're right."

"What do we do?"

"Wait twenty more minutes and then call the cops."

"Good idea," Reggie said sarcastically. He didn't like this at all. Instead of calling the cops, he would go find her. He knew where Tommy lived. He knew where her friends lived. He knew where she and Tommy were going to meet so he could drive her home. If he found her friends at any of those locations without her, then he would worry.

He waited for exactly twenty minutes, then climbed the stairs to let Rebekah know he was going out to look for Taleah. She kissed him good night, waiting for just the right time to let go. Then Reggie slinked out into the night to search. He first checked the park. It stood vacant, as was the most likely route to and from the park. He drove by Tommy's house and observed his car parked on the street. Reggie parked and stomped to the front door. Tommy himself answered it. The look on his face alone was enough to confirm that she wasn't there.

"Where is she?" he demanded.

"I thought she went home," Tommy said.

"You thought wrong."

Reggie stormed away, worry replacing anger with every step. Driving a little too fast, he stopped by all of Taleah's friend's houses. Each friend told him the same thing—that Taleah had returned home. Worry turned to panic. This didn't look good at all. He would have to call the police, but a nagging feeling in a dark back corner of his mind prodded him, suggesting he should try other avenues. "Damn the FBI," Reggie whispered, shuddering. Taleah wouldn't run away because she had no reason, but if someone desired to kidnap her, Reggie knew only one possible suspect. But then again, the FBI would have nothing to do with this. Reggie would be considered just a step below paranoid and this was a local issue to be solved by local authorities. He got it in his car, took a moment to drain his emotions, and then conjured the faith to bow his head in prayer. The panic melted away and plans of action prevailed.

2
Expired

The treetops swayed in the breeze, their trunks rattling an array of groans as if the woods themselves were at last giving in to the pains of solitude. In situations like this, there always had to be someone or something to blame, but the only person Sandra could heap the responsibility on was herself. She lay on the trunk of a fallen tree. Its knotty protrusions dug painfully into her back. Her muscles trembled and hunger churned in her stomach. She was notably conscious, trying to remember exactly what had transpired during and in the horrifying moments after the crash. Her brain didn't seem to work efficiently, as if the lull of sleep were a drug that deprived her mind of clarity and detail.

The whole scene reminded her of a softly distorted, hazy artistic photograph where hard lines and sharp corners were blurred into simple whispers of concrete existence. She moaned and then clapped a hand to her mouth. Once again, she was looking up at coniferous treetops. Though the river had vanished, the sound of babbling water still echoed, providing a haunting wisp of memory. Precisely how much time had passed away since the accident was a guessing game, but she consciously decided that it had to have been days or maybe even a week. Yet the pain was still fresh, and to her knowledge, no drugs had been administered to her.

Her rescuer had to have been in these woods nearby. Through the fog of her waking thoughts and the wind rushing through the trees, she thought she heard shuffling nearby. She craned her neck and tried to roll over when the sound penetrated her ears again.

"Try not to move," sounded a voice in the darkness. She thought she recognized his voice, but the fact was that details like that one, while once perceived, were now nothing more than the mind trying to fill in missing details. "You're in pain."

She looked up, silently wishing he were at her side so that she could see his face, but he was neatly obscured in the darkness. Now that she was starkly conscious for the first time in what she guessed was days, a steady stream of questions prodded at the front of her mind.

"Where are we?" she asked.

"As far from civilization as either of us wants right now," the voice rasped.

She tried to moan but stifled it at the last second as her next question formed at the tip of her tongue. "Ugh, what do you mean by that?"

A gust tore through the canopy and she thought she felt a raindrop strike her forehead. Indeed, a very light drizzle had commenced, but after time it faded and dried up. The trees creaked from the force of the wind.

"You're safe."

"Safe from what?" she asked with a little more force. "I need a hospital, and...Trees. Oh, this is no hospital."

"Alternative medicine." He shuffled a little more to straddle the log behind her and then his silhouette appeared over her. He shoved a bottle to her lips, but she turned her head in distrust. "It's just water. Drink. The last thing you want is to be dehydrated."

Giving in, she took a few gulps from the bottle as he held it for her. His grizzled hair brushed against her forehead, but his facial details remained hidden. She coughed and then took one more swig from the bottle. He withdrew the bottle and spun the cap back on.

"How long has it been?" A knot dug into her back and her exhale turned into a painful sigh.

He didn't answer. Instead, he stroked a hand through her hair and observed her body. She tried to scoot away from him, but it was no use. Both of her legs were immobile, but at least she felt them, even if the feeling was something just short of hellish pain. She moaned once again.

"I told you not to move."

"Please don't touch me," she whispered.

He chuckled softly. "Ah, you don't have any choice, Rosie dear."

"My name is Sandra."

"Maybe in some other life far, far away that's what you were known as. I like Rosie better so that's what we're calling you."

This proposition sounded daring, but just to be sure she wasn't imagining things, she asked him a question she knew he would deny. "I have to use the bathroom. Can you please take me to your cabin?"

He exhaled, as if trying to explain lost logic to a child. "You are nowhere and everywhere, I'd imagine. So if you want, you can conjure your own bathroom. I'll just disappear for a few minutes."

She didn't care much for the riddles. "Where is it?"

"No cabin here. We're roughing it tonight."

"Where is your car?"

"The truck is parked," he said. "About sixty meters from here, uphill, and I still have the keys."

"Are you saying I can't leave?"

"You could if you were able." He sighed again. "The way I see it, you don't have a choice." He paused to allow the grim reality of the situation to sink in. "I'm afraid both of your legs are broken. Once your energy wears off a little bit more, I'll apply some splints so that the repair process will go smoothly."

"You don't sound like a doctor, but you seem to know what you're doing. What did you just put in the water I drank?"

"You seem to have trust issues," he growled.

"No I don't. I'm just smart. You wanted to me to drink, and the best way for you to make me calm enough to do some orthopedic work is to give me a numbing agent."

Again, a chuckle escaped him. "You'll come around." The shuffling noise returned as he stood up. She heard him walk away as a nearby tree croaked. A pang of uneasiness crept over her, making her want to flee. He *was* a kind man. He had rescued her. Then again, the middle of nowhere was not high on the list of prescribed destinations when nursing multiple broken bones.

The pain was agony that rolled upon her like icy tides, corroding the fabric of her very being and slicing away at the reality behind her consciousness.

"You never told me your name," she told the shadow, which was withdrawing into the night.

The breeze carried his voice, brushing it and polishing it to sound something like melancholy brimming in the darkness. "You can call me Art."

With a volley of complex pains bordering on insanity, she willed herself to roll off the log. She fell upon a sharp, shattered stump, which dug into her side, sending shards of agony through her midsection. The warmth and dampness of blood trickled toward her navel beneath her shirt. Instead of screaming, she clawed at the muddy, needled forest floor toward a subtly rising incline. The calming harmony of the wind in the trees became a fearsome growl that echoed as if through chasms where time was nothing more than a bleak node of infinity. The spectacle of the darkened world around her became a landscape of liquid paint, black, gray, and blue. Spatters of red joined in the procession.

Her body began to convulse with such rigor that it surprised her. What he spiked her water with was taking a drastic toll, wearing her mind to little more than weightless streaks of projectile paint. She wanted to vomit, but her muscles were not tense enough to give her that (satisfaction). Her fingernails dug deeper into the earth. She inched her way toward where she perceived the incline to be. One of her nails snapped. Instead of waning, the pain somehow became a more sinister proclamation of agony that was simply less real than the kind she'd been feeling.

Her first impression of Art had been completely wrong. Shame abandoned her as her muscles shut down. Her mind thrust a frenzy of tattered emotions and fraying reminders of thoughtful memories. This horror would last until little more than a pile of lifeless bones remained of her. Deep in her subconscious mind, she uttered a terrorizing scream that sounded as if hell had suddenly spawned another dimension inside her mind. It created a dark hole through which she seemed destined to travel. A pinprick of light appeared in this tunnel-like spectrum and grew. Her body was like a vine craving the nourishment of the light. "Come to me," a calming voice whispered. "Come home."

Tears splattered on her cheeks as the light caressed her skin, revealing purity and perfection. The pain began to fade. And before the thought registered that she was dying, there was nothing. Only death. Finally, Art was nothing more than a dark spectator to her demise.

3
Suffocation

Momentum leaned Taleah's body to her left. Her mouth was gagged with what seemed to be a rag or an old sock soaked in some sort of cleaning agent. Cheap twine bound her hands and feet. A course matte of sandy dirt covered the rigid metal bed of the truck she was riding in. Faith graced her with a genuine reflection of this situation. Confusion and torment, however, provided a more real, more sinister portrait of the world around her.

Moaning as loudly as she could, she struggled against the twine with her hands and kicked at the windows of the shell covering the bed of the pickup. The windows flexed when her feet connected with them. She used the truck's force of acceleration and a worm-like wriggling motion to scoot toward the tailgate. The latch on the shell appeared to be something she could operate with her feet. She would open the hatch, call out for help, and then, if necessary, jump from the vehicle whether it was in motion or not. She shuddered when she imagined the pain of falling from a moving truck onto concrete, but the chance to feel the pain never arose.

The tailgate was locked. Desperate tears flowed down her face. Instead of celebrating victory with her father, hanging out with Tommy, or sleeping, she was trapped in a moving truck. This was sadly all she was capable of remembering. The events leading to her kidnapping were fuzzy memories further frayed by the passage of time and what felt like a blow to her head. She felt the sudden impact and then the grave silence of nothing—just snow and white noise—for what seemed to be the next forty minutes. In reality probably only a minute or two had passed, which gave her kidnapper more than enough time to secure her hands and to stuff her mouth with a rag.

When she realized that escaping wasn't going to be as easy as she thought, she violently thrashed her body and rolled around on the bed of the truck. The metal ribs and loose rocks shot jolts of pain through her back. As trying as this ordeal was, its memory was neither vivid nor devastating. She had plenty of time to think matters though. Judging by how much time had passed and the uncertainty of how long she'd been out, she guessed that the truck had travelled about twenty miles. Yet, without a real handle on the direction or speed of travel, she had no way of knowing where she really was or where the truck was headed. Time stretched. Reality gelled in her mind.

She rolled to her left when the vehicle turned again and then seemed to quickly pick up a lot of speed. This could signal that they were entering a highway. She pressed her hands against her pants to feel for her phone. He must have taken it from her. Then again, he was probably a pro and knew what to expect and when. At any rate, he would never make it that easy to escape. Since she had 'butt-dialed' friends many times before, she knew she could do it when she actually tried. How difficult could it be? If they answered, she would loudly bang a rock around the metal bed of the truck and kick the fiberglass windows. Having no cellphone seemed to eliminate too many options. What did hostages do before the advent of cellphones?

Tears streamed down her cheeks as she thought about the prospect of never being found. As good as her father was—as *lucky* as he seemed—he stood little chance to discover who had her and where he was going in time. Before the unthinkable.

Just what is the unthinkable? Perhaps that was why they called it the unthinkable, but she found herself at a loss. She had some ideas, but she truthfully didn't want to know. His motives could be few or many. The most likely she guessed to be sexual abuse, followed closely by ransom, but those two options presented only many variable tangents. If they couldn't find her, the end result would probably be death. But how long would it take?

She stopped herself from thinking about the potentially ghastly consequences of this ordeal. Instead, she sat still and thought about the quiet confidence of her father. Though she knew little of how he'd grown that confidence, she understood that its basis was upon a simple faith in the Lord. It couldn't hurt to pray. And that she did. But at some point, prayer would become useless because faith without action did not identify faith at all.

Thinking about the possibilities of escape offered a fresher prospect on the reality of the situation; it kept the misery at bay. When he tried to untie her, she would fight him away. She had a plan. In fact, part of her plan had already been set in motion.

The kidnapper wouldn't just keep her phone would he? No, he probably left that behind near the dark street she walked when she he took her. But something else was missing as well. The ribbon she'd used to tie her hair after the game had at some point been removed. That could have provided an obvious clue to investigators if the ribbon rested near her phone. With any luck the police could determine which direction the vehicle travelled.

As time slipped away into the void of the past, she thought about her father, and of Tommy. He'd probably hear about this some time or another, but what if he didn't care and decided to break up with her over it? *Where is he?* Was he aiding in whatever search party may have already been sloppily assembled? Was he still in the park waiting for her? Tommy could have been comfort, but her father could give both comfort and safety. She wasn't sure if much faith could safely be exerted in Tommy. Even though Taleah lived with her mother, she knew Dad to be stable and dependable. He was a better man than she ever gave him credit for—until now. He would find her for better or worse.

Reggie studied Anna's posture. Her face was buried in her hands and she was sobbing. Reggie slowly scooted his chair closer to her. His heart ran with an odd rhythm like contrasting drum patterns spliced together against an entourage of ambient classical music. He wrapped his arm around her, trying his hardest to feel warm and encouraging. She cried harder.

Watching Anna, Reggie's wife Rebekah looked down at her loosely folded hands. She squinted and a lone tear squeezed from her eye and dried on her cheek. Reggie scanned her expression for reinforcement on what he should do in attempt to comfort Anna. He was no mother, and so couldn't possibly understand such a relationship. Rebekah expressed a different story.

She had met Reggie a couple of years after the Art Rassine debacle. She knew about Reggie's triumphs and his sorrows. Taleah was almost like a daughter to Rebekah. Almost. But Reggie knew that even she could not understand, and therefore her ability to help Anna cope was stunted.

Reggie tried to steady his hands as he comforted his ex-wife. Her entire body trembled as if she were thawing from a deep freeze. A low moan escaped her lips and her tears puddled on the table. Reggie reached for the tissues and slid the box to her. She didn't attempt to retrieve one from the box, so Reggie did it for her. With her head still down and her face still in her hands, she took the tissue from him. She used it to dry her tears, but for each tear absorbed, another took its place.

Still, she was beginning to calm. Reggie whispered. "They'll find her."

Anna's voice squeaked. "That's wishful thinking."

"Hopeful," Reggie corrected her.

"How can you have hope?"

Rebekah looked up. "There's always hope."

"Hope?"

"It's what teaches us that there is a God who loves us." He paused to draw in a deep breath. "But you already know that."

Anna didn't say anything. She lurched her shoulders, opened her eyes, and almost started to laugh when she observed the mess she was making of the table. She grabbed a handful of tissues and tried to wipe away a puddle of tears mixed with other bodily fluids.

Reggie grasped her hand. "Don't worry about anything. I have a bad feeling about this, but if my previous experience taught me anything, these guys are trained and skilled investigators. They can find almost anyone."

"Almost."

Rebekah silently nodded, and then lowered her eyes.

Instead of arguing, Reggie let his expression droop. Trying to form a retort of some kind, he glanced to Rebekah and then back to Anna. He came up empty. Of course, she was right. It had been eleven years and the FBI still knew nothing regarding Art Rassine's whereabouts.

Rebekah shrugged, nonverbally agreeing with Anna. Although she didn't have much faith in the government's tactics, she had to trust them. They didn't have much to work with.

Reggie understood why finding him had proven such a difficult task. The man (if Art Rassine could even be considered a man) had been off the grid for years. If he even had a cellphone or other electronic device, it would prove easy to track him. Art Rassine dwelt in shaded canopies, which made satellite or thermal scans unreliable. If the man truly wanted to disappear forever—and it was clear that Rassine had—he could do it.

Silence pervaded the desperate atmosphere in the room until a knock came at the front door. Rebekah stood to answer it. After the police showed her their badges, she welcomed them in. "Please come in," she told them.

"You're Mrs. St. Clair."

"Yes, but I'm not Taleah's mother."

Reggie and Anna entered the room. Anna's knuckles whitened as she clutched the box of tissues. She let her red-tinged eyes momentarily meet the police officer's. "That's me."

"Do you have a picture of your daughter?" Officer Lendl asked.

Reggie withdrew his wallet, unfolded it, and handed the photo to him. The officer studied it before stuffing it into a plastic bag.

"The first thing we'll tell you is to be calm and let us do our jobs," the other officer said. He removed his hat and stared at Anna as if he didn't know what else to say. Reggie eyed her as she nodded slowly.

"Any information you can give us about Taleah would be helpful. How old is she? How tall? Who are her friends?"

"She's five-seven, maybe five-eight."

"Five-six and a half," Anna corrected him. "One hundred and twenty-one pounds."

"She hangs mostly with softball buddies," Reggie said. "I don't know all their names, just her best friends. And her boyfriend."

"Softball," Officer Cody repeated. "Who is the coach?"

Reggie shrugged. "I forget his name." He glanced at Anna.

Anna shrugged. "Campbell, Carter, Crane..."

"We can get that info from her school," Lendl said.

Cody sighed and stared at the photograph. "How old is she? She a junior?"

"Yes," Anna replied. "Seventeen."

"Can you tell me about her emotional state or her relationship to her boyfriend?"

Reggie and Anna stared at each other. Rebekah nodded knowingly but kept silent.

"Any tension between them or the boyfriend and you guys?"

Reggie chuckled, but his laugh was not founded on humor. "You know, I hate the kid, but what father doesn't hate his teenage daughter's boyfriend? It's a rite of fatherhood."

"To answer your question," Anna said, brushing a fresh tear from her cheek, "No she would not run away."

"Even if she did," Lendl asked, "have you any idea where she would go?"

"Skip town with her friends?" Reggie said. "But let me save you the trouble. She didn't, I already checked."

"We appreciate your diligence," Cody said. "Anything else you need to mention?"

Issuing what he intended to be a blank exhale, Reggie bowed his head and sunk into the sofa. He let go of Anna's hand. "Ten or eleven years ago, I was an unlucky witness to a gruesome kidnapping and murder case. I was holed up in the Adams County Sherriff's office for more than a week. They found out who did it, but he killed a senior deputy and escaped. I couldn't stop him." Reggie rubbed his temple, remembering the traumatic headaches and emotional devastation that accompanied the investigation.

"Do you think this man is involved?" Cody asked.

"The man knew me. I don't know if or how he could find out about my daughter, but it wouldn't surprise me. He was a beast, but he was smart. Very smart."

"Can you describe this man?" Lendl asked.

"It won't do you any good. The FBI has searched high and low for eleven years and hasn't found anything.

Officer Cody eyed Rebekah. "Anything to add, Mrs. St. Clair?"

Rebekah shook her head and replied softly. "She may not be my daughter, but I love her."

"We will get in touch with the FBI and perhaps Adams County," Cody said. "We'll get on board, but rest assured, we will find her."

"Thank you." Reggie wanted to believe Officer Cody. Deep in his soul, he desired faith in the law, but no matter how much he tried, he could not conjure the belief. The FBI was failing, and if this had anything to do with Art Rassine, the local police would be helpless. He scooted toward his wife and flung his arms around her, partially in defiance and partially in haste. His own heart was once again becoming an enigma. Disbelief poured soot across his thoughts and emotions, tinting them black with the temptation of discord. He hugged Rebekah tighter and began to cry.

4

Vacuum

Pinned to the office wall behind Special Agent Torrance Marks of the FBI were side-by-side photographs of the gem-encrusted compass and its creator, the man simply known as Art Rassine. Agent Marks was for the moment oblivious to everything going on around him. He temporarily had his back to his desk while emails chimed on his computer. Studying the photographs felt oddly cathartic. Whether or not he wanted to believe it, Rassine had slipped through his hands. It was maddening.

Rassine seemed like nothing but a shadow. The sheriff's deputy he had killed prior to his escape was still a sore subject. Marks had taken ownership of that misstep and meant to correct it, but Rassine skillfully evaded capture.

Over the last eleven years there had certainly been leads. Eight months ago, a Montana store owner called the most-wanted hotline and reported having seen Rassine. The shopkeeper didn't know of the reward offer, which had slowly risen. In truth, Marks didn't know how much the reward was. He adhered to a policy not to discuss those matters with callers claiming potential leads. Then again, the reward was for information directly leading to Rassine's capture. Marks had learned the hard way not to expect too much and the lead had proven minor. One person reporting having seen him supported a reason to search satellite footage of the area in question, but that had turned up no evidence of Rassine being there. Marks had ordered searches of the nearby woods, which he understood would not turn up anything new. He believed his profile of Rassine to be stout and correct. The searching agents discovered nothing—not a single gem, footprint, or fingerprint. Not even a hair.

The FBI had all the forensic evidence they needed. They had his DNA samples, his fingerprints, his blood type, his facial scan, and an extrapolated rendering of what Art Rassine would look like today versus twenty years ago. The file on him was large. What they didn't have were financial records. They didn't have a real name (Art Rassine was an alias). The 'art' of matching the facial scans, fingerprints, and blood type to those in law-enforcement or legal files had returned nothing of significance. They had even received 'illicit permission' to hack for medical records, which again led to nothing.

Marks had come to doubt whether Rassine was really as good as he seemed. After all, he was off the grid. His skill at evading capture, while not overlooked, was precisely accidental. Sure, Marks deemed him clever. To some extent, all criminals were. But was he really clever enough to avoid everything they could use to get a handle on him?

The FBI's law-enforcement resources were second-to-none with the possible exception of the CIA or NSA. But even they would probably have no luck in finding Rassine.

Agent Marks stroked his chin, rocked his chair back and forth, glared at the only photograph they had of the man, and then slowly turned his chair. His phone rang, but he ignored it. He paid close attention to emailed leads regarding a case unrelated to Art Rassine. While true that the FBI had officially limited resources regarding the Rassine case, Marks had a special interest at heart. Several of them, in fact.

Sheriff Toyovich of Adams County, Idaho, had made it a habit of calling Agent Marks monthly to demand updates and request information on new leads, even though he knew fully well that he had no legal authority to continue hunting for Rassine. They had no right to investigate, even on the extremely miniscule chance that Rassine was still in the county or even a neighboring county. Agent Marks had grown frustrated with the process just as Toyovich had.

During a struggle between the deputies, the witnesses, and the shadow, Rassine had injured a key witness. Marks owed Willis Ralston an explanation. He owed Vera and Mindy Caldwell, Rassine's only surviving victim, justice. He owed Reginald St. Clear reassurance that the hunt for Rassine would come to a conclusion. The problem was, he had nothing new to report to any of them.

What Marks deemed the FBI's federal manhunt program was not going well. Officially, they had all but given up on finding Rassine. Of course, they did give him a token designation on their most-wanted list, but active investigation had been suspended indefinitely until more concrete leads came to light.

Just this morning had come yet another lead that would invariably lead nowhere. Still, through obsession Marks chose to pursue it. This time, a Montana rancher claimed to have come in direct contact with Rassine, who was hiding out on his land. Of course Rassine escaped. A small team of agents had been dispatched to the ranch to look into it. And just an hour ago, they had called in their report. They believed what the rancher told them but found a significant lack of material evidence that he'd even been there. Marks had cursed.

He vaguely formed a thought in his mind that he would telephone St. Clair to update him on the progress. It had been years since he'd spoken to Reggie. What did he have to lose? Marks had vowed to Reggie that he would find Rassine. He had promised it to be only a matter of time, and his commitment to that end remained strong.

Agent Marks's phone began ringing again. This time, he answered it with an impatient grunt. The secretary explained who it was and then patched the call through to him. He sighed while he waited.

"Mr. St. Clair," Marks said. "What can I do for you?"

He let a moment of awkward silence pass, waiting for Reggie to speak.

Trying to find a way to articulate what he needed to tell Marks took longer than Reggie wanted it to. "My daughter. She's missing."

Reggie hoped that Marks would surmise that this case involved Art Rassine, but feared that Marks was going to pass this off as something completely out of the FBI's jurisdiction. After all, this whole ordeal smacked of Rassine. Instead of acting careless, however, Marks seemed genuinely interested.

"Bad news," the agent remarked.

"Mabye *good* news for you," Reggie said.

"How so?"

Again, Reggie subconsciously rubbed his temple as if it were pulsing with pain. There was some sort of discomfort, presumably nothing more than a lingering morning headache after a long, sleepless night. He swallowed. He hated to phrase the 'good news' as he was about to, but he figured it would prompt the FBI to help him. "It means you have a new lead."

"Any idea where it might lead us?" Marks asked.

"Hopefully my daughter."

"What is your daughter's name? Have you brought this up with your local police?"

Reggie frowned. What kind of a question was that? "Of course I have. And her name is Taleah."

"Taleah St.Clair?"

Reggie didn't need to verbally answer the question. He simply nodded as if Marks could see everything Reggie was doing.

"We'll get in touch with the Meridian Police," Marks said hastily. He sounded as though he were scribbling a wealth of information on a tiny notepad to be perused later.

Filled with a sense of rage, Reggie slammed his fist to the table. A dull ache enveloped his hand for a few moments. He let it subside and then continued as calmly as he possibly could. "I want you to find Art Rassine. Today. If he harms Taleah..." He trailed off as a new vein of thought replaced his calculated tirade.

"We will as soon as possible, Reggie."

Marks was suddenly being more personal which, as far as Reggie saw it, was an admirable trait for a professional federal agent.

"But understand that the FBI is an investigative law enforcement agency. We will investigate and hopefully find the truth in due time. I have to ask you to depend on the state and local police as we hunt for Rassine."

Instead of relief, Marks's statement offered only a sense of despair. Reggie's heart rate quickened. He leaned closer to the edge of the couch without noticing that Rebekah was standing right behind him. "Rassine has my daughter. You have to help me with this."

"We are," Marks offered. A muffled thump that sounded like a door closing fortified the momentary silence between Marks's sentences. "In fact,

I've just personally assigned an agent to gather the materials we need and make contact with Meridian. He won't go home until it is done."

"Today?" Reggie asked.

"I have to be honest," Marks sighed. "The chances of this all coming to a close by the end of the day are remote. I know what you are going through, but please try to be patient."

Patience is a virtue.

"I can't do it...Her life is at stake!" His voice quivered. He paused to massage the pain in his forehead "He's going to drug her! He's going to rape her and then...kill her! And then he'll add another gem into a Goddamn wooden compass."

"Relax, you know we are not going to let that happen."

Reggie swore. "If I don't see acceptable progress by nightfall, I'm going after him myself."

"Be patient. You'll get in our way. Be smart, damnit!"

"Don't you dare." Reggie's heart rate throttled him. He began to shake more.

"Don't be a fool, St. Clair. You know the consequences of taking that action yourself. Remember what happened last time? We are here for a reason. I can't stop you from doing something stupid. But if you want to see your daughter again, you'll cooperate."

Reggie raised his voice another notch. "Is that a threat?"

Marks didn't answer.

"Is it?"

Again, silence sliced a gaping hole in the argument. Reggie felt as though he could strangle Marks.

Rebekah tapped him on the shoulder. He turned quickly and glared at her. A frown prowled at the corners of her face. She looked older, yet more delicate like petals of a rose cut off from its source of nutrient. Helplessly, she raised her palms in the air.

Reggie slapped the phone closed and threw it across the room a little too forcefully. "What?" he demanded.

"Please be patient. I can't live with you like this."

A deep, sorrowful sigh escaped Reggie's lips. Of course Rebekah was right. She was always right. "It's not that easy."

"I know it isn't," she responded delicately. "This isn't your fault. Don't make it be."

He frowned. "Was there something you needed to tell me?"

She nodded. "Anna's coming. And so are the cops."

Again, Reggie let out an exhausted sigh. There was no way the FBI had followed up with the Meridian Police Department already. After all, such swift action would have been like an indictment of bureaucracies throughout the Federal Government. As Reggie sat in silence, Rebekah massaged his shoulders. He had given in to his anger, and for a brief moment darkness was beginning to contort calmness into spiraling chaos. Reggie was falling into oblivion and the invisible hand that stretched forth to bring him to safety began to grow distant. For the last eleven years, quiet had penetrated the tempest, making it feel as if it had ended. The darkest of storms always had those pockets of deception—days without rain—but the blackness would invariably return.

5
Devils

Officer Cody was discussing the findings of the Meridian Police Department with Agent Bill Coles of the FBI. Since Art Rassine's escape, Coles's role in the investigation diminished, so his knowledge of the case was spotty. He set his feet squarely and stretched his hands across the table in front of him. He'd just hung up the phone with Marks, who had rushed him off to the Boise area earlier this morning. Reginald St. Clair was not yet informed of his arrival, but he would be in due time. The first task Coles needed to undertake was questioning the Meridian Police.

Two items of importance sat in clear plastic bags on the table. Coles quickly put on a pair of latex gloves. He examined each of them slowly before unsealing the bag containing Taleah St. Clair's cellphone. During the past eleven years, Coles had been trained in computer forensics. He would examine Taleah's phone more carefully when he had a few minutes to himself. For now, the evidence itself would have to suffice. He placed the bag holding the ribbon back on the table next to the phone and stared at it. "And you're sure this belongs to the girl?" he asked.

Cody nodded and rolled his chair closer to the table. "The fingerprints don't match those you sent to us this morning. It would be safe to assume they belong to Taleah."

"In the FBI we have a special term for assumptions."

"They matched fingerprints on the phone, but we lifted another set of prints. They matched your perpetrator's fingerprints exactly." Cody leaned back and laced his fingers behind his head as if to show satisfaction in his work.

Instead of congratulating Cody on a job well done, Coles continued to grill him. He meant to intone impatience with his speech but had a feeling he was coming off as nothing more than arrogant. "And the ribbon...no prints from our mystery man on it?"

"None," Cody answered.

"What about skid marks? Drops of blood? Surely you've collected more evidence than this."

"You think we didn't look?" Cody said, irritated. "No blood. If an altercation took place, it wasn't rough."

"Hair samples?"

"Our forensic detective found one or two but let me save you the trouble. Nothing belonged to your perp. I'd assume the FBI has the resources to send its own forensic team up from Salt Lake."

"This is a preliminary visit," Coles said. "Everything you find will go through me. If for any reason you are not able to contact me, you will get ahold of Agent Torrance Marks, are we clear?"

"And the witnesses?"

"I'll take it from here. The notes from your meetings with the parents will be included in your package I *'assume'*. Hopefully detailed notes. And Miss St.Clair's photograph. Please tell me you have obtained it."

Cody turned around, opened an email, punched a few keys, and printed the latest photo of Taleah.

"I'm going to question the boyfriend and the girl's mother. It might seem redundant, but in my experience, when agencies team up on investigations, further questions will need to be answered. Also, I like to record questionings, as long as witnesses give written consent. That is not a common practice of local police detectives, but trained federal agents can detect lies from audio recordings."

"I wouldn't say that," Cody lied.

"Please enlighten me."

"Forget about it."

"Based on the evidence we have here, we have the authority to take over the investigation entirely. But we like to have help on some cases. We'll take the lead on this one. You just cooperate."

"We have been." Cody spun his chair in a half circle to regard Agent Coles, who was already beginning to stand.

Coles snatched the bags from the table as Cody slid his notepad to him. "We'll be in touch."

He left the Meridian Police department headquarters and pulled onto the quiet side street thinking about his next task. Driving perhaps a little too fast, he mentally planned his questions.

The next stop was the boyfriend's house. Of all the questioning he would need to do, he looked forward to this visit the most. Teenagers had certain 'tells' when they weren't being entirely forthcoming. Coles had a taste for practicing the lingo, which for some reason had ways of making teenagers uncomfortable. Whether or not he believed them to be implicated in the crime, he loved making them squirm.

When he arrived, Agent Coles knocked sharply on a heavy, paneled wooden door with a small window near eye level. After a moment of waiting, a red-haired woman approached the door and opened it.

"Agent Bill Coles, FBI. I need to speak with Thomas Britton."

"My son," the woman said. "We've been expecting you."

Coles nodded knowingly. When she welcomed him in, he stepped into the waiting area and followed her to the living room. She called for Thomas and entered the kitchen.

The boy exited his room down the hall, walking with a haughty saunter, his arms dangling loosely at his sides. There was no smile on his face. Coles took this as a sign of 'meaning business', which he appreciated. It also showed respect, which he did not anticipate.

"Thomas Britton," he commented as the boy took a seat in a recliner across from him. He glanced out the window and then commenced staring at Coles.

"Tommy, man."

Coles tried to smile. "Mr. Britton. Agent Coles, FBI." He showed the boy his badge, just as he had shown his mother.

Tommy looked a little bit too relaxed. Coles was already becoming unaccustomed to the boy's style. If he was in the mood to show respect, he might have commended him on it.

"You want to talk about Taleah," Tommy stated.

"Where were you last night?"

"The park, waiting for her. She never showed."

Coles leaned back slightly and continued to study Tommy's demeanor. A subtle shrug here and a sly glance there were signs that the boy was unusually confident. He'd been in this kind of situation before.

"No?" Coles continued. "Must have ticked you off."

"At first it did. Then I got worried. You're going to find her, right?"

He stared at the boy. "How long have you been dating?"

"I don't know, a month maybe. My friends think I'm a wannabe going out with a softball player."

Agent Coles uttered a humorless chuckle and kept staring. So far, his idea of breaking the boy wasn't going as prescribed. He half-heartedly attempted to change his tactics. "You a skater? I saw your board outside."

The boy flung his raggedy blond hair away from his face. "It's my old one. I'm fixing it to sell online."

"How long did you wait for Teleah?"

"More than an hour."

Coles checked his notepad and mentally checked an item he wanted to verify off the list. Moving onto the next item, he looked up into Tommy's eyes. "I understand you made a few calls while you waited."

After another effortless shrug, Tommy answered. "Yeah."

Coles frowned and nodded. "Your girlfriend's phone confirms it. Several of them from you."

"Like I said, I was worried."

"And then you called a few other numbers. What were those calls about?"

Tommy shifted his feet. "I called some of her friends, see if any of them saw her."

"Had they?"

"Well, yeah. She was hanging out with them after the game. The plan was she'd meet me at the park for like a mini-date and then I'd drive her home."

"Who won the game?"

"Taleah."

"All by herself?"

"Pretty much. What do you care?"

Coles shrugged and glanced down to his notepad. "Small details. You'd be surprised how those can bite you in the butt or save your bacon. What time did you leave the park?"

"About 10:30, 10:45."

"Small details."

Tommy cracked his first smile of the conversation. "Ten thirty-eight, I guess."

"Who can verify that?"

"Are you kidding? You got my phone calls, the mileage on my car. All your evidence is accurate, dude."

Agent Coles chuckled again, this time while glaring at the boy. "Some manners."

"I care about Teleah, *sir*. I'm trying to help."

"Of course you are."

Somewhat abruptly, Agent Coles stood up and strode toward the door.

"Let me know when you find her," the boy called after him.

Coles didn't turn around. He nodded at Tommy's mother, who was sweeping the entryway.

"Thanks for stopping by," she said.

Instead of offering a friendly reply, he closed the door and walked to the car. He got all he needed from Tommy. Every answer was honest, but his body language was even more honest. He had nothing to do with Art Rassine.

He drove to the park where Tommy had waited for Teleah. He examined her phone carefully, including all of her text messages, photographs, and data usage. The girl lived like a teenager. There were 47 congratulatory text messages with 51 replies, eleven phone calls, spotty internet connections, and a whopping 93 pictures each featuring herself, her friends, or her father. He shut the phone down and remembered Reggie St. Clair. The man had a terrible attitude about being a key witness in the murder case eleven years ago. Some untold emotional distress had been eating him alive. Though Reggie never talked about it with the FBI or the Deputies, Agent Coles could see it. The memory was a dark cloud painting the details with dingy strokes of peril. He was not in charge of Reggie, but he wanted to question him anyway.

After replacing the cellphone in its bag, he started the motor and drove away. He drove slower this time, taking extra caution to obey all traffic laws. The next interview was going to be much more difficult.

The next stop was Taleah St. Clair's mother's house. Anna answered the door almost immediately, like she had been expecting him. Coles silently wondered if Officer Cody warned all of the interviewees.

He showed her his badge. "Agent Bill Coles, FBI. I need to speak with you about your daughter."

She swung the door open and welcomed him in without so much as saying a word. A scant remainder of a tear touched the corner of her eye. A box of tissue and a garbage can were strategically placed near the recliner. He scanned the room for items belonging to Taleah. A baseball glove sat idle on the couch along with her red cap. No books. Probably everything she owned was in her bedroom. For the moment, Coles didn't need to see it, but he might ask later if he felt the situation warranted it.

"What time did you suspect something was up the other night?" he started.

"I don't know," she said. Her voice seemed strained from the aftermath of crying.

Coles didn't intend to show concern, but his expression leaked it anyway. "Understand that these small details can be very important in a case like this. Got an educated guess?"

"Um, thirty minutes or so. After her curfew. But not really until after I talked to Reggie."

Nodding, Agent Coles continued. "How many times did you try to call her?"

"About ten."

"What did Reggie say?"

"I assumed she was there still. At his house." A fresh tear rolled down her face. Instinctively, she reached for the tissue box. "Sorry," she squeaked.

"I'd be more worried if you didn't show any emotion," he stated softly. "How long did you wait before calling the police?"

"Reggie did after he searched town for her."

"We'll ask Reggie when we get a chance, but I think the Meridian Police already did."

"They asked all of this already," she sniffed.

"I know." Coles decided to shift gears and go directly for the most tantalizing answer she could possibly give him. For the moment, he didn't care about the consequences. He looked up with a dull frown.

Anna's expression drooped and the corners of her mouth folded down to reveal a paralyzing frown.

"Reggie mentioned something about a kidnapping and murder case he witnessed several years back. He recounted the story to the police on their first visit. Can you expound on that story from your own point of view?"

She sniffed again, and dabbled at her cheeks with the tissue. "Reggie was a mess. Abusing drugs. Headaches. And I was being so cruel."

"How so?"

"We were getting divorced. I worried about Taleah, so I wouldn't let him see her. At least until I figured his addiction was gone."

This information came as a shock to Agent Coles, but he did his best to suppress the surprise on his expression. This was one of those 'small details' that would probably morph into a huge turning point in the case.

"Do you think Reggie would relapse?"

"He's clean."

"What was it? Pot? Meth?"

"Painkillers. I found out about it before the divorce."

"Why did you get divorced?"

"We just grew apart. The drugs enhanced it. He was turning into a man I didn't know. One I didn't want to know."

More tears spilled on her cheeks as she attempted to force them back. She was too weak. Her hands shook as she slowly raised the tissue to her cheek. Her frown made Coles want to look away in shame. Though he'd dealt with grieving parents and partners before, something about Anna caused him to react differently.

"Must have been difficult," he said after swallowing.

She didn't answer.

"I didn't know about the murder until almost a year later. He opened up to me. Explained. Something had changed in him for the better."

"What did he tell you?"

"That the man was a monster. Didn't even seem human."

Coles simply waited for more, which took longer than he expected. Instead of pushing, however, he let the conversation take a pace more natural to Anna and her complex emotions.

"He killed three women, but one got away. They ran into a trap in the mountains. One of the deputies was killed. Reggie shot him, but he got away. And now Reggie thinks this..." she searched her memory, raised her eyes, and searched some more. "Art. He thinks Art is Taleah's..." She couldn't finish. She sobbed and buried her face in the crook of her arm. In the midst of an abrupt lurch, she dropped the tissues on the floor.

"I know you don't want to hear this, but he is. Evidence confirms it. Did you ever see this Art? Anyone suspiciously lingering in the neighborhood? Any unusual messages or friend requests?"

She continued to sob but forced herself to shake her head.

"Disturbing phone calls?"

More tears, but no answer.

"Did Taleah mention anything about her friends meeting a strange person asking about her?"

"I can't...I can't believe this is happening. Why? Why her? Why? Oh, God."

"Ms. St. Clair, I know this is hard, but please try to help me out here."

She nodded.

"We're going to find her. If you think of anything else call me or Agent Marks right away." When he noticed her looking up at him, he leaned back, glanced down, and tapped his pen on the notepad.

"He's going to kill her."

"He's not," Coles assured her. "We have good information, good leads. He won't get a chance because there are good people in this world, and Art Rassine is a most-wanted."

Though part of his statement was an outright lie, he believed everything he told her. He said goodbye before leading himself from her home. He needed a heart-to-heart with Reggie now more than ever. The bottom line was that, like Tommy Britton, Anna had been completely honest. He wondered whether he'd get the same kind of honesty from Reggie, but believed that Reggie would try to hide the problems he experienced during the divorce. Then again, Reggie would not just hand over his daughter to a madman who had caused him years of heartache and grief. If such a thing had happened, Reggie had to have been fooled. Yet, of all the things Coles believed Reggie to be, foolish was not one of them. Reggie understood the situation and its pitfalls better than anybody on the planet, with the possible exception of Art Rassine himself.

6
Recluse

The tan, sun-yellowed pickup rolled to a stop after what had seemed like hours of motion. The panic of not knowing where she was had begun to transform into thought and plans of escape. Taleah struggled against the rope binding her hands and feet. The rag in her mouth somehow was beginning to taste even worse. In effort to dilute the flavor and to keep from gagging, she tried to keep the cloth moist with her saliva. Whatever the chemical was would get into her stomach, and it was likely toxic, so she was careful not to swallow. A trickle of drool escaped her lips. The remaining moisture from her tears was drying into folded lines across her makeup.

The time spent in the bed of the truck could prove beneficial. She felt confident that by now she could describe the exterior of the truck, though she couldn't visually recall what it looked like. It had to be a model from the 70s or 80s. It was beat-up, rusted, and had oxidized paint, but it ran. That was all her kidnapper cared about.

She scooted to the front of the bed while trying to remain quiet. She inadvertently kicked a loose rock and then ducked to pretend she was lying down. After a few minutes passed, she lifted her head to peer through the window, leaning her face against the glass directly behind the stranger. Through the rear-view mirror, she studied his face.

It appeared dull and leathery, as if it had been exposed to the elements for too long. A mane of wiry hair lined with grease and dust protected his face from further damage. His huge jawbone curved to a blunt chin and his muscles were meaty. As she watched, he looked through the mirror and stared at her until she ducked her head.

"Nothin' to see anyway," he growled.

She squirmed against the rope and tried to scream a curse word at him, but all that could come out was a dull, muffled moan.

He ignored her.

She thought about his face for as long as her mind would let her. The depth encapsulated in his facial hair distinguished a trait of wildness that seemed both unnerving and entrancing. And those eyes. They were what truly set him apart from all the other men she'd ever met. They were dark and mysterious, completely devoid of emotion—cold and senseless but touched with evil. They reflected no light; they were completely empty.

The eyes alone made her want to cry. On a normal day she would simply cringe and look away. Today, terror gripped her.

When the truck proceeded, it bounced up and down four times in rapid succession. He had just driven over railroad tracks. Another clue. She categorized that in the invisible mental file marked 'important', but in reality, the chance to use this information would probably never come.

"Getting a little suspicious back there," he growled above the increasing wind noise.

She kept her head low but imagined that she looked desperate and perhaps even helpless. For now, he stood in the position of power until they reached their destination. She had a plan in place for when that time came.

Instead of letting emotion and despair tower over rationality, she tried to make sense of the blurred landscape. What direction were they headed? She squinted in the morning daylight, which struggled to penetrate the fiberglass windows. Rather than detail, these windows to the outside world, both figurative and literal, showed only shapes and distorted hints of color. Desert and mountains were all she could see. North. But then again, virtually the entire Intermountain West was composed of that exact ecosystem. If she was wrong, they could be in Southern Nevada by now.

With this line of logic came a problem of reasoning. If they were heading north, they should have been almost to Canada by now. The landscape in that region was far different than the one she observed. They'd stopped somewhere for the night, but she didn't seem to remember it. She didn't get much sleep, or so she thought. But for traveling for so long, they certainly hadn't gone very far. If the opportunity ever arose to properly study the landscape, she would get a better picture of what it looked like. Every little detail she could pick up on was important.

She wiggled her feet back and forth, then her hands, and then her feet again. She felt the rope loosen ever-so-slightly, but not enough to wrestle free. If her plan of escape was to be successful, she'd need the use of her limbs.

After another twenty minutes of staring and thinking, she closed her eyes as if to feign sleep. But instead of faking it, she gave in to the dark, wispy clouds of thoughtless oblivion. Her dreams revealed only herself and the kidnapper. Nothing but captivity and freedom. The core of every subconscious thought lingered with the captivity. Still, the very idea of freedom construed hope. She clung to it like a lover.

Reggie frowned when his phone rang. The phone identified the caller as simply 'FBI.' He promptly answered it. There was no hope that this conversation would offer more than insignificant details.

"Tell me you found her," Reggie said.

Marks sighed. "Can't do that, Mr. St. Clair. I'm sorry."

"Don't apologize." His voice was harsh and abrupt, but he had nothing more to offer.

"We got a break this morning while Agent Coles was running around Meridian questioning people."

"Where is she?"

"I think you remember Coles. He'll be meeting with you this afternoon."

Reggie's heart sunk, but its beat quickened, inducing pain. "More damn questions? I'm not answering any more. Just once answer me. Where is she?"

"We found the cabin where Rassine lived back when he was friends with Lance Harrison. Rustic old place, full of history. A couple owns it now as sort of a summer home. It's near the inlet of the Salmon River canyon up towards Riggins, Idaho. Not much there but unkempt pasture and some rotting wooden fence. The couple came in from Arizona for the season a month ago. Our team went in and searched the place an hour ago."

"What did they find?"

"Part of an old title stuffed in a box and hidden. It was frayed and crumbled. Our mobile forensics crew is taking a look. It contains Art Rassine's legal name, James Bullock. I think Art Rassine has a better ring to it. What do you think?"

"Don't give a damn!" Reggie barked.

"The man bought it back in 1977. Couple says they think it was built sometime around '71. Papers from that far back are somewhat unreliable, but I think we got us a decent lead. It's going to lead us to financial records, which can only help."

"How long will that take?"

"Could be hours or days. Your guess is as good as mine."

"You know what I told you the other day?" Reggie asked, all at once a little too thoughtfully.

Marks didn't answer.

"It's still a promise, if she isn't located in twenty-four hours."

"Our people are working on it."

"Tell them to work faster!" Reggie bit his lip, trying to keep from yelling, but it wasn't working. He could feel his soul blackening.

Marks let silence sour the emotion. "That's all I wanted to tell you at this point. Expect to hear from Agent Coles within the hour."

"Whatever," Reggie grunted. He dropped the phone on the table. During his conversation with Agent Marks, he had become partially aware that Willis had entered the house and was sitting in the chair across from him, staring. Rebekah had left the room.

"Doesn't sound good," Willis admitted after a moment of silence. He had been watching Reggie frown, and if Reggie knew him well enough, he aimed to correct it.

"They could have a hundred agents searching the woods for her right now, and they're busy examining papers form 1977. It's going nowhere."

"I'm here, my friend."

Reggie stared at him, not meaning to look so dour. It wasn't a look he could fix by simply flexing his facial muscles. It would take an outside influence, a trait with which Willis was perfectly blessed.

"Think of it this way, they're covering all their bases."

"Still on that baseball thing?"

"Sliding into home. What's it to you?"

"We both know it isn't for the money. What did you say it paid?" Reggie glanced to the entryway of the kitchen. Rebekah rounded the corner carrying two tall glasses of water. She smiled at Willis, paying little attention to Reggie.

"Thanks," Willis told Rebekah. Then he turned to Reggie and added, "I lost track."

Reggie didn't smile. "Funny."

Willis nodded. "I know what the mood is but who said I couldn't try to lighten it?"

"A wild man has my daughter. God knows what he's going to do to her. And you're sitting here making jokes?"

"It was uncalled for," Willis admitted, still smiling.

"Cut him a break, honey," Rebekah chimed, cozying up next to him. "He's only trying to help."

"Great job," Reggie said. His lip quivered. For a moment, he wanted to pummel the couch but held his fist. "I...*can't*...take this."

With that, Willis's expression changed to a simpler form of concern. Reggie got the feeling he was about to belt out another choice proverb which he knew nothing about.

"If you love someone..." He shrugged. "Got to let them go."

Forcefully, Reggie shifted his focus to Willis. "We've been friends for a long time. Been through a lot together. But if you ever say anything like that again, I'll kill you."

Instead of smiling, Willis's face drooped into a frown. He shifted his weight to his left, considering Reggie with a sad, but curious look. "You know, buddy, I'd laugh if I didn't actually think that was true."

"Oh, shut up," Reggie said.

"Boys!" Rebekah flung her head back and raised her palms. "I don't understand men sometimes!"

"Feeling's mutual," Willis cracked, still not smiling.

Inadvertently, Reggie glared as if he were going to choke Willis. A warm, but nonetheless uncomfortable silence commenced. Reggie was getting restless waiting for the FBI. He wanted to hunt for Taleah and Rassine. Even if he had no chance of finding them, it would offer a different perspective and a breath of fresh air. Reggie inhaled slowly and then sighed.

The sound of the door knocking snapped him out of it. Rebekah rose to answer. She welcomed Agent Bill Coles into the living room. He took a seat in the other recliner next to Willis. "Good afternoon Mr. Ralston," Coles said.

"Didn't you learn anything eleven years ago?"

"Ah, Willis," Coles corrected himself. "And Reggie. Can we have the room? We need to talk."

Rebekah looked confused, but a knowing glance flashed across Willis's face. He subtly nodded at Reggie as he stood up to leave the room.

"Take me back eleven years," Coles started. "Tell me everything."

"We were flyin—"

Coles cut him off. "Before that."

"You talked to Anna," Reggie guessed.

Coles didn't answer. He stared, waiting for an answer.

Reggie glared at the ceiling and then began to stare into nothingness. He sighed. "Then she told you everything you need to know."

"You didn't think it was important back then? That my key witness was abusing pain pills?"

"None of your business," he groaned. "Besides it was Adams County's case."

"That's not what's important."

"Yeah, I had a problem. My life was falling apart. And no one intends to develop a tolerance for pain medication. It's just that Vicodin is addictive as hell. The doctor prescribed it."

"When did you change?"

"Call it a change of heart."

"Was it when Anna let you see her again?"

"Before that," Reggie croaked. He glanced to the floor and then looked up. A stray tear formed at the corner of his eye. Coles was dredging up painful memories, but memories that brought to mind the power that had changed him. "I finally understood the plan of salvation—that I could be saved."

Coles nodded. "But it was troubling you. It was getting worse and worse. I could see it. And that friend you were talking to on the phone wasn't making it any better."

Reggie studied his memory. While true that age was beginning to wear on him, he thought his memory was still solid. He simply couldn't remember if Coles had witnessed any of his conversations with Richard Kerrin. "You know about that?"

Another nod.

"He was trying to help. I was just too stubborn for it to make any difference."

"And now this anger is returning."

Reggie scowled and looked away.

"Don't let it derail us," Coles warned. "Who knows, it could be the difference between seeing Taleah again and—"

"Don't you dare lecture me," Reggie interrupted. "This is a waste of time." A flicker of a tear rolled down his face and he clenched his fist. Go. Find her. Get the hell out and find her!"

After a thoughtful sigh, Coles stood and strode to the door. He placed a hand on the knob and looked back at Reggie, concern touching his investigative demeanor. "You're an honorable man. But be rational."

Coles left the room and closed the door behind him leaving Reggie with the shambles of his tattered thoughts. He wiped the tear away and decided to forge a plan. *Coles and Marks have no idea what they're talking about.* Reggie had to protect his daughter. It was his job and no one else's.

What Coles had just said sounded like something Ted Brickshaw had told him all those years ago while assigning Reggie the surveying job. Even now he could hear it echo in his head like fragments of a shattering dream: *Everything happens for a reason. Don't let this become the reason.*

7
Tombs

Thinking about how late spring almost magically transformed this landscape from an icy world of white to something resembling beauty, Art navigated a network of roads from nearby New Meadows. Deep underground at the old Lance Harrison ranch, where once sat morbid secrets, the blood of three victims dried into the hard, clay-like floor of 'the tomb.' Carved from an abandoned well, this chamber served as not only a grave, but as a hiding place. Without the knowledge of old Lance, Art had hollowed out a portion of the earth 12 feet beneath the surface and had driven stakes into the walls. The new room was small, affording only close quarters for three women.

The process of converting the well was painstaking yet rewarding. Harrison himself barely knew the well existed, it having been covered up and sealed since long before he inherited the property. But damn if Lance wasn't a thorn in his side. It wasn't worthwhile to dwell on the past; Lance Harrison was dead and that was the end of the story.

Art had coveted the property ever since he laid eyes upon it. He'd studied it meticulously, watching the overgrowth and the lack of grazing cattle, and hoping Harrison was going to sell the place. It was beautiful country, but also isolated. Recreationists had neither real access nor reason to trespass. While prime recreational lands existed just over the mountains to the west, this area was seldom seen. Only one road led to the property. A couple of spur routes branched off of the main road, but these were nothing more than old logging roads and faded away to nothing more than ruts in the undergrowth after less than a half mile.

Harrison and his wife had flown to Montreal for a week. Art already knew about the well. He'd even been at the bottom, had felt its cold, hard walls, and had decided that converting it to a secondary bunker was not only a smart idea, but more importantly, a realistic one.

The actual digging took much of the week. He had to take careful considerations when hauling away the soil and the stone, so as to not disturb the lay of the land and to leave nothing behind. Several locations had served as dumping sites, but the other underground bunker—the one where he'd kept the bear tied up—had served as a sort of storage vault. Lance actually did know about this bunker but had no reason to access it.

The other bunker had been created as a bomb and fall-out shelter sometime during the Cold War. The Harrison family first acquired the ranch when the original owner had been forced to sell during the recession of the 1970s. The younger Harrison didn't use the shelter and so had not mentioned it to Lance. But Lance was a capable rancher and knew his property inside and out. The bunker wasn't necessarily a difficult point in the ranch to find. It was nestled in a heavily wooded area that wasn't used for cattle grazing or open range, thus it was largely unused. But not to Art.

Several wine casks lined one of the walls within the bunker. There was plenty of clutter. Lance had stashed a few items of little value in this bunker, but it was neither an attic nor a cellar.

Still eyeing the scenery, Art turned down one of the back logging roads. There would be plenty of police presence at the ranch. If they were smart, they'd have already linked the disappearance of Reginald St. Clair's daughter to him. And if any of them were smart, it was Reggie. Reggie had almost been the end of his era.

Reggie was the reason the police and the FBI had so much 'dirt' on him, so much evidence. They had everything they needed to nab him, put him away for life, and probably even to execute him, but they didn't have him. He was careful at avoiding that.

The landscape seemed oddly still. He studied the beginning few steps of his trek through the hills, and then opened the tailgate of the truck. She was awake.

She wildly flailed her limbs, kicking Art in the gut as she went. She kneed him in the face and then attempted to use her head as a weapon. *The silly girl.* Instead of ducking her barrages, he simply gripped her throat, held her tight to the side of the vehicle, strengthened the knots, and then slammed the tailgate shut. She moaned, but little sound could escape her gagged mouth.

He let silence enhance the tension and chuckled. "You still got some fight in you."

Another dull, muffled moan, followed by more thrashing of limbs. He ignored it.

The trip was only a quick jaunt. Since he'd left 'the tomb' a lot had happened, but he felt fairly confident that he left an important gemstone buried somewhere. The diamond. He focused on the task at hand, which would prove to be difficult.

The gate to the ranch formerly owned by Lance Harrison was fitted with a new lock and guarded should Art Rassine come snooping around his old stomping ground. Two teams of FBI agents switched off guarding the property. Before that, they had one more look inside Rassine's makeshift burial tomb where St. Clair had found the bodies of two victims. The only problem with the action of staking out the entrance was what to do when the couple got home.

Agent Torrance Marks was uncertain what to do when that time came. He thought about letting them access their home to drop off their belongings, retrieve mail, and feed their pets, but that was a bad idea because Art Rassine (whom he liked to call The Shadow) was a dangerous man. Instead, he considered hiding them in a nearby motel. But the nearby motel was a sad shanty in downtown Council, population 816, a good hour away from the ranch. That wasn't a good idea, either. Bur Marks was clever. He would find some worthy alternative.

Agents Clark and DeLaren were sitting in the unmarked car debating about whether Marks was right to assign them this duty. Marks had selected Clark because she had experience at this ranch, having headed up the forensic crew all those years ago. DeLaren was a fresh, promising young agent who had a good attitude and got along well with everyone, even the usually frosty

Agent Clark. She'd married a good man eight years ago. The small talk focused on her husband and daughter for a few minutes before switching back to Agent Marks.

"Doubtful he comes back," Clark was saying. "Even if he knows we got everything we needed out of his hiding places."

DeLaren was perhaps best known for his unusual profiling technique. He shrugged. "He was a serial kidnapper, serial killer. They get off on visiting their own crime scenes."

"Since when?" She bit her lip and stared into the brush at the side of the road. "And it was eleven years ago. Even if his first victim was held here, which she wasn't—"

He cut her off. "*Especially* if it was his first victim. I wasn't involved in this case eleven years ago, but the hell if I don't know what I'm talking about."

"For a black guy with a French name," she teased.

"You know what I'm saying. They say Rassine was no fool, but they also say he used this vicinity as a sort of sanctuary. He could be anywhere in these woods right now. All we're doing is guarding the most likely access point to the ranch."

"And he knows the area good enough to get around without a map," she agreed. "We'd be better off with aerial surveillance. If Marks is so good, why don't you think he realized that our best chance is flying circles around the place? That's how the original crime scene was discovered."

"Accident," DeLaren interrupted. "It wasn't us."

"We got everything we need, we just can't catch the bastard," Clark lamented. "I remember doing some spelunking where the women were found. It was terrible, but we didn't find info on the killer there. We lifted his fingerprints from the compass thing he made, the loose gemstones in the grove, and then matched them to some we found on the chains in the well. The ridge where St.Clair shot Rassine...we got his blood type and DNA from the blood trail. Everything a perfect match, but we still couldn't identify him. Know why?"

"Let me see," DeLaren pondered. "I'll tear a page out of Marks's book. The man was essentially a shadow."

"Off the grid for at least twenty years before Mindy Caldwell went missing. Add eleven more to that. Had no record, criminal or hospital. Well, besides from his actual birth, which never turned up, and rarely does it ever."

"Marks is just covering his bases." He glanced at her, leaned back against the headrest, and studied a fallen tree in the forest. "He don't think Rassine will be back, or he'd be flying, like you say."

"I agree he probably won't come back, but we still should be flying just in case. Cover our bases,"

"So what was the motive?" DeLaren asked.

She grinned and chuckled. "Eleven years and we still don't know that. But seeing as how he's made off with St. Clair's daughter, I'd say the motive has changed. Revenge."

"Revenge for shooting him," DeLaren agreed.

"And for bringing him within a whisker on his own face of justice."

"Men like this laugh in the face of justice."

"But it still bites them in the ass," she said.

Agent DeLaren let the silence stretch. Now instead of focusing on the fallen tree, he let his focus drift and wander, both optically and mentally. Some said that not focusing was a sign of vacantness, but it was his way of doing things. You could never see the whole of the solution without looking at the whole of the problem. After five minutes, he broke the silence and looked at Clark's face.

"Do you think Rassine would bring St. Clair's daughter here?"

"No. Somewhere else, far from here. But just as wild."

"Speaking of wild, I have another idea," he pondered. "What if St. Clair himself turns up? Marks says he's getting awful impatient and who can blame him?"

"If he comes, we'll just have to forbid him access, isn't that right?"

"I know what I'd be doing if it was my daughter."

She nodded. "I'd do the same thing. But we're feds and it would hinder us catching him."

DeLaren simply stared as if into oblivion. Gathering somewhere in the darkness of his subconscious mind was a void that should have been filled with action. He thought about what a moral man would do in this situation, not what a cop would do. He would be helping St. Clair even if it would turn out to be his undoing.

8
Lure

The television screen flickered and turned to snow when Rebekah flipped past a series of channels for which reception was limited or prohibited. She stopped on a sports channel and stared at highlights of the day's baseball games for as long as she could tolerate it, which was about thirty seconds. That wouldn't do. She flipped a few more channels and stopped again. Some sappy romance flick. She wasn't in the mood for that. The down tempo music that accompanied the poor acting provided background noise. She glanced to the stairs when she heard a series of bumps from upstairs.

The dullness of the evening was alarming. Instead of watching television, she should be at least helping Reggie cope, and probably helping him to devise a strategy. The news from the police wasn't good. She let the movie run and thought about the earlier conversation she'd had with Reggie.

"What did the FBI want?" she had asked.

Reggie looked down to his palms and uttered an exhausted sigh.

"Had to be something personal or else he wouldn't have had me leave the room."

His voice cracked when he attempted to speak, but all that came out was a muffled croak. He stammered. "Something that happened to me eleven years ago."

"But you told me about that already." She stared at him, waiting for an answer.

"Besides that." He thought about it, looking dismal, and then revised his statement. "Well, in addition. Something I haven't talked about much, even with you."

"Which is?"

He glanced away for a split second and returned his gaze to his hands. "I told you about the headaches I used to have. But there was more to it than that. There were nightmares, and pain. The doctor prescribed Vicodin, which helped. But the effects wore off too fast, so I took them more often. I built up a tolerance."

She tilted her head. "You mean...?" Then it dawned on her. Her hands shook and she stared at Reggie, in search of something more, something comforting. But all that came was darkness. "I thought we told each other everything."

"I meant to tell you years ago. It was a big part of why Anna and I divorced. Why she didn't let me see Taleah."

"You didn't trust me?"

"I did," Reggie started, "it's just..."

"You didn't."

"Well...it was a long time ago. I thought...thought that if I didn't talk about it the pain would eventually wear off. But that's the easy way out. There was a better way but I didn't know. Or care. Then Rassine got in the way and all of it escalated."

The memory broke and faded when the sappy show cut away to a commercial break. She sighed of boredom and tried to think about Taleah. Blankness arrested her thoughts. She picked up the remote and clicked through at least ten more channels before falling on the local channels. The late news was running. She thought about changing channels again until they put up a photograph. She froze. It was Taleah.

"Reg," she called. "Reggie come down here."

"Just a minute," he called.

"Get down here now! They're talking about Taleah."

A monstrous thump vibrated the upstairs floor, followed by a steadily increasing thunder as Reggie bolted down the stairs.

The photograph of Taleah lasted just long enough for Reggie to take a seat next to Rebekah.

"Local authorities have teamed up with the FBI to search for a man believed to have kidnapped and murdered at least three women," the news anchor started. "A fourth escaped."

The newscasters cut to video of Agent Bill Coles explaining the case.

"Obviously, this man knows what he's doing. He intentionally left clues behind eleven years ago. We believe he'll try the same thing this time."

"How quickly do you envision apprehending the suspect?" the interviewer asked.

Coles turned terse if not crimson. "He's not a suspect, he's a perpetrator. Before long, he's going to come to us, either by coming out from hiding or leaving more clues behind. We've allocated all resources to finding this man and bringing him to justice. But finding Taleah St. Clair remains our primary goal."

Reggie flushed as he listened to Coles make a martyr out of Rassine. He balled his fists as a frown etched its way ever deeper into his face. Rebekah stared at the screen as if in disbelief. She didn't even glance at Reggie.

A chord of anger pulsed through his veins. "You gotta be kidding me," he growled.

"To aid in the ongoing manhunt for Art Rassine," the news anchor continued, "The FBI has requested your help. Should you see anyone resembling this man..." They flashed the only photograph of Rassine anyone had. "...Please call the number on your screen immediately. The FBI is offering a reward for any information leading to Rassine's arrest."

Reggie grabbed the remote and wrestled it from Rebekah's hands. He glared at everything he set eyes upon. His heart was a beating like a runaway jazz tune about to careen into landscapes of heavy metal. His muscles spasmed.

"They're just sitting on their—asses."

"Reg."

"I'm done being patient."

She wrapped her arm around him, but instead of comfort, her embrace only provided the fire of impassioned rage. He trembled and his lip quivered.

"Honey, please don't do anything..."

"Irrational? No, that's what the FBI is good at."

"I want Taleah back as much as you do."

"I want Rassine," Reggie muttered, his voice rising. He pulled away from her. A fowl, painful scowl engulfed his face in shades of misery. He clenched his fists and tightened his jaw muscles. Though Rebekah attempted to hold him from the brink, it wasn't working. He continued to ramble as his face turned redder.

"Don't…"

"I'm not waiting anymore." The timbre of his voice rose to a violent crescendo. "I'm not going to just sit on my ass and let them kill her trying to bait Rassine. It isn't going to work. They know what Rassine is capable as well as I do. I won't just stand by…"

"Please."

"I'm going to find him!" His jaw muscles tightened, invoking black emotions of the past. "I'm going to find him! And I'm going to kill him!"

Reggie's whole body trembled. Rage glued his eyes shut for a moment before he pried them open. Upon realizing how far he'd just ventured into dark thoughts, he attempted to change the contorted expression of anger into a simple, blank stare. Tears were streaming from Rebekah's eyes. He wrapped his arms around her to let his troubled heart calm.

"Sorry," he whispered.

She lurched in his arms. "Don't do it."

"I have to go after her. My duty. You'll understand."

She let go of him, wiped her tears away, searched her thoughts, and then gave him a nervous glance. "Maybe he does deserve to die. But it isn't your job."

He meant to say he knew but didn't have the heart to lie to her. Instead, he nodded and looked to his hands.

"Don't kill him."

"I might have to. Last time, when I shot him…It was self-defense."

"Please don't put yourself in that situation."

"I'll do what I have to," Reggie said, passion rising up in him once again. "Rassine won't hurt anyone again. I can't allow him to tear families apart. I'll make sure."

"And if you don't get to Taleah in time? What then?"

Reggie paused as if to consider, but the very prospect of that happening was more than he could handle. He shuddered at the thought. His heart rate climbed another notch. He couldn't blame her, because she aimed to help. Yet, sometimes when a caring person whose heart was truly in the right place attempted to comfort a grieving parent, the desperation somehow grew only thicker and the tears heavier. He couldn't let her go. She had so much left to experience. Her relationship with Tommy "the Terror" was only in its infancy. While true that Reggie was uncertain whether he could trust the boy, Taleah liked him. She had more championships to win on the diamond.

Gemstones. A ruby, a sapphire, an emerald, and a star garnet. The list of stones Rassine had used to make his compass conspicuously lacked the most valuable gem of all. To that end, what if kidnapping and killing Taleah (who, in this case, represented a diamond) was in his plan all along? The diamond was the hardest known substance on earth, and Reggie vowed to make it 'hard' for Rassine to abuse her.

Darkness spilt into his soul as he imagined her, tears running down her face, and struggling against ropes that could burst into flames at any time. He imagined the ferocious wilderness that Reggie had once described Rassine's eyes to be consumed with. With that darkness in his heart, he was ready to take the plunge. It was now or never.

"Don't go alone," Rebekah said after a long pause.

"You won't come with me?"

"You'll need someone stronger than me. Someone who knows the wilderness better—someone more fit. But someone who can lend you emotional support."

"I'd already signed Willis up," he said. "He'll refuse at first, but I can be good at talking him into things." He studied his hands and thought about this journey some more. How productive could blindly searching the mountains near New Meadows actually be? He would also need help on the home front, and possibly a little bit of law-enforcement assistance. Just not from the FBI. Deputy Smith Monaghan was probably still under the employ of Adams County.

"Good," she said.

"Can you and Anna do me a favor while I'm gone? I know it won't be easy, but I need someone to keep an eye on the FBI and report back to me."

"You want me to spy on the FBI? That's impossible."

"I said it wouldn't be easy. If you can't hack them, try going through the front door and finding someone sympathetic to talk to. They can't all be...*hacks*."

She stared at him. Her eyebrows furrowed together and her forehead wrinkled. When she realized that Reggie was indeed serious, she looked down and offered a subtle nod.

"Can you do that?"

"Mabye. Will Anna cooperate, or will she go completely off the deep end? She's a wreck right now."

"Maybe she will improve when she finds she's doing something productive to get Taleah back. Wasn't always easy to console her with action, but I always found it to be worth the price."

"The price of what?"

"Effort."

"Okay," she said. "When do I start?"

"Tonight."

"It's 10:30. At least give yourself some daylight."

Reggie fought it but surrendered anyway. In at least one aspect, she was right. Driving out of town, especially with the day Reggie just had, could be an exercise in disaster. But then again, it would give him something useful to do with the inevitable insomnia. Add that to the fact that it was likely he'd find Rassine at night, when it would be easier for Rassine to ambush him. This business peddled danger, but it was a risk worth taking. He would need a weapon, but at 10:30 pm, the means of acquiring one legally were severely limited. While truly a matter of life and death, this task could more immediately endanger his life. If he was right that Rassine would try to ambush him, Reggie might never get the chance to rescue Taleah. *You can't rescue anyone when you're dead.*

Rebekah opened her mouth to speak again, but a knock at the door interrupted her. Reggie arose to answer it, expecting to find an apologetic FBI agent standing there. Instead, he found Willis.

"Speak of the devil," Reggie said. "I was just about to call you."

"Phone's dead," Willis explained. "I saw the news."

"Think they've gone insane with the *lazzaiz faire* technique?"

"Actually, that's why I wanted to talk to you. I understood you'd be angry. Come to think of it, you *do* look pissed."

"Can you blame me?"

Willis lowered his voice to a whisper and leaned closer to Reggie, a sheepish smile tingeing his lips with a little too much lightheartedness. "I know as an ump, you're not supposed to pick sides. But I'm a fan of Taleah."

Reggie couldn't offer a witty retort. He simply glared at him. "So you will help me."

"Sure, with what?" The sentence made it halfway out of his mouth when what he was agreeing to dawned on him. He quickly revised his statement. "Absolutely not. You're crazy."

"Maybe," Reggie said. "But the FBI isn't about to do anything useful. So I have to find her. I need some help. Rebekah and Anna are going to monitor the FBI and the cops, and I might call up Smith to help, too. It'll be easier to find her the more people we got searching. Common sense. And I'll need a source of emotional stability just in case I go bats."

Willis suppressed a grin. Over the last few months, he'd grown amused with the term 'bats' and its related euphemisms.

"You gotta help. I'm out there all alone, and who knows what could happen. Rassine might kill me before I can get to her."

"So I'm there as a shrink and a medic?"

Reggie nodded.

"Sign me up."

"Already did."

Willis's expression soured. "What the...Why you impish...*prick!*"

"Nice," Reggie said. He wasn't in the mood to smile. He was in the mood to plan. His anger and frustration flooded the back corners of his mind, allowing positive energy to flow through his brain once again. Wrapping himself around a productive task eased the burden of the blackness and stifled the din of terror. Yet, this time, even with the light of rational thought, the darkness of carnal emotion lurked just beneath the surface, ready to attack at a second's notice.

9
Confined

Darkness encroached upon what appeared to be a perfect wilderness. An eerie breeze whispered in the conifers, invoking solemn memories of a life long forgotten. After promising herself that she'd deny sleep's temptation and thinking about the day she'd just had, she allowed herself a lucid moment to stare into nothingness. Taleah's thoughts became muddled and sparse, then reduced themselves to nothing more than quiet, subconscious sparks drifting up into the night. When thought ran out, all that remained was sleep.

Taleah found herself wandering on a gravel road that cut through alternating stands of lodge pole pines and sagebrush. She stared to open marshlands, wondering how far she'd gone, when it dawned on her that she couldn't remember where she'd been. She stopped atop a subtle incline to observe a wide meadow dotted with sage at one side of the road. A small pocket of aspens crowded the other shoulder, giving way to a patch of sage and a gradually thickening grove of lodge poles and tamaracks beyond. She turned around. The landscape behind her, while breathtaking, offered no clues as to where she'd been.

As if remembering a memory from only yesterday, she observed the scene as the present. But something didn't seem right about her or the surroundings. Inside, she was very much the same athletic seventeen-year-old, yet the shape of her body and her clothes indicated that she was thirteen. How had she traversed so many years in such a short amount of time?

The shade enticed her by promising cool relief from the sun. She took two steps toward it and froze. The breeze seemed to utter some sort of spiritual incantation that carried neither pitch nor rhythm. Something about the landscape seemed familiar, but at the same time, none of it did. It was all wrong.

The pockets of trees revealed subtle hills beyond, while jagged mountains towered over the sage-ridden grasslands. If she was thirteen years old, this could be somewhere near Island Park. The memory of the trip tickled her subconscious mind, provoking further thought. For the first time in years, mom had allowed her to spend time with her dad. Together, they'd travelled to Island Park for camping. No friends, no mother, no step-mother—just father and daughter. She'd found that she loved spending time with him. She didn't understand why mom was so hesitant to let her go.

Camping. Of course. There had to be a nearby campground and presumably, dad was out looking for her already. She spun in a slow circle to observe the land around her. No smoke drifted up from behind thickets of pine. Odors of bitter sage and rustic pine permeated the warm, humid atmosphere. She blinked in the sunlight. This landscape was devoid of human activity, other than herself and—and her captor.

Terror gripped her. The breeze whispered again. She stared into the trees as her heart rate escalated. The silence and the beauty of nature was one thing, but she was not alone. A pinecone dropped from a nearby tree and culminated in a hollow clatter against the needle-strewn ground. And then a shadow moved. She forced her eyes to focus, but the shadow had merged into deeper shade behind a thick tamarack.

Instinctively, she ran in the same direction she'd been walking. Descending the gravelly incline was easy; looking behind her was not. No one pursued her. She stumbled but regained her footing. A stream of sweat coalesced at her bangs, intensifying the glare and heat of the sun. Adrenaline was giving her a workout.

It took more than two minutes for her mind to conclude that the intruder to her dream world was either imagined or not near enough to pose a real threat. She stopped running and leaned over to pant in a shallow ditch where a stray sage grew. Another grove of pines gently brushed against the azure sky three hundred yards in front of her where the road doglegged left.

The gravel dug into her feet. She looked up and winced. Then she began to stare at the trees. The shadow lurked there, looming as large and grizzled as ever. He stood at rest against a slender aspen and studied her. A tear squeezed itself from her eye. She darted into a patch of sage, zigzagged, stumbled down a steep embankment, and flung face-first into a patch of sooty dirt. She rolled over, groping at her painful knee. A single sapling grew next to a fallen, sawed-off log. The remains of a cold, ashen fire ring marred the ground next to her. Was this the campsite where she and her father had been?

Where was the car? Where was the tent? Where was he?

"Dad!" Her voice sounded oddly hollow as if composed of only the memory of her voice. "Dad, where are you? Dad? DAD!"

The wind whispered a precursor to her answer.

"Right here, sweetheart," a low voice grumbled.

Her heart leapt. She turned and faced the shadow. His mangy hair framed his face in otherworldly contempt, which somehow fostered only icy strands of reality. The world around him spun into chambers of gray, like blanketing thunder clouds with no end in sight.

She screamed and ran anywhere but here. But she didn't make it far. A stray remnant of firewood sent her stumbling back to the earth.

He seized her throat as she tried to claw away from him. His grip was vice-like and insane. He flung her forward as if she was nothing more than a tiny doll. She flipped several feet through the air and landed on her shoulder.

Again he came at her, this time wielding what appeared to be an uprooted tree trunk. Growling indistinguishable comments aimed at how pathetic she seemed in his...*shadow,* he seemed to smile. But it was cold and merciless. He stepped forward, about to kill her, but then—

Taleah's eyes snapped open. Her breathing was heavy and erratic. A series of chills seemed to douse her entire body with ice water. Her eyes darted in every direction before coming to focus on a deep shadow etched into the night. The shadow moved. Taleah uttered a nervous, wavering whimper that should have been an outright scream.

Though her hands and feet were still bound, she thrashed in violent spasms to worm away from him. He approached. The night darkened his shadow, and then his eyes appeared as faint white slits that seemed cold and opaque. They reflected no light.

"No. N-n-no!"

"Relax my darling," he growled. His voice was steady and firm, but sterile.

"No!"

"You'll find it'll suit you." He seemed to back away a half-step.

Her muscles remained tense, but she ceased struggling. She avoided focusing on him. Her father had taught her to focus on the solution rather than the problem. Her captor was the problem. Avoiding eye contact, while not offering much relief, proved a method of focusing on a solution. For now, the only viable solution was to look away. He could not look so menacing when she refused to look at him at all.

Upon observing her subdued body language, he exhaled. The sound resembled a sigh, but more calculated and less submissive. "That's the spirit."

"Don't...don't talk to me."

He chuckled. "A good idea, but a tactic others have failed at. Problem was, they went crazy."

"You're crazy."

"I'm not crazy, sweetheart—"

"Don't call me that."

"I'm resourceful." He finished and carved a gap in the conversation long enough to allow the elusive presence of reality to at last sink in.

She eyed the black shape of a pinecone on the ground. Darkness coiled its way around the tree trunks like black serpents in search of the moonlight. A humid draft descended into the forest and her muscles tensed. She trembled.

"I wonder what your father would have to say 'bout that."

She didn't answer. Tears rolled down her cheeks and dripped to her collar.

"Reggie always was clever. In too deep now."

"He's coming for me. He's gonna find me."

Another cold chuckle. "Thought that topic might come up. I don't doubt it. Not at all." His shadow loomed in the darkness, growing and leaning in on her. "But he's walking into a trap, just like last time."

"A..." She intended to coerce him into explaining his point by responding with a question but decided that his comment didn't justify response. She squirmed against the ropes and scooted through the dirt until her back rested against a lodge pole. A spasm caused her neck to flinch.

"He didn't tell you about that night, it seems. He shoulda died. Shot me instead."

"And you...got...away with murder."

"Not yet." He paused. His voice began to drone as if he were deep in thought but retained its gravelly texture.

The pattern of his speech was unsettling. She shifted her focus upward into the canopy. Thousands of distant eyes stared down at the scene, providing just the proper silent audience. She exerted every ounce of energy she could muster into taking charge of the situation. She leaned forward and let her gaze fall on a stump of wood at the shadow's feet.

"He almost missed," her captor continued. "But he got just close enough to derail my plan of escape. All the while the FBI runs around on their hapless manhunt..."

"They'll never find a *man*."

"Hope not."

"Go...to...hell," she whispered.

"That's not a new demand."

"He won't miss next time," she said. "He'll put one through your head while I watch."

Silence resumed but lasted for less than 30 seconds. "That's not like you."

"Now he knows where to aim, because he knows you'll run like a coward." She exhaled sharply and struggled against the ropes. Her motion was careless and too calm. Instead of offering hope of freedom, her struggle only served to kick up a tiny puff of dust from beneath the fallen needles.

"If that's true you ain't got nothin' to worry 'bout."

A sharp stone pierced her hand. A tiny yelp issued from her mouth, but she suppressed it before it could gain enough steam to be audible against the whispering pines. She grasped the rock and ran her thumb along its serrated edge. If it could draw blood, it would be sharp enough to loosen the binding at her wrist. She mentally kept her motion slow and methodical so that she could spring him with a surprise he couldn't recover from.

The shadow retreated a step or two, falling back into thicker darkness. He reached down and grasped something that could have been a weapon.

The sound of rattling and crunching paper forced its way into the humid wind before dying. He approached her again.

"You'll need something to eat, so you'll have the strength to do what I ask you to."

She swore. "You need me to be weak."

He chuckled again. "Just as smart as your pathetic father."

"Don't you dare call him that. You don't even know him."

"I know him," he corrected. "And you. I've spent years studying."

"You don't know jack." She reached deep inside herself to withdraw a string of profanity unlike any she'd uttered before. She forcefully kicked at a pinecone just beyond the reach of her bound feet.

"Jack. Must be what you call that fool Willis."

"Wha—?" She couldn't bring herself to intone surprise, but the freedom of her speech had already done the damage. She was becoming weak. He was breaking her down without even trying.

"I told you." He scoffed. "And if your father is smart, he'll enlist the fool's help. That's another fellow that refused to die, but at least he got to burn."

"You're so much smarter and so much stronger than my dad," she mocked. "And you're doing this to prove it? Even if they catch you?"

"If I was so worried about being caught, I wouldn't have made it so easy for 'em."

Another curse word ejected from her mouth, but she didn't care. Strong or not, her determination would propel her will to outlast his. Yet his strength seemed unlimited.

"What do I want?" He let his voice trail away and shifted. "Let's just say..."

"You want to murder my father. But your trap isn't going to work."

"All traps work if they have live bait, sweetheart."

"Don't...you...*dare!*"

A cold laugh escaped his lips and wafted on the breeze like a foul, pervasive scent seeking new victims. "He beats the FBI, it'll be just another unfortunate hiking accident, and I go underground. And if he doesn't..." His laughter intensified. "No one'll ever see you or me again."

Though his words touched her with chords of explicit rage, they intoned undeniable threads of truth. Taleah silently gasped, wiggled against the rope, and stared at the food he'd placed at her feet. She was starving but would not give him the satisfaction of winning his ridiculous game.

His heavy footsteps retreated. The shadow once again morphed into the surrounding blackness. The stars peered down with baleful silence. More tears splashed onto her cheeks. The light from the stars began to flicker and fade as if turning to negative pulsars ticking down to extinction. Similarly, the glimmer of hope would soon become nothing more than a vapor of human though without definition or form.

10
Inception

Time was an illusion Reggie could ill afford. Its passage fused his heart with a concoction of molten rage and torment. When he awoke from sparse, but dark dreams, his heart exploded with tremors of confusion. He blinked twice, rolled toward Rebekah, and pretended to attempt sleep. Though his muscles soured on the concept of getting up, he suddenly found himself wide awake. There was no time to lose.

The blue, pre-dawn glow of the room emitted a provocative, sullen moment of reflection. Reggie softly kissed Rebekah's lips and swung his feet to the floor. He rubbed his eyes and temples. Visions of Art Rassine torturing Taleah served as the catalyst to spring him from the bed. He punched his fist into his hand and walked to the bathroom.

The man behind the mirror looked as if the night had frayed him beyond recognition. His cheeks were long, and his frown punctuated. Deep lines dug into his forehead and bruised the corners of his eyes with shadow. Reggie peered into his own dark eyes and turned away. There was nothing worse than seeing himself stretched to the brink of demise. The darkness that so suddenly had taken residence in his soul was breathtaking and disheartening. He thought about it and attempted to will the darkness away, but a small voice in the corner of his mind altered his reasoning.

There will always be darkness.

"And I need light," he mumbled.

Use the dark.

Reggie looked back into the mirror. A spark ignited his eyes. Although he still looked dreadful, the echo of fire in his pupils constructed a degree of hope. Instead of sorrow, his emotion exuded contempt; instead of hopelessness, his mind was set on resolve.

He washed his face in cold water and then halfheartedly brushed his teeth. Before returning to the bedroom, he shaved quickly. His suitcase was ready, packed with only the bare essentials.

After unplugging his phone from the charger, he dressed and slowly descended the stairs. His first call, while preparing a hasty breakfast, was to Willis.

"Umpire," Willis said. "For hire," he added.

"Bottom of the ninth," Reggie grunted. "Down four to one. Time to get going."

A long pause drifted between them. Reggie believed that Willis was uttering a silent sigh while staring at the alarm clock.

"It's 5:30 a-freaking-m."

Instead of vocally urging him to action, Reggie emitted a low growl.

"But I get it. First thing we need to do is get us a gun."

"Not likely," Reggie said. "What time do you think the pawn shop opens?"

"Eight," Willis answered. "There's supposed to be a background check involved, but this place is known to bend the rules once in a while. We *are* in the Gun State."

Reggie understood the humor Willis intended, but consciously chose to ignore it. "Are you packed?"

"I got what I need. You too, or did your wife pack your bag?"

"Funny," Reggie panned. He leaned back in the chair and flexed his arm muscles. He didn't have anything to add, so he allowed silence to resume.

"So we gas the car, grab some food, make some calls before the pawn shop opens. After we shake down the place, we hit the road. Is that the sketch?"

"The sooner the better. We got a lot of driving to do."

"Next question," Willis said. "Where the hell we supposed to go?"

Willis had just touched on a point Reggie had spent the better part of the night pondering. Where to start indeed? He had some ideas. Rassine was but a fragment of the extensive Idaho wilderness. There were countless nooks and mountain retreats in which he could hide. Trying to narrow down exactly where he would go was akin to tracking down an alley cat loose in Tokyo.

He shrugged. "Maybe we start at Lance Harrison's ranch. He's got a couple of hideouts there. I doubt he'd risk it, but we might get a clue as to where he would go. We can also visit his old cabin. The FBI knows where the property is. Rebekah and Anna should be able to get that info without any problem."

"Hacking the FBI?" Willis asked. "You think that's even possible?"

"It will have to be. If they don't budge, she'll have to dig deeper. Rebekah's good at this stuff."

"I know," Willis chuckled. "Every time I called a strike in that championship game, she'd already used a laser to measure the pitch."

"I see. But maybe your vision isn't perfect."

"The Ump is always right," Willis lamented. "You have to have some final word, or the rules become meaningless and fall by the wayside. I don't have to tell you twice what breaking the rules entails."

"You're still on about that trespassing excursion eleven years ago?"

"You got caught. Consequences ain't always pretty."

"Whatever." Reggie stroked his chin and thought about it. Rebekah would succeed at getting information not because she was good, but because it was what she did. When indebted to someone, her drive to succeed in her endeavor waxed stronger than almost any hurdle that could be haphazardly lobbed at her.

"Then where?"

"We use our intelligence to follow leads. That's what the FBI is supposed to be doing but they suck at it. We're going to find Taleah and Rassine. A hundred bucks says we do before the FBI."

"What if the FBI doesn't have any leads?"

"We find our own."

Willis sighed. "This could take over a week with all that busy work, even with your wives helping us."

Reggie allowed himself a moment to think about how Willis had just offered a silly little retort on his favorite false aspect of the Mormon Church—polygamy. By now the joke was tired and worn out, but he used it with such grace and fluidity that its surprise was enough to draw a smile on any normal day. Today, however, was not a normal day. Reggie frowned.

"And then we still have the elements and the night to battle. Long process."

"You're right," Reggie said slowly. "Time is of the essence."

Willis paused for a second, allowing the essence of his emotion to punctuate the conversation. "That's what they always say."

Instead of furthering the conversation on time and how it seemed like an illusion, Reggie let silence carve a crater in the discussion. Neither of them hung up the phone for at least thirty seconds. Willis seemed to be concocting a reassuring sentence but couldn't arrange the words. Instead of speaking at all, he let the seconds pass.

"So hurry up," Reggie said.

Willis remained silent, then started to utter a sentence, and then fell silent again.

"Spit it out," Reggie bolted.

"I just...this requires careful planning. Like what the boss, old Brickshaw, always used to say." He imitated the boss's gravelly speech perfectly as he explained. "To do it the right way, you have to be prepared." Then after a few seconds' hesitation, he added. "Isn't that a Boy Scout thing?"

"Sure," Reggie verified.

"Yet you still want to hastily run off to save the day."

"Someone's got to and hell if the FBI will." Reggie paused, collected a deep breath, exhaled, and then continued. "Sometimes haste is the only alternative to watching from the sidelines, or in your case, behind the catcher."

"Haste makes waste, my friend. Ancient Chinese proverb."

"No it isn't," Reggie argued.

"Whatever. The point is, the waste might be your life. Or Taleah's."

"What?"

Willis sighed. "Think about this. Without planning carefully, you might just walk into a trap. Provoke Rassine to hurt Taleah, or both. Rash decisions are your worst enemy."

"I don't want to hear it," Reggie growled.

"Just trying to help. Besides, isn't that what you signed me up for?"

Willis had a point. Instead of verbally expressing how right his friend was, he shifted gears.

"I need to make a couple more calls before we leave. Get your suitcase, a breakfast bar, a coffee, and get over here."

"Will do," Willis said.

Reggie doused the conversation with a grunt, looked at his watch, and decided to wait a few moments before waking Rebekah and Anna. He shook his head. Thought invaded. Why did Willis always have to be right? While true that some advice was built upon solid principles and other tips riddled with holes in logic, Reggie's friends were always full of wise counsel. Even as far back as Ted Brickshaw's *'don't let this be the reason'* remark and Richard Kerrin's spiritual promptings, Reggie was being steered in the right direction. Whether their words were helpful or not, they were true. All Reggie had to do was listen.

He buried his face in his palms and uttered a quick prayer asking for protection, but most importantly pleading for Teleah's safety.

Then he grabbed his phone, climbed the stairs, and sat on the bed next to Rebekah. She always looked beautiful when she slept. Reggie leaned to kiss her just as her eyes opened. She tried to smile, but the pressure of the situation prevented it.

"Good morning," she said.

"Maybe not," Reggie admitted. "Ready to do this?"

She shrugged.

Reggie looked away as he dialed Anna's number. When it began to ring, he put it on speaker. She answered after four rings. As if strained by a long night of tears, her voice sounded rough and erratic.

"I'm heading out in a little while," he started. "What I want from both of you is cooperation and teamwork. I want to know what the FBI is up to, where their investigation is leading them, and whatever isolated ranch they intend to search. You both have outstanding computer skills, so I think a little bit of digging will go a long way."

"Illegal digging," Rebekah noted.

"They'll figure it out," Anna lamented. "Eventually. It's... a felony?"

"Are you saying you don't want to help get Taleah back?" Reggie scolded.

Silence. Reggie had touched the right nerve.

"But as long as it all ends well, it's a forgivable offense," Rebekah noted.

"Will it end well?" Anna asked, sounding unsure whether or not she wanted to hear Reggie's answer.

"I don't know," Reggie concluded. "Problem is, I don't know what Rassine is up to or what his real motive is. Maybe he knows I'll come after him, maybe not. I just have to think two steps ahead of him. Which, I'm afraid to say, is easier said than done."

"Got that right," Anna said.

"Call this the execution phase of my plan," Reggie continued. "I think you can figure out how to listen on the FBI's radio frequency and maybe even tap their calls. I'm hoping this hasn't boiled down to volleys of emails dictating action to each other, because that's when nothing gets done. I'll need some immediate action."

"Okay," Rebekah sighed. "Is there a certain order you want your information in?"

"I want to know what the status of the Lance Harrison ranch is, and then I want to know if they have set up camp at Rassine's original dwelling. On those two places I want every bit of evidence they have not shared with us."

"I think we can do that," Rebekah said. "The FBI uses a lot of technology and their firewalls are not as solid as those of the CIA or NSA."

"Still stronger that everyone else," Anna said. "Even for someone as skilled as you."

"I know it won't be easy," Reggie said. "Don't waste time trying to cover your tracks. If they're going to investigate you, they're going to investigate you. But they have to get through Rassine first. If my plan goes off correctly, I'll get to Taleah before the FBI has a chance to botch the whole thing."

"I know you will," Anna said. "She loves you. Trusts you."

"So do I," Rebekah whispered.

"Get on it," Reggie said with a stroke of finality.

Rebekah hung up the phone, sat up, and stared with a glum expression. She shifted her shoulders and waited.

After a moment's pause, Reggie scooted closer to her. He held her in a close embrace that somehow could not warm his soul or last long enough. He shuddered at the thought of being alone in the wild without her. While true that he had Willis, his best friend was no match for the closest love he'd ever known, with the exception of Taleah. He didn't want to think about the task, but it was impossible to ignore.

"I don't want you to go," Rebekah whispered.

"I know. But I have to."

"I know you do, just…"

Reggie waited, but she seemed to be taking her time constructing the proper phrasing so that what she wanted to say would have the desired effect.

"Just…be careful," she finished.

Reggie nodded.

"And use the help you've got. A good friend can go a long way. Remember that."

A wild idea smashed its way into Reggie's mind, yet instead of cowering from it, he welcomed it. He studied it with careful consideration. If the FBI wasn't going to be forthcoming, what better help would there be than a friend in law enforcement?

He picked up his phone and dialed the number to the Adams County Sheriff's Office by memory.

A woman picked up after two rings. "Adams County, how may I direct your call?"

"Deputy Smith Monaghan," Reggie said, his nerves calm.

"One moment." She put him on hold.

Rebekah stared at him as if with pondering disbelief.

He frowned.

Smith answered the phone after at least 45 seconds. His voice sounded like forced patience. "This is Deputy Monaghan."

"Smith, this is Reggie St. Clair."

A long pause cut a seam in the conversation like a jagged knife. "Reggie. Long time. What can I do for you?"

"I need your help," Reggie started. His blood pressure ticked up a notch and heat rose to the top of his forehead. "My little girl has been…taken. Art Rassine is the culprit."

"Rassine? That's terrible. Haven't heard a thing about him in years. All I know is the FBI's treating it like a cold case now."

"It's not cold anymore," Reggie said. "It's red hot."

"And the FBI, they know?"

"That's why I need your help. You're about the only person in law enforcement I can trust. My wife is keeping an eye on the feds, but it wouldn't help to have your support as well."

"On watching the FBI?"

"And tracking my movements as I search for Rassine and my daughter."

Silence. It made Reggie want to scream. "This is a bad idea, Reggie."

"Everyone says that. But put yourself in my shoes. What else can I do? Wait for the FBI, who is sitting on their hands and expecting Rassine to fall into their lap while Rassine rapes and murders Taleah?"

More silence.

"What? Talk to me!"

"I know what you're going through, Reggie. I can help if I can believe beyond a reasonable doubt that Rassine is an Adams County."

"I don't care about your jurisdiction."

"Sheriff Toyovich does. He's retiring after this year. He might look the other way because of that, but I'll still end up in hot water with whoever is elected to replace him."

"It's all about you, isn't it?"

"Of course not."

"I'm going to find her," Reggie continued. "I don't give a damn about whether you think I should or not. Just back me up. Leave the county if you have to."

After another long pause, Smith sighed. "I'm not gonna stop you."

"Got that right."

"And 'to serve and protect'—that's the law enforcement creed. So technically if I'm not protecting you, I'm not doing my job."

Reggie allowed himself a moment for that to sink in.

"Reggie, keep this on the downlow. Don't tell anyone else you're going. Don't give the FBI any reason to investigate you. Be careful."

"As careful as I can be."

"You think Rassine has any idea you're coming?"

"Maybe," Reggie said.

"Don't go alone. Take a friend."

"I've already thought of that," Reggie said.

Smith paused. "Let me guess. Willis Ralston?"

"Yes," Reggie said tightly.

"I guess I need a word with him, then. I'll give him a call right away and tell him to take good care of you."

Reggie listened for more.

"One more thing, Reggie. When you're hunting through forest, leave some space between you and Willis. Keep in contact and within shouting distance and keep a good line of sight. That way if Rassine surprises one of you, he can't get both of you."

"Fine," Reggie said.

After a moment of waiting and exchanging goodbyes, Reggie dropped his phone to his lap. He pulled Rebekah closer to him in one last embrace and tried to form more meaning behind his whispered 'I love you.' It was a simple phrase, but without emotion, nothing more than three small words built the sentence. With Rebekah it always meant more than that. Same with Taleah. But somehow, saying it this time meant less permanence and used less heart.

She sensed it. A tear rolled down her cheek. She whispered back, "I love you too."

He pulled away from her with a blank expression spanning his face. Reggie grasped her hand and placed it on her knee before he stood up to descend the stairs.

The journey on which he was about to embark was like defining two sides of a coin. The familiar life with Rebekah and Taleah began to spin away from view, replaced by the shadow of desperation and despair. Rassine was the darker side. Tails. This task promised to be much more dangerous than searching the woods for clues to the murders of three women he'd never even met. And since Taleah was, in contrast, his whole world, the trek would meander into much darker territory. Whether or not Reggie anticipated that, it was coming. Some tales had darker endings, but alas, he could only hope that this coin revolved back to heads.

11

Ignition

Like tan and ecru brush strokes painted against a coiled sky, the golden grasslands swayed in the west wind. As Reggie and Willis traveled north, the grasslands intermittently wove between wild sagebrush and flat farmlands. The mountains loomed on all sides, provocative, yet immovable. As with the lay of the land, Reggie had little power to control the course of events leading to this moment. Instead of gently guiding his life to where it was intended to go, Reggie found himself a passenger simply watching the events unfurl around him.

This trek was pummeling Reggie with bad memories. As if the inside of the Adams County building in Council wasn't bad enough, the promise of once again finding himself near Lance Harrison's Ranch was yet another threat to his fickle sense of comfort. Reggie stared at the gun in his lap. The last time he had handled a firearm he was aiming at Art Rassine and pulling the trigger. He remembered the pain of that moment well.

Disturbingly, the pain was not caused by shooting Rassine, nor by watching blood seeping from Rassine's side. Prior to the shot, Rassine had surprised Reggie by hurling a huge chunk of granite into his back. The despair over his divorce and being forbidden to see Taleah had complicated matters.

These days, Reggie somehow found himself to be a simpler man. The valleys and peaks of his emotions were less defined and the slopes not as steep.

Willis was maneuvering the car through a series of sharp bends in a steep, basaltic river canyon that gave way to green farmlands with stunning mountain vistas surrounding. Rolling hills folded the landscape near the bases of the mountains as if warning of imminent turmoil.

Peering to the gun, Willis asked, "You remember how to shoot that thing?"

Reggie vacantly nodded and reached a hand to his temple. "Do you?"

"Nothing to it. I still don't understand why they'd only sell us one. It isn't like we were about to knock off a bank or shoot up a mall, right? Even if one of us does look the part."

"What's that supposed to mean?" Reggie glared into nothingness.

"Flip that visor down. The owner's manual claims there is a mirror behind it. Look in the mirror and tell me what you see."

"You think I want to play your game?" Reggie meant to sound cool but came off as hot and aggravated.

"Then let me try to describe what you look like."

"Can't wait," Reggie said sarcastically.

"You look like a pitcher staring down an oh-two count with the bases loaded."

"Brilliant," Reggie lied. "Do I have to listen to these stupid baseball metaphors all day?"

Willis took a moment to think about it. "You remember last time when we were driving to the helipad in Payette? You looked miserable then, too. I'm trying to cheer you up, but..."

"But my attitude is like the mountains," Reggie finished for him.

"Was about to say you're not in the mood for it. I'd be inclined to agree with your version if I understood what the hell it means."

"Forget about it," Reggie said.

Silence stretched for at least five miles. Reggie stared blankly at the gun between stolen glances at the mountain grandeur. Just watching the landscape change was like a page torn from one of his nightmares, only this one was real. The only way Reggie could describe the events of eleven years ago was as a bad dream whose memory faded slowly.

Reggie had changed since pulling the trigger that night. His life had wandered back on course. Once again he knew where he was going and how to get there. Destination was a metaphor Richard Kerrin had used on Reggie, and Reggie had played along. Now, the idea came full circle. Somehow, the destination described in that conversation was the beginning of it all.

Knotted. Rassine had carved that into one of his 'Era Sinistra' clues...

Reggie's phone started ringing. He quickly extracted it from his pocket and glanced at the caller identification. It was Rebekah.

"Hey honey," Reggie said.

"The FBI has been snooping around Harrison's place. Apparently a couple owns it now. They're guarding the gates in case Rassine feels inclined to revisit. As far as we can gather, there is no activity at Rassine's old cabin."

Reggie considered the news and frowned.

"They are also questioning a store owner near Missoula who claims Rassine was a recent customer, though there is no video footage proving it."

"Right now, they're pretty much forced into believing it, though," Reggie surmised.

"Exactly. They are operating on that premise. So they're backtracking all nearby routes into Idaho."

"They thinking his port of entry is Salmon or the route down to Lewiston?"

"Can't tell. If I was to guess I'd say the Lewiston route. I'll listen to the chatter and try to verify that in the next few hours."

"Good work."

"How is the drive?"

"Scenic," Reggie answered. "Since we're having this conversation, Willis hasn't killed me yet, so we have that going for us."

"Are you still headed to the ranch?"

"Probably," Reggie admitted. "There's a lot of land there and I know of a few ways to access that property without going through the front gate."

"Be careful, my love," she pleaded.

"Sure," Reggie said. "Keep up the good work and keep me posted."

"I will. I love you."

You too," he affirmed.

When Reggie shoved the phone back in his pocket Willis stared at him between glances at the road. Reggie didn't say anything for more than five minutes. Instead, he watched the landscape change with the miles. The Seven Devils Mountains loomed to the northwest, while the backside slopes of Tamarack Mountain prodded at the eastern skyline behind a range of foothills. He admired this spectacle until Willis slowed to enter the tiny town of Midvale.

Even at twenty-five miles-per-hour, the town was gone in a flash and Willis was once again accelerating to 65. He rounded a slight bend in the highway and glanced back to Reggie to wait for an explanation but didn't verbally ask for one.

"The FBI is staking out Harrison's old ranch," Reggie droned.

"Sounds delicious," Willis joked.

Reggie rolled his eyes.

"They expecting Rassine to show up with Taleah or something?"

Massaging his temple, Reggie stared at the road ahead. "He's not that stupid. The FBI might be, but Rassine is going to steer clear of that place."

"Why, do you think?"

"Something is bothering me about this whole thing. You know last time, we found the blood-soaked recliner, the 'era sinistra' notes, the compass—and it all happened within a few days. We're talking about a man who purposefully leaves clues behind. Yet here he is, completely silent."

"Maybe they're not looking hard enough," Willis replied. "Besides, they found Taleah's phone and her ribbon. That's evidence."

"But it wasn't intentional," Reggie argued.

"Rassine could have kept her phone."

"That wouldn't do him any good. Probably has less chance of being caught without it. Do you watch any of those crime shows on TV? They can always track cellphone signals. Him leaving the phone wasn't a 'catch me if you can' taunt. It was a well-conceived evasive maneuver."

"What about the ribbon?" Willis asked.

"Rassine didn't leave that behind, Taleah did. Either way it wasn't intentional. What I'm looking for is intentional clues—the ones meant to stand out."

"Maybe we'll only find them in the woods," Willis guessed.

"Yeah but where do we start?"

Willis focused on the highway for a few minutes, using his keen line of reasoning to build a response. Reggie stared at him briefly, but then allowed himself a moment to stare into oblivion. Staring into nothing sometimes brought a sense of relief or even peace, but not today. Today, the fragments of his mind were assembled into a monolith of chaos. Winds and black clouds were coiling in the dark corners of his mind.

"You know, Rassine probably expects us to visit Harrison's ranch. Figures we're at least that smart. Maybe it's a false lead. If it is, don't you think we'll be able to find something?"

"I think Rassine wants to disappear forever," Reggie said, his voice drained of color and his tone flat.

"So what's his end game?"

"I don't know," Reggie admitted. "Rassine is nothing if not confusing."

Willis grinned. "He's like a woman."

Reggie forced a smile, but Willis could always tell the difference between a 'faux grin' and a real one.

"You didn't think that was funny," Willis commented. "But give it time. I'm betting a real one illuminates this car in three...two...one..."

But it never did. Reggie reached into darkness on all sides. It bled surreal colors and frightening shadows into a single potion of despair.

Use the dark, Reg.

"To disappear," Reggie mumbled.

Willis snapped his focus to Reggie so sharply that it should have given him whiplash. "Excuse me?"

"What?" Reggie bolted.

"You're talking to yourself again. That's not a good sign."

"Sure it is," Reggie lied. "The best people do it all the time. It helps us retain mental clarity by separating us from the outside world and, by extension, our own problems. If we can't focus on solutions, all we'll see is the problem."

"You're bright," Willis said, "but bloody horrifying."

"I get that a lot, especially from you."

Willis smiled. "I'll give you that one. But what is the solution?"

Wispy trails of cirrus clouds floated high above the landscape in an expanse of deep blue. The sunshine was bright, even energetic.

Though Reggie was weary from the drive, he was hardly tired. He watched stands of lodge poles roll past, remembering how they looked like three-dimensional barcodes bleached with the sun's rays. After allowing himself a moment to close his eyes, he looked up and stared at the gravel road.

Willis was pulling to a stop about a mile from the gates to the Harrison ranch. Because the road crested a subtle incline and veered right, the gate was not in view. Here there was no sign of FBI presence.

"This a good place to stop?" Willis questioned.

"As good as any," Reggie answered.

"I don't like it. They come out, they'll see the car, identify me as the owner, connect me to you, and then come to arrest us. Only this time we'll go to federal prison."

"Got a better idea?" Reggie asked.

"How about the road to Rassine's old hangout, the what-did-you-call it?"

"Sanctuary? Interesting idea. And I bet that's not on the FBI's watch list, either."

Willis backed into a careful three-point turn and drove down the dusty road perhaps a little too fast. During the two-mile jaunt to the abandoned logging road leading to the sanctuary, they shared little conversation.

The sanctuary was a thick grove of ponderosas surrounded by jagged rocks that punctuated the edge of a meadow-like clearing. The last time he'd ventured into this territory, Art Rassine had carefully laid a trap that snared Reggie, Willis, and the Adams County deputies. That night was dark and rainy. Chaos. Rassine had defeated all four of them. The memory of that night punctured the landscape of burdensome emotions with a needle of pure black. So much had happened, yet Reggie now seemed to recall every detail about the last conflict with Art Rassine.

His lip quivered.

The drive to end of the logging road lasted between five and ten minutes. Reggie extracted the phone to check for messages the way he usually did and then slid it back into his pocket before exiting the Subaru.

"Ready to do this?" Willis asked.

Reggie shrugged.

As if reading his mind, Willis nodded. "I think we'll be a little better prepared this time." He opened his trunk and examined his stash of laser survey equipment, accurate to within six centimeters over 300 yards. The tripods were tucked in the corner of his trunk, but he ignored them.

Mixed in with the array of surveying tools was a coil of rope, a backpack, two canteens, and a first aid kit. Reggie was impressed with Willis' preparation. It seemed almost as if time had taught him to be a better outdoorsman. Eleven years ago, Willis hardly knew the wild existed.

"Came a little over-prepared this time. Can't risk a disaster like last time."

"Nice assembly," Reggie said.

They carefully stuffed the bag with the canteens, the rope, and the survey equipment. Upon securing his canteen, Reggie discovered a pair of small flashlights. He withdrew one of them and examined it.

"Fresh batteries?"

"Sure," Willis said. "Just in case. But I sure as hell hope we're out of here by nightfall."

"Good thinking. It seems like you thought of everything."

"Got the gun?"

Reggie placed his hand over his pants pocket and nodded slowly.

"Let's go hunting."

They shared sparse conversation for the next ten minutes. By Reggie's best recollection, the sanctuary was located in a wide gully between larger hills just over a mile beyond the end of the logging road. He didn't remember the way, but even if he had, the last trek to this locale was under the cover of dusk. Willis guided them through a series of bends around fallen logs and slabs of granite.

Cutting through the undergrowth thankfully proved to be easier than Reggie had anticipated. A recent thunderstorm had carved trails of runoff erosion through the foliage on the hill. The remnant of the rutted road had long-since disappeared, but the ruts were still visible in some places. They followed these ruts to the top of a ridge overlooking a wide valley. Reggie stepped onto a rock at the precipice, which formed a shallow cliff, and gazed over the valley.

This was the place.

Willis led the way down the incline, stepping carefully around pockets of poison ivy and underbrush. They zigzagged between dozens of fallen trees. After five more minutes, they arrived at the edge of the clearing. They quietly made their way across the clearing toward the dense grove of trees. Taking this precaution seemed useless to Reggie because he already knew Rassine wasn't here. Because of the length of travel, Rassine had to have been driving a car or truck. There weren't a lot of places in these woods to stash a vehicle, especially under the watchful eye of the FBI.

They stepped over the chunks of jagged granite and immersed themselves in the deep shade. In this grove, only a few patches of desert grass poked up through the needle-strewn floor. Reggie swept away eleven years of debris, searching for footprints or any other sign of human activity. Following his example, Willis began to do the same.

Reggie watched him through his peripheral vision. He crouched lower to the ground and stared at the roots of the trees, the sharp protrusions of granite, and the countless rocks and pinecones that littered the ground. This place showed no obvious sign of human presence.

But what about animal presence?

Reggie swept the confines of the grove twice before coming to the conclusion that countless animals had used this place as shelter from the elements. He groaned as if in pain.

After a few minutes, Willis stopped moving. Reggie understood what this might have meant and turned toward him. He was staring at something at eye-level on the closest tree.

A glint of reflected light caught Reggie's eye. There was no mistaking it. He stood and approached the tree.

Strung between tiny twigs protruding from the bark was a white string. A small metal clip that resembled a modified bobby pin dangled from the center of the string. And attached to the metal was a shiny stone. Reggie studied it. A diamond.

"Son of a bitch!" Reggie yelled. "He's been here. And we missed him."

"How long, do you think?" Willis's voice droned flat and careless.

"Don't know," Reggie answered.

Willis turned in a circle and then slithered between the trunks of two trees. He stopped again, withdrew a knife from his pocket, and carved a chunk of bark from the tree. He eyed the bark for a moment and then looked into Reggie's face. A healthy dose of perplexed silence towered over the conversation.

"What do you make of this, Reg?"

Reggie grabbed it. A tiny shape of a house was tanned against a smooth surface on the bark.

"It was loose," Willis said. "And a corner of paper was sticking out from behind it."

"Let's see the paper," Reggie demanded.

"Nothing on it. Just used to mark the spot. Think this is something he left behind way back when?"

Reggie repeated his request to see the paper. Willis reached down and picked the tiny sheet of paper from the ground. It was devoid of yellowing, was still crisp, and carried no sign of water saturation.

"No," Reggie said in response to Willis's question. "It's fresh."

"What does it mean?"

"Nothing," Reggie said. "It's just another damned clue. We should know all about his clues by now."

"We're not going to follow it?"

"We don't have a choice," Reggie replied. "If we want to find either him or Taleah. Tips from the FBI will only get us so far."

"Where do we go next?"

Reggie thought about it a moment. He stared into the darkness of the shade. Desperation was beginning to fill the darkness of his spirit. *Desperation*, and he'd covered so little ground. A pulsing headache began to hammer away at the inside of his skull like a wild heartbeat attempting to flee into the night. But the shell of Reggie's inner emotion was far too dense for it to escape. A tear of rage dripped from his eye. His lip quivered again.

"You're scaring me again," Willis said. He was watching Reggie coil like a serpent rearing for attack.

Reggie said nothing and let only the darkness of his soul seep out into the shadow. There was nothing left to find here. They'd found everything Rassine intended them to find. The fact that Rassine had correctly guessed Reggie would visit his sanctuary was disturbing. Rassine was playing him again and only a rash decision founded upon anger would break him from the spell.

Willis stepped toward the entrance to the grove, indicating that it was time to move on. Reggie followed, slowly at first, and then let the passion of his search arouse his muscles into more structured action.

The hike back to the car was uneventful and quiet for most of the trip. Heeding Smith's advice, Reggie stayed between fifty and one hundred feet of Willis, keeping him within his line of sight at all times.

"What do you suppose he meant by it?" Willis asked. "Another one of his 'catch me if you can' taunts?"

"Possibly," Reggie replied, "But I can't see how his procedure and intent can be the same this time."

"Taleah's unique," Willis agreed. "But don't you think he was daring us to find him way back then?"

"No," Reggie said. "I've had eleven years to think it over. I think his clues were nothing more than a game of deception."

"So why don't you think this is deception?"

Reggie thought about it. "It just doesn't feel like it. Something seems wrong about this whole thing and I'm going to figure it out."

"You think his game could be revenge this time," Willis stated.

"I do."

"Maybe he's luring us."

"I don't doubt he is."

"But why?"

"Don't know, but we have no choice but to pursue because not doing it will only end badly."

"True," Willis agreed. "But following these clues could end even worse."

"It's the 'could' factor that keeps me going," Reggie said. "When you play the lottery, it's implied you *could* win, which is why people play. If the only possible result is a loss of money, nobody would buy lottery tickets."

"Sure. Except when you chain smoke, you *could* get cancer, but that doesn't seem to stop anybody. It's a different example, but a similar circumstance."

"We're dealing with life and death here," Reggie snarled. "Any chance we take is worth it."

A gap in the conversation signaled a change of course. Reggie's frown grew deeper.

After a few minutes, Willis spoke again. "Any idea what the diamond means?"

"Only that she's the most precious," Reggie said. "Priceless even. Maybe that's all, maybe not."

"You know what else is shaped like a diamond?"

A third voice answered, "A baseball field."

Reggie quickly drew the gun from his pocket but was not fast enough. A tall, athletic black man emerged from behind a tree pointing a gun squarely at him. "Drop it, St. Clair."

Reggie hesitated.

"Drop it! Or you get a bullet in your chest."

Slowly, Reggie reached down and placed the gun in the dirt at his feet. Willis appeared flabbergasted.

A second agent appeared nearby to Reggie's left. He recognized her as the agent that was in charge of the forensic team that unearthed the skeleton eleven years ago. Willis glanced to his left and smiled at her.

Agent Clark dangled a pair of handcuffs from her left hand while aiming her gun with the other hand. "You're under arrest for obstructing a federal investigation," she started.

"Let me go," Reggie growled. "Now! Or my daughter is going to die!"

Agent DeLaren cuffed Willis and the two agents approached their car. Once in the backseat, Willis whispered. "Nice job."

"Shut up."

"There's a solution to this," Willis said. "You know there is. But what is the solution to the bigger problem? The one you alluded to earlier."

Reggie gritted his teeth and narrowed his eyes as if thick black smoke was pouring from the openings of his skull. "We kill Art Rassine."

12
Centripetal

For the two minutes during which Reggie and Willis shared clipped, terse conversation, Agents DeLaren and Clark stood in front of the left front door of the vehicle and conversed quietly. Reggie strained his ears to listen but could only hear the sound of two voices.

Willis glared at him for a few moments, and then raised his eyebrows. He opened his mouth to speak but before he could utter a single word, Agent DeLaren swung open the door and kneeled in the front seat so that he was facing the captives.

For a moment, none of them spoke. DeLaren looked inquisitive and pondering. The light in his eyes was subtle, yet alarming in the fact that it revealed his interest, but not his real emotion. The man was good at hiding it, which was probably the primary reason he was a federal agent to begin with. He focused his attention on Reggie.

"Not sure what you were getting at by coming here, St. Clair," DeLaren said.

"Why should I talk to you?"

After subtly raising one shoulder, the agent's eyes darkened. "You're thinking you're going to find Art Rassine all by yourself. Be the hero. Sure that's what your daughter wants, maybe expects it too. But you're a damn fool."

Reggie felt his expression droop further. He stared at DeLaren as if the darkness were about to shoot out of his soul, launch itself at DeLaren, and then penetrate his skin. DeLaren only stared back, but in comparison, his eyes seemed blank.

"You're already shutting yourself off. That's good."

"What about this right to remain silent thing?" Willis asked with a disheartened shrug.

"You don't have to say a thing," Agent DeLaren coaxed. He glanced to Willis, then back to Reggie and continued. "Running off after Rassine ain't bravery, it's plain stupidity."

"You don't have kids," Reggie said as if choking on his own voice. "So you can't possibly understand what it's like."

"I don't," DeLaren confirmed. "I might be inclined to do the same thing, except one thing. I'm an FBI agent."

"And you won't go rogue." Reggie lowered his voice even further and looked out the window. Agent Clark was pacing back and forth in front of the car and hurriedly speaking into her phone.

"Nope. But I can help you out."

"You'd do that?" Reggie asked, the timbre of his voice rising. "Risk your career for someone you don't even know?" He was intrigued, but careful.

DeLaren narrowed his eyes and thrust his head left in a careless sweep. "Nah. Helping a brother out ain't even against the rules, per *se*. Only if that conflicts with our investigative duties. And we do intend to ensure your daughter's safety."

"Then why the hell are you sitting on your ass lecturing me and following pointless leads?"

"We're not so different from one another, know that?" DeLaren almost smiled at Reggie, but creased his lips downward at the last second.

"Whatever."

"You're so hell bent on finding Rassine, why you wasting your time searching a place you already know he isn't at? I heard about how smart you are, but damn. You don't look so convincing right now."

"Had to start somewhere," Willis interrupted. "So we started as his sanctuary."

"And we got lucky," Reggie barked.

Agent DeLaren opened his mouth to offer a retort but stopped cold with the surprise. "Say what?"

"Rassine wasn't there," Reggie explained, "but he had been. We needed a clue on where to go next, and guess what we found?"

"It wasn't lucky at all," Willis said.

"Right," Reggie agreed. "Rassine anticipated me showing up there and gave me a clue to bait me."

"Why'd he want to do that?" A skeptical frown skewed DeLaren's face.

"I don't know," Reggie said. "That part bothers me."

"So you're going to follow it anyway?" DeLaren raised his eyebrows and leaned his head back a few inches. "Still not convincing."

"Don't have a choice," Reggie replied. "Following pointless leads isn't getting me anywhere. The good news is I'm a trained surveyor, so if I have a starting point, I can follow anything."

Willis tried to smile, but winced in the sunlight that was flooding through the windshield. "He's a dangerous man."

A dull pause carved a crater the size of the Yucatan in the center of the conversation. Reggie's eyes glazed over as he continuously stared at Agent DeLaren with occasional glances to Willis. If he were to guess how he looked, 'contemptuous' would have been the first word to spring to mind.

Willis sighed, stretched his arms, and leaned back against the seat. He eyed Agent Clark amorously as she continued to pace in front of the car. Such body language made Reggie want to retch. They were wasting their time, and everyone seemed so relaxed!

After what had seemed like hours of little more than thought racing through Reggie's brain, he looked out the window away from DeLaren. Agent Clark closed her phone and stuffed it back in its holster at her hip. She briskly walked to the passenger door of the FBI vehicle. She opened the door, got situated, and then turned her head to stare at Reggie.

"Did you tell him?" DeLaren asked her in a hushed voice.

She shook her head. "Did you tell them?"

"Negative."

"Tell us what?" Reggie demanded.

Agent Clark straightened her neck and pretended to intimate concern with the motion of her eyes. Her posture was as proper as a Catholic school girl's. She didn't so much as glance at Willis. Instead, she went for the fatal blow to Reggie's conscience.

"Know how we knew you were here?"

Reggie shook his head.

"We saw your dust trail. Thought someone had to be approaching. Even though we were certainly on the lookout for Rassine, we intended to stop anyone who approached the gate. We watched. Your dust trail faded away, indicating you changed your mind. Rassine wasn't dumb enough to try visiting again. Owners wouldn't just suddenly decide not to return from vacation less than a mile from home. That left only one person. So we waited long enough for the dust to fade, then followed it slowly. When we found your car you'd already gone."

"Looking for Rassine is incredibly stupid," DeLaren commented. "If Rassine came back, consider yourself lucky to be alive."

"He did come back," Reggie croaked. "Long before we got there."

"To his makeshift hideout," Clark interrupted.

"His sanctuary. He left us something."

"That a fact?" DeLaren asked, amused. He smiled, nodded subtly, and leaned on the front seat headrest closer to Reggie.

DeLaren's demeanor made Reggie want to punch him, but alas, he was cuffed.

"What did he leave?" Clark asked. She sounded irritated. She closed her eyes just as she started her sentence, twitching her head from side to side and clasping her hands on her lap.

Reggie thought she looked too tense for the situation, but then again, he valued such intensity because of the situation. As the old saying went, time was everything. Her body language suggested she was making the most of it, all the while being frosty and filled with quiet intellect. DeLaren and Willis were languid.

"Another gemstone," Reggie said through clenched teeth. He allowed his jaw muscles to slacken and frowned at her. "I'd show it to you, but..."

"Uncuff him," Clark demanded, glancing to DeLaren.

"Ten-four ma'am."

She shot him a merciless glare, which he quietly ignored and pretended he didn't even see.

After DeLaren opened the car door and removed the handcuffs from Reggie's wrists, he slipped his hand into his front pocket and slowly withdrew the diamond. It was a least a full carat and probably worth more than Willis's car. He turned it over slowly in his palm while the other three carefully examined it.

"We'll need to extract prints from it," Clark said vacantly.

Willis detected a slight smile creeping onto Agent Clark's face, which caused him to smile. If Reggie understood it right, Willis saw this as the ice beginning to chip away. It made her look more personable and even more alluring.

"Will you marry me?" Willis joked.

As if nonverbally confirming that the diamond in her ring was just as big as Rassine's she lifted her left hand up and shoved it toward Willis's snout. He made a motion to bite her hand, but she recoiled at just the right instant.

"Sure," she said, scowling at him. "Right after you're done rotting in a federal prison."

"Whatever," Willis said. "The feds may be strict, but you still don't lock someone up thirty years for screwing with an investigation."

"What do you care?"

"I don't. Reggie's on my time. I'm just bunting."

Reggie shook his head and frowned in disgust.

"Be my guest and dust it right here," Reggie said.

"No, we have to take it to the lab," DeLaren jabbed.

"No way, sir," Willis cracked. "I'm making a necklace out of it for wearing on the diamond."

Reggie suddenly erased his frown and looked up to Willis. His stare lasted less than two seconds before Willis dropped his spar with Clark and began to stare back at him, perplexed.

"You're a genius."

"Tell me something I don't know."

"Sorry, how do you come to that conclusion? I only see a clown." Agent Clark leaned back, tossed her hair at her shoulder and looked out the window as if to obviously avoid eye contact.

"It's a diamond because Taleah is a diamond."

"And she plays on one."

"What are you getting at?" Agent DeLaren asked.

"Dominates, actually," Willis added.

Reggie closed his eyes and looked toward Agent Clark, who was refocusing her attention on the conversation before them. "Softball."

"Of course," DeLaren said. "Should have seen that one coming."

"Hit you like a fastball, did it?" Willis said.

Now playing along, Reggie said, "You're the Babe Ruth in this car."

Willis shrugged, smiled, and fixed his stare on a spot just below Agent Clark's neck. "Maybe Yogi Berra."

"My grandfather met Yogi one summer," DeLaren said. "Said he was the nicest guy in baseball but confusing as hell. He even popped out one of his 'Yogi-isms' on gramps. The old man said it was a riot."

Agent Clark glared at him. "Let's get back on topic. St. Clair and Ralston, Agent Marks does not yet know you showed up here. Don't make us inform him. We can't stop you from searching for Art Rassine. But refrain from getting in our way again or you will go to jail, clear?"

Reggie nodded.

"And we are ordering you to leave the vicinity of this ranch. Sign on the gate says trespassers will be prosecuted. The owners will be home anytime, and we've given them written permission to shoot anyone who enters their property."

She stood from the car, opened the back door, and removed Willis' handcuffs.

"I'll take the rock," DeLaren said, holding his palm out to Reggie.

Reggie shook his head and dropped the gem in his hand. The diamond itself was only a small piece of evidence which Reggie already knew implicated Art Rassine. He didn't dwell on the striking irony of the clue as much as he perhaps should have been. Instead, he closed his eyes and tried to reconstruct the events of that fateful night eleven years ago into a cohesive timeline. Every image he'd catalogued was intelligence he could use to conquer Rassine, but perhaps most important was which way he'd gone when he fled from Reggie.

He tightened his muscles as he tried to remember. He'd passed out before Rassine disappeared from view. Art Rassine was sliding down the slope of a ravine that zigzagged between the hills near the Harrison ranch. He was leaving a blood trail. When he reached the bottom of the incline, which way had he turned? East or west? Upstream or downstream? Reggie settled on a guess before long, but the decision was loose and not convincing enough to be the foundation of his next course of action. He still needed his wife to prop him up. He needed to know what Agents Clark and Marks were discussing on the phone.

Reggie staggered toward Willis' Subaru as the agents looked on. Before taking the last step to the passenger side door, Reggie stopped, squinted in the sun, and turned around to face Agent Clark.

"Can I help you?" she asked, somewhat nervously.

"Maybe," Reggie said. "Eleven years ago, I shot Art Rassine. I injured him and he ran, but not before sliding down into the ravine. The FBI must have investigated the whole scene of what happened on that ridge. What direction did your evidence suggest Rassine ran when he hit the bottom?"

"I'd have to look over the file," she said, shrugging. "In Salt Lake. But I'm pretty sure we determined east."

Agents DeLaren and Clark returned to their seats in the FBI vehicle and shared some small talk before starting the engine and backing away.

Reggie leaned against the car. The warmth of the body's metal painted a stripe of odd comfort across his legs and midsection. The day was heating up. In the city the temperature would be reaching close to a hundred degrees. He stared eastward into the pines that were huddled together in a tight clump in the crook of a bend in the rutted road. Here in the mountains, it felt closer to ninety but that was warm enough. Sunscreen was one thing he failed to think of in packing for this trip.

A pang of uneasiness crept through his bones like a tiny predator through dry grass. He allowed it to slither into darker spaces before centering his focus on its layers. As if expecting the feeling to dissolve into nothing, it slowly grew more complex and more concrete. A growl churned in his stomach. Pain knotted his muscles.

Thinking about the diamond was only slightly cathartic, both because it was a direct clue from Art Rassine and because it implied greater danger for Taleah. He groaned. The beginnings of a silent prayer formed at the fringes of his mind but were quickly erased as if by a sudden, subtle breeze that flitted against his skin. At this stage of the (what was it, another investigation?) journey, the diamond was starting to look like a key cog in the structure of this crime. It was a pinion around which the entire chain of events seemed to spin.

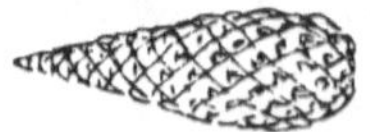

Anna and Rebekah had assembled an advanced system of monitoring the FBI's communications. Of course, no one within the Bureau suspected that the mother and stepmother of a victim to a federal criminal were listening. That made their jobs somewhat easier. Still, the task was daunting. Tapping the FBIs cellular signals had proven difficult, but not impossible. By nature, cellular signals are much easier to intercept than older land lines. Rebekah had the technology readily available to eavesdrop on almost any conversation. But the FBI's cellular signals incorporate an extra couple layers of encryption. She was not able to list phone logs without illegally searching through FBI databases. This required low-level, but still highly illegal hacking. When she found information in the database and cracked the encryption, she used a program on her laptop to reproduce the calls with stunning clarity. She didn't miss anything.

When a call was made to Agent Marks's cellphone, Rebekah offered a smile. Anna, sitting across the dining room table, cringed as if she were expecting the worst. It was definitely true that a federal agent could show up at the door any minute, but Rebekah doubted it.

"Marks," he answered.

A short pause convened before the caller identified herself. "Marks, its Clark."

"Clark. What's the problem? Agent DeLaren giving you trouble?"

By the tone of her voice, Clark sounded somewhat amused, yet the pattern of her speech seemed to indicate a certain degree of stress. "DeLaren? He's like a lamb. Pretty much agrees with me that Rassine will not try to access the ranch. Took some convincing, but with him, everything does. He's a good agent."

"Indeed," Marks said. "It's why I assigned him as your partner. I understand he's angling for an undercover position."

Clark ignored the suggestion. "News?"

"Good news," Marks confirmed. "Reggie St. Clair isn't privy to this info, so let's keep it between our team."

"Give me the bad news first," Clark quickly demanded.

"Bad news is we're running a little thin out of the Salt Lake office. Washington doesn't want to send us any help, because the bureau is busy nationwide. So we're stuck with four field agents, including Coles. With your forensics expertise, I need you to stay at the front lines of every new lead. So we're sending you to the town of Salmon. Chopper picks you up in an hour just outside of New Meadows. Be there."

"Copy," Clark said. "The good news?"

"The good news is we have a new lead. This one looks nice and juicy."

"I can handle anything," Clark bolted.

Agent Marks cleared his throat before delving into the story. "Salmon police department just arrested a drug dealer. It's due to hit the Eastern Idaho papers by tomorrow morning. Señor Martin Huerro is the thug. They busted him on a sting that was based on a tip suggesting that Huerro was dealing or manufacturing drugs in his basement. As red-handed as he was, he wasn't about to admit it, but it just so happens that he saw a poster of one Art Rassine inside the station. Said he knew him and quickly tried to use it as leverage to 'get off easy' as they put it."

"Knew him how?"

"Sold to him."

"Heroin?"

"Heroin," Marks confirmed. "Gave us approximate dates for their visits, and this thing goes back almost twenty years. Long time for a local dealer to sneak around unsuspected."

"Are they going to give him lenience?" Clark asked.

"Lawyers will try to swing that when this Art Rassine case goes to trial, if it does before Señor Huerro does. It's just kinda out of our hands right now. What is in our hands is investigating him to make sure his story stacks up against the facts of our Art Rassine case. It will give us a clue as to where he's been, which will lead us to a more localized search area."

"Salmon's a long way from our interest zone," Clark commented. "Why would Rassine need to travel all the way there?

"In the drug dealing business, longevity is a strong selling point," Marks explained. "And twenty years is nothing to sneeze at, especially for a man who thrives on flying under the radar. Rassine is accustomed to being off the grid, and no drug dealer in their right mind is going to put him on the grid."

"Any idea where the money came from?" Clark asked. "That will give us another angle to the lead. Money's easy to track. Even cash if spent in large enough quantities. Street value on heroin is high. If the volume Huerro claims is high enough we'll be able to find where the money came from."

"I'll be working that angle," Marks said. "Get on your way to New Meadows and be on the lookout for Reginald St. Clair."

"Copy," Clark said.

Rebekah wiped her brow at the conclusion of the conversation. This was a huge break. She glanced at Anna, swallowed hard, picked up her phone, and dialed Reggie's number.

13

Onyx

Light and dark intertwined and wrapped around each other as if painting the world around Taleah in alternating stripes like a zebra's coat. Her vision was hazy; she could see only black and white. A warm, pungent trickle of blood leaked down her forehead. She had passed out and was just now regaining consciousness.

The extent of her audial perception was somehow enhanced, yet instead of clarity, she could only hear the noise of a roaring cacophony. She struggled to make sense of this perception until she remembered how it sounded when the man who called himself Art had taken a side road and parked in the forest to retrieve something.

Part of her wished she knew what the object of his attention was, but mostly she didn't want to know. She momentarily struggled against the ropes surrounding her while trying to remember the events that led up to her fainting. Art was a monster. Nothing more and nothing less. He seemed to have an abundance of intelligence and the brute strength of a grizzly bear. Physically, he was terrifying and intimidating. She tried with all her might not to take anything he said too seriously. She never once doubted that her father would emerge victorious—until now. Now she even questioned whether Rassine would ever suffer defeat.

A flash of red brightened the world around her just as she closed her eyes. Her vision fluttered like puffs of red dye dribbling into clear water. She squeezed her eyes shut tighter. An eruption of blues and yellows spread across her artificial vision. The memory of the struggle seemed to be coalescing visually, piece by piece. The bindings around her wrists slipped loose enough to slither out of as she frayed the middle of the rope with the sharp stone. As the air in her lungs became heavy, she sprinted between a pair of trees. A wash of pain flooded over her. Blood trickled down her face. This deception surprised Art, but not starkly enough for her to escape into the wild.

Art, it seemed, didn't even need to run to catch up with her. He lobbed something heavy and rough as she turned to get a glimpse of him. In a dizzying spectacle of convulsing pain, it connected with the side of her forehead. Spasms of sharp pain jolted through her body and a cool scent of dry pine wafted into her nostrils. Her world faded from black to pure white and back to black.

Art was both strong enough and smart enough to ward off her assault. She punched and kicked and clawed at him when she broke free, but somehow none of the blows she delivered seemed to do much damage. In the confusion he had let go of her for a couple of seconds, which was enough to amass some ten yards of separation. Even as athletic as she was, he was still able to catch up with her. The distance he had thrown the stump of pine had to have been around six feet. Less than that and the force of acceleration would be negative and thus the damage would have been minimal. Instead, it knocked her cold. She had actually learned something in physics. *I thought I would never have use for that junk.*

For the moment, she lay alone. When she opened her eyes, her vision regained enough color and clarity to determine her surroundings. Not only that, but everything around her seemed silent—*too* silent as a matter of fact. She listened closely for birds or splashing water or rushes of wind. She heard nothing but a little bit of sloshing water that could have been a duck in a pond. It was nothing that could indicate human movement. The field of her vision in front of her was a spectrum of yellow and orange puncturing deep greens. To her left a void of sheer black punched a hole in the distorted image. Trembling, she turned to face it. Somehow the abyss promised safety.

Quietly, she immersed herself in the shadow. A swell of cool air brushed against her arms and legs. This shadow seemed to be the entrance to another world. It was a cave. Though the imagery around her continued to appear blurred, distinct shapes were beginning to emerge. Pine trees of several species guarded the mouth of the cave. Underbrush and poison ivy provided depth to the forest floor. A dull shadow slowly crept toward her as if encroaching on the opening. The sun was beginning to set above what appeared to be a ridge.

The earth beneath her feet hardened as she stepped into the dark. Instead of a carpet of pine needles and loose soil, the den's floor was hard and clay-like. It was also moist. Trembling, she stepped further into the den. As she retreated, the outside world began to fade to darkness. The setting sun began to be only a faint glimmer protruding into the shadow.

Here she had no friends, no father, no Tommy, no Mom or Rebekah. They were nothing more than a memory that brushed against the back wall of her conscious mind.

Like the fading light, hope began to dim. Exactly what was taking Dad so long? And where was she? The list of questions she began to ask herself seemed endless. She was becoming less and less certain of herself, less confident, and more frightened of Art. Perhaps in this dark, he would fail to find her, but then again, when he returned it would only be obvious where she'd gone. And in this cave, there was no escape.

Her hands were bound behind her back. Her face was red, filthy, and scarred from the fight. As the questions continued to come and her doubts climaxed, the terror escalated. She could feel it in her bones like tremors from an unknown, but powerful source. A stray tear splashed onto her cheek. All was bleak.

She glanced toward the fading light, opened her eyes wider, and then attempted to add a dash of theology to her thought. The fading light was like hope. As long as she kept it in sight, she could never lose it. She forced herself to think about her father. She imagined him running toward her in the forest, with blood on his face and sweat oozing from his pores. In this vision he was a champion. This momentarily kept the despair at bay. But hope did not come without its price or its opposite.

With a dull thump, she winced in pain as she bumped her head on an overhanging chunk of rock. As she tried to regain balance, her foot twisted against something hard at her heel. She tripped, bounced off the rock, and fell to a heap on the clay floor of the den. When she pried her eyes open, the light was gone, replaced instead by a silhouette of utter black.

Somewhere distant, a rock moved. And then another one, closer. The eerie silence was only a precursor to the feeling of eminent dread—hope's opposite. It came at her like a shadow at dusk. More rocks moved, rolled, and scattered. She attempted to remain as silent as possible. Art approached.

Reggie hung up the phone and placed it back in his pocket. An expression of victory, still fringed with concern rippled across his face. He craned his neck sideways, offered a coy glance to Willis, and then halfheartedly attempted a smile.

Willis saw this and reacted. "Faux grin."

Reggie quickly shook his head and looked away, focusing instead on how the sun was beginning to shrink toward the peaks of the Seven Devils Mountains. The glow was fantastic, even artistic. Reggie pondered on how the landscape looked in comparison to the early masterpieces.

The color of the lighting, the massing of the sun against the azure backdrop of distant mountains, and the rugged lines that formed the scene were staggering. He stared at it, allowing it to sink in until the scene seemed viewed through a translucent purple film.

If he were in the mood, he would have been amazed and maybe even pleased. But Art Rassine's masterpiece was like a sour aftertaste that simply could not fade.

After all this time, he could admit that this crime was indeed a masterpiece. It had to have taken plenty of study and determination to pull this off with such precision that he could make it hundreds of miles before anyone had a clue where he'd gone. It was a job well done, but Reggie's mood was dour.

This masterpiece of a crime could have been as beautiful and breathtaking as the forming sunset, but Reggie was determined to destroy it—to wipe out its colors and pervert the meaning behind the endeavor.

"Nice sunset," Willis commented, keeping his focus on Reggie.

"No, it isn't," Reggie croaked. "It's pitiful."

Willis shrugged and leaned his head slightly to the left. "To appreciate beauty in even the direst of circumstances is a gift given to man for joy."

"Save it," Reggie jabbed.

Willis seemed to recoil but remained steady. He focused on the rotting wood siding of the cabin once owned by Art Rassine. His silence seemed to stretch a moment too long before he said something.

"Sounds like your wives have been busy," he said.

"They're doing their jobs well," Reggie replied blankly.

"It seems reckless for the FBI doesn't it?"

Reggie squinted his eyes in the sunshine, considered it, and then frowned. "They've got bigger fish to fry."

Somewhere beyond the cabin snaked the waters of the Salmon River preparing to wind its way through the canyon country to the North. "Probably loads of big ones in that river," Willis pondered.

"How can you think about fishing at a time like this?" Reggie hoped his scowl could drill a hole in Willis' skull. "Focus!"

"I'm focusing." Willis retorted. "Some people do things differently than others. And we've known each other a long time."

"Yeah."

"So if you ever say anything like that again, I'll kill you." Willis said this with a sly grin as if to communicate that we was mocking Reggie.

Reggie understood it and narrowed his eyes in disgust. "Jerk."

"I think I heard that name being yelled out at least seventy-eight times the other day at the game. Though I doubt any of them came from you."

Reggie ignored him. "Let's go in."

"Ten-four," Willis said, swinging open the car door.

Together they walked the hundred yards between what appeared to be the end of the driveway and the house. A narrow, washboard road curved around the northern edge of the property like a ribbon in the wind. The gravel from the lane had preserved the outer reaches of the driveway for years, but closer to the house, it disappeared into tall thickets of dry grass and thistles. A lone sapling pine attempted to force its way up through the gravel, but with measured success.

The plank siding of the house, pried loose from years of wind and rain, shook when Reggie carefully ascended the rickety wooden steps to the screen door. A piece of the door trim had fallen off and lay in a garden below a small window that was covered in plastic. A ribbon of police tape was wrapped around the door handle and tied through a gaping hole in the screen. The wood door stood slightly ajar.

Drawing the gun from his pocket, Reggie pressed his index finger against his lips and moved slowly. His hand vibrated from nerves as he slowly eased the screen door open. When the door was open wide enough, Reggie kicked it open with enough force that it smashed against the paneling inside. He stared into the darkening haze for a moment before diving into the room. His knees painfully collided with the stone entry way. Still firmly pointing the gun, Reggie rolled toward the center of the room.

There was no one here. He loosened his grip on the gun, but still held it ready.

"What are we looking for?" Willis asked.

"Clues."

Willis nodded and made his way along the perimeter of the room away from the small kitchen area.

Reggie cautiously stepped between stones and weeds that were growing through the floorboards of the kitchen. The floor structure strained as he stepped over it. Several nails worked themselves loose from Reggie's weight.

"Clues," Willis repeated.

"Anything?"

"Bass," Willis said, eyeing a stuffed fish trophy on the far wall.

"Great," Reggie said. "Keep searching."

Taking a couple of heavy steps, Willis stopped and looked at the trophy from a different angle.

Reggie resumed his search by swinging open several cabinet doors. Cobwebs caked the interior of these cabinets. Lost in the cobwebs were a few dishes left behind after Rassine abandoned the place. He wasn't here looking for clues as to why Rassine left, but for possible direction on where Rassine lurked now. It seemed entirely possible that he was in the vicinity.

Darkness was beginning to fill the cabin with shades of shadowy gray that seemed to petrify everything in sight. But for a lot of footprints and fingerprints in the dust, the inside of the cabin appeared undisturbed.

He worked his way past an alcove where a small refrigerator once stood and to a corner in the wall, which led to a short hallway. Reggie held the gun against his cheek and slowly curled his finger around the trigger. He peeked into the corridor, withdrew a deep breath, and then took a giant step into the hallway. He came to face a doorway leading to a tiny bedroom. The light from the sunset spilt through the window, illuminating planks of rotting wood. A film of dust framed the perimeter of the room.

Without lowering the gun, Reggie stepped into the room. Something moved in the corner. He wildly swung the pistol in the direction and fired a round through the wall. A mouse scurried from an opening in the baseboard and into a rectangular, black shadow in the corner of the floor. The sound of the gunshot rang in his ears. Footsteps thundered through the living room approaching the hallway as Willis uttered a curse word.

"It's nothing," Reggie said, lowering the gun.

"Scared the bejeezus out of me."

"Best to be ready than sorry," Reggie said.

"You can say that again."

Reggie didn't respond. He nodded toward the shadow and approached it. It was a hole in the floor, where two sections of planks were removed. Rusted and twisted nails littered one side of the opening. The missing planks were nestled against the wall in such a fashion that they appeared to be loosening baseboards. The FBI had not left this room particularly well. It appeared almost as if they had found the evidence they needed, and then hurried out.

Willis knelt down next to the hole and reached his hand into the darkness. After a moment, he slipped the flashlight off of his belt and shone it into the opening in wide, sweeping arcs. Reggie observed lots of cobwebs, but nothing notable.

Willis sighed. "Nothing. Unless you want to take out the whole floor to the house."

"That's not a bad idea," Reggie said. "But we don't have time for that. Besides, if he would have left a piece to the puzzle, he would have put it somewhere we can easily find it."

Willis shook his head and looked down. "You got this sonofabitch all figured out, don't you?"

"I think he's got a surprise or two in him," Reggie said.

"In a game like this," Willis said thoughtfully, "surprises can be deadly."

"I know that. But it's not myself I'm worried about."

"Shucks," Willis said. "I don't know what to say."

Annoyed, Reggie bit his lip and continued to stare into the hole. This was likely the place where the FBI had found part of the deed showing Art Rassine's real name. At any rate, the opening had been scoured clean. There was no chance the FBI left anything behind, and they had obviously been here more recently than Rassine himself.

Reggie stood up straight and stomped back into the front room. Willis calmly followed him. "Nothing," Reggie said. "Nothing but a goddamn fish!"

"Doesn't it seem out of place to you?" Willis asked.

"Everything is out of place!" Reggie pounded his fist in a near-by wall, holding the gun loosely in his other hand, his grip quivering. "Damn FBI!"

Willis approached the trophy again and flipped the flashlight on, illuminating the pine plaque. The entire relic seemed untouched. A thick gauze of spider webs spanned between the fish's fins and tail. A cake of dust covered the whole thing.

Reggie started at it from afar.

"Doesn't look like anything meant for us," Reggie surmised. "It's been here too long."

"Probably," Willis answered. He quickly changed the subject. "Where did Rebekah say they caught the drug dealer?"

"Salmon," Reggie said.

"Right," Willis replied. "As in not Bass."

Willis shook his head and closed his eyes for a second. "That's not what I'm getting at. Look, that river right there is the Salmon River. One of its forks begins near that town, but it flows away from Montana."

"Of course it does," Reggie said impatiently.

"So maybe that means by coming here, we're going the wrong direction."

"What makes you think that?"

"Nothing, just deception. You say Rassine was pretty good at that game."

"I don't think that's his game anymore," Reggie argued.

Willis turned toward Reggie and let the light illuminate a dusty cone in the center of the room. The light made Willis' face appear dark and threatening, yet he hesitated. "Hear me out," he started. "The FBI says someone claimed to have seen Rassine near Missoula. One guess what Idaho town Missoula is closest to."

Reggie didn't answer. He stepped closer to Willis and frowned.

"Salmon," Willis finished. "What does that tell you?"

"Nothing."

"It means we have to hit up Salmon."

"Missoula," Reggie corrected. "If you are so sure about Rassine's deception game, then logic would have it that we're supposed to be checking out Missoula. What's the fastest way to Missoula from here?"

"From here, you head up to Grangeville, take Highway 12 to Kooskia, then turn left onto the 99." Willis knew his way around Idaho better than Reggie did. In retrospect, it was impressive. This made him thankful that he had Willis at his side.

"Kooskia?" Reggie said.

"Say, isn't that the town where...:"

"Rassine's first victim became available," Reggie finished for him. "Conveniently on the way to Missoula."

"Maybe you're right," Willis agreed. "We should head to Missoula next."

"No," Reggie said quietly. "This stupid fish isn't a clue."

"It would be if you let me tell you what river this fish was pulled from."

Reggie growled. "I don't care about that. I want to know where Rassine is now!" He stomped. "And somehow I don't think he's bringing Taleah on a damn fishing trip."

"Take a guess," Willis shouted. "Stop yelling and take a guess where the fish was caught."

"The flippin' Salmon!" Reggie shouted. "What difference does it make?"

"Can't you see?" Willis fought back. "This is the clue we needed. Whether he intended on us finding it is irrelevant. The fact that it's a fish isn't even important."

"So you think we search up and down the Salmon River?" Reggie guessed.

"Nope," Willis grunted. "You might not want to hear it, but…"

"Spit it out," Reggie demanded.

"The Lochsa. It parallels Highway 99 almost until the Montana border. That's where we search."

Reggie stood idly, staring into the dust at his feet. He nodded slowly. Whether or not he wanted to admit it, Willis' idea had merit.

This was the wild. It had been Rassine's hangout for decades, ever since he went off the grid. He knew it better than Reggie did, understood it more thoroughly, and adored it more fervently. To Reggie, this warned of inescapable danger, especially in a place he'd never been. It was unforgiving, but most importantly, it was right where Art Rassine wanted them.

14
Coordinates

egotiating what seemed to be a maze of sharp turns, Willis steered through the canyon of the Salmon River with the precision of a trained performance driver. Willis elected to admire the scenery every chance he got. North of New Meadows, U.S. Highway 95 steadily descends into a rugged canyon and meanders through turns that should be taken at speeds slower than the posted limit. Instead of slowing, Willis seemed to be challenging the highway to give him a better thrill. For nearly thirty minutes, he did not speak—not until the coniferous trees started to thin just before reaching the town of Riggins.

After finding nothing but a stuffed fish at Rassine's old home, Reggie had removed some of the surveying equipment from the back of the Subaru and placed it on the dashboard for his convenience. He laid out a laser measuring unit and a small tablet that functioned as a triangulation device. By using a known origin point, the tablet kept an accurate tab on exactly where they were. This was important, because in a landscape such as this one, GPS was of little use.

Reggie balanced the tablet device on his knee and meticulously watched the headings change. The device was accurate to within inches over a distance of more than a mile. In the world of surveying equipment, it was top-of-the-line. Exactly how Willis had convinced Ted Brickshaw to loan it was a mystery to Reggie. At any rate, he didn't care. All that mattered now was that it served as a tool he could use to track down Art Rassine.

Recognizing an error, he dropped the pencil in frustration. Willis glanced at him. Reggie picked up the tablet and punched some icons on the screen with a little too much force.

"What exactly are you doing?" Willis asked.

Reggie scribbled down a series of polar coordinates and examined them briefly. "I'm breaking down some—damn it!" He scribbled out the coordinates he'd just written and hit some more icons on the device.

"You break it, you bought it," Willis said, only half-joking.

This device was worth as much as Willis' car. Before Reggie employed its use, Willis had warned that Brickshaw would string him up if the device was damaged.

"Keeps malfunctioning and I might break it," Reggie panned.

"User error," Willis said. "It only does what you tell it to."

"Right," Reggie said. "So how do you explain that it gives me the finger?"

Willis chuckled. "It might be accurate as a razor, but probably isn't capable of removing any digits."

"It's removing plenty of *digits*," Reggie growled through clenched teeth.

"Show me the finger."

Reggie waited for the screen to give him the same error it had given him the last three times he had tried to calculate the equation. And then, magically, it worked. Reggie shook his head and sighed.

"Having that much luck, are you? What's the point, anyway? Even if we did know exactly where Rassine is, all that thing's gonna do is pinpoint the location and give you the nearest monument. GPS is useless."

"I'm looking for patterns," Reggie explained. He dropped the pencil and stared out the window into the blue twilight. Majestic pines seemed to float by atop the mountains instead of blurring. The silhouettes and shadows of the peaks were at times dizzying. During the night, the canyon was dark because the moon was hidden behind mountains.

"Patterns," Willis repeated. "Such as?"

"We know where Rassine has been," Reggie started. "Some alleged locations and some confirmed. We have the park he took Taleah from, Harrison's Ranch, the Sanctuary, his old cabin, the canyon near Kooskia, the town of Salmon, and Missoula. I thought if I could work out a trajectory of his route, I could guestimate his destination."

"It isn't working out?" Willis asked.

"He's all over the map," Reggie stammered. "Figuratively."

"That means he's one step ahead of us," Willis lamented. "Figuratively."

"You think he knew I'd try this?" Reggie asked, already certain of the answer. He paused, yawned, and looked outside. On the left they were paralleling the river. The fading light was reflecting the white crests of rapids. The surface of the water sparkled like glitter in bright sun. If Reggie was in the mood to appreciate beauty, he would have noted it. Instead, he only examined it from a purely objective point of view.

Willis let the pause linger as he steered around a huge boulder that rested twenty feet from the shoulder of the road.

"It's a guess," Willis said. "He's proven to know plenty about you, so it wouldn't be surprising if he knew you'd use a few tricks of the trade to try and locate him. The dude is smart."

Reggie shook his head and glanced at the dashboard clock. "It'll be good and dark long before we reach Kooskia," he said with a frown.

"And after that, we still have to wait for where the Lochsa branches off the Selway." Willis finished his remark with a subtle grunt.

"How far is it between the confluence and the border?" Reggie asked, hoping the number would be low. The longer the distance, the more miles of darkness they would have to search.

"About eighty miles," Willis stated.

Reggie groaned.

"And change."

"That's a long way," Reggie said, an air of sorrow soaking into his voice. He lowered his head and attempted to search for a sense of solace that was nothing more than a shapeless vapor. The intangible nature of this expedition drove him mad. There were too many variables and he needed guidance of another kind.

Staring out the window proved cathartic at times, distressing at others. When sitting quiet with only his thoughts as company, time stretched until there seemed to be more of it. With every passing mile, Reggie became more and more worried about where the trip was taking them, and about Taleah. The wait was stretching toward an invisible horizon. What horrors Rassine could unleash upon Taleah seemed unfathomable, but starkly real.

After at least an hour of cross-checking data and scribbling calculations on the legal pad, Reggie put the equipment and the notepad away in frustration. Instead of doing anything he would have considered productive, he slipped into memories of eleven years ago.

Echoes of voices replayed in his mind as if stretched across time and space. *Don't let this become the reason. You are not yet as Job. Come to me, Reggie.* In the savagery of the remembered emotions, the voices sounded again and again until Reggie believed he could no longer tolerate it.

He still remembered what Taleah was like eleven years ago. The sweetest, most innocent person alive. Pills for pain, sleepless nights, and despair had taken their toll. The fact that he'd built up tolerances to those medications had its way of plunging his heart into further darkness. But the past was in the past. He'd learned his lessons and moved on.

The lessons from eleven years ago seemed too numerous to think about from a positive angle. In life there were always lessons. And the hardest ones were often the most valuable. The thought made Reggie shudder as if a sudden chill swept through his spine. The fragments of yesterday now seemed like howling ghosts trapped in a merciless prison of futility.

The light that eventually broke through the clouds eleven years ago had been the light of Christ. Richard Kerrin was right. He had become a good friend. Reggie thought of calling him, but decided not to. Best to preserve battery power in case there was an emergency.

The moments seemed to fade into deeper darkness as Reggie and Willis rolled north on Highway 95. Willis drove in thoughtful silence. Reggie turned to him with a deep frown etched across his face. Willis glanced back and lowered his expression.

Instead of saying anything, Reggie stared out the windshield into a pair of distant taillights painting a red streak across the center of his vision. It looked almost like blood on damp undergrowth.

"Back when," Willis started. "You know...did you ever wonder how Rassine sprung that trap on us?"

Reggie hesitated as if he didn't hear Willis. He continued to stare at the blurring taillights. A few specks of rain splashed onto the windshield but could not sustain enough vigor to wet the pavement or the car. "He knew we were headed to the sanctuary."

"Yeah, but the trap itself." Willis paused to construct a cohesive theory. When he spoke, he posed the idea as a question. "Like he knew we'd be in the clearing all along? Do you think he set up those traps knowing exactly where we'd walk?"

"I don't know," Reggie said. "Long time ago. In light of what's going on here, I can't see how it's relevant anyway."

"I have a bad feeling," Willis said, "that it actually is relevant."

Reggie scowled and snapped his focus back to Willis. "What?"

"If that night taught us anything, it's that Rassine was an expert at setting traps. Hell, he probably did it all the time on wildlife. Man's gotta eat."

"What are you saying?"

"I'm saying we should be on the lookout for these kinds of snares when we're in the woods searching. Try to sniff for gasoline, look for ropes tied to trees, things like that. I hate to say it but I think this monster is clever if not horrifyingly intelligent."

"Figures," Reggie grunted. "But you're probably right."

"I think he knew the most likely path we'd use to get to the sanctuary. All he had to do was make sure his initial trap covered enough ground so that it didn't matter if we ended up ten feet left or right. He had all the tools at his disposal and it wouldn't surprise me if he did again."

Reggie shook his head and glanced to his lap before recommencing his stare at the taillights, which were beginning to look like a pair of cars. Not realizing what he was doing, he glanced at the dashboard. Willis was driving five miles over the speed limit.

"Only now he doesn't have a storage shed to store all this stuff in," Willis guessed. "Maybe in his truck, but he'd have to lug it around. I think he needs to be more mobile this time."

"Probably," Reggie said. "He knows how to hide and he knows he's the one being hunted. And maybe he figures if I find him I'll kill him."

"Isn't that your plan?"

"Can't go down without swinging," Reggie said.

Willis smiled, but Reggie ignored it and continued to stare at the vehicles ahead. They were beginning to slow down.

Over the next five minutes, a dark blue haze began to settle over his vision. His eyes were slivers. He could still see the headlights brushing brilliant red strokes against the darkness, but the scene was colliding with the abstract in his subconscious mind. More minutes passed and he at last gave in to sleep, even if was to be brief.

A ribbon floated in the wind against a sullen, charcoal backdrop. Like tears freefalling to the ground, a shower coalesced. The darkness in front of him shimmered like a thousand fragments of broken glass dancing in twilight. The ribbon stained red and became an oblique, textured shape slicing open the flesh of Renoir's greatest work. As rain began to fall the colors remained solid. But the red flowed like diluting blood. On the banks of the river stood a mysterious shadow with the shape of a man but the heart of a creature. Sparks of fire stapled his eyes shut. And the faintest dot of red punctured his midsection. An image of Taleah flashed across the night like lightning. She was beautiful and serene, yet bathed in despair.

15
Dependence

The sunset over the valley and the town of Council was almost breath-taking. Thin, high clouds painted the horizon in opalescent shades that were nothing short of mesmerizing. Agent Bill Coles of the FBI simply glanced at it and grunted. This day had shown him enough and he wasn't about to sit and admire the sunset in this remote area. Besides, Salt Lake had sunsets, too. Almost as good as this one.

Within ten minutes of each other, four cars entered the parking lot of the Adams County administration building tucked away at the north end of the town about a quarter of a mile from Highway 95. Each of the vehicles carried only one person. Following Agent Coles, the next car was that of the building maintenance and operation engineer. The car following him was a tan and white GMC truck belonging to Sheriff Mark Toyovich. Five minutes later, a bookkeeping secretary pulled into the lot. Fashionably late, County Comissioner Glenn Burks parked his black Lincoln. When Burks exited his vehicle, he looked just as perplexed as everyone else.

If Coles was in the mood for pushing people around, this would have been fun. Instead of smiling, he simply nodded toward the commissioner in an effort to acknowledge his presence. Burks wore a face resembling that of a seasoned politician. He looked hopeful, yet skeptical. His expression seemed to exude patience even through the lack of understanding.

The only person brave enough to approach Agent Coles at this hour was the sheriff. He looked like he'd aged fifteen or twenty years since Coles had last seen him. Most of his hair was missing and his face drooped in slabs of flesh that looked over-ripe and wrinkly. His frown only deepened when he observed the heartless stare of Coles.

"FBI," Toyovich scoffed. "Surely couldn't have waited for morning."

"Matter of life and death," Coles said, as if passing Toyovich's frustration off as nothing more than a slight annoyance.

"Whose life?"

Coles raised an eyebrow and squinted. The last of the sun began to sink beneath the ridgeline. Gathering all of these people seemed stupid, given the circumstances. The hell with protocol. But Agent Marks insisted they do this the right way. And of course it had to be Coles' job to round them all up like stray cattle. He regarded it as scrub work. During the drive from Salmon a logging truck nearly lost its load, causing Coles to slam on the brakes in a flurry of panic. He didn't want to answer Toyovich. "It's need-to-know."

"Figures," Toyovich said, still scowling.

"Pardon the hour," Coles said, not really meaning it. He shook his head and clasped his hands as if ready to dig into a pile of messy paperwork. "This is something that has to get done tonight." He stopped and turned toward the maintenance man. "Let us in, Mr. Abbott."

Abbott did as instructed. The four of them followed him into the building. He flipped on the lobby lights for them and stood beside the door like a sentinel. Agent Coles was the last one in. He thought about shaking hands with Abbott but, upon looking at the man's hands, decided he wished to keep his hands clean. Instead he offered the same courteous, if not half-hearted nod he'd just given the commissioner.

When they entered the corridor, Commisioner Burks turned his head. "What can we do for you, Agent Coles?"

"You can take me to the properties database," Coles demanded.

The surly blonde secretary smiled. "Right this way."

She led them into a room with a half-dozen cluttered desks arranged in two columns. Without speaking, she pulled a chair out from behind one of the desks, took a seat, and logged into the server. After quickly typing her password, she clicked through some files and brought up the appropriate folder. "Address?" she asked.

Agent Coles slid the photograph of Rassine's old cabin to her. She examined it and flipped it. The 'suspected' address was written in black ink on the back.

Sheriff Toyovich only needed to glance at the picture to understand what was really going on. "Sonofabitch," he said. "Don't tell me that man is still on the loose."

Coles glanced at him, shook his head, and watched the secretary open a file.

"Ten—eleven years and you FBI clowns still can't find him? This needs to be resolved now!"

"We're working on it," Coles said, impatiently biting his lip and lowering his eyebrows. A muscle twitched. Instead of expounding on his idea, he simply stared at the photograph and uttered a careful sigh.

"He killed one of my deputies!" Toyovich continued.

"One of our finest county employees," Burks agreed. "Deputy Jamison might not have been the most personable man alive, but he was a good friend and a fine cop."

Coles wasn't in the mood for the barrage of attacks from both sides. He slowly closed his eyes. When he opened them, he was staring at a similar photograph of the same building on the computer screen.

"Gather 'round," he demanded. He didn't wait for them to give him their full attention before he started to speak. "This is the former residence of James Bullock, also known as Art Rassine. On the FBI's most-wanted list. Suspect of serial kidnapping, rape, and murder. Four deaths are attributed to him, though one appears to have been an accident. A fifth victim managed to escape before Rassine himself disappeared. The case went cold, until a few days ago."

"What's caused it to be reopened?" Toyovich asked, still sounding irate.

"Another victim."

"Who?"

"Classified," Coles said. "We need to know everything about this property from construction to completion, to occupancy, to condemnation.

The secretary scrolled down and carefully scanned the document. "Built in 1971, Original deed owner Stedson Construction."

"Stedson went bankrupt in '74," Burks noted. "They had at least half a dozen properties listed on the market before they sunk."

"Who purchased it?" Coles asked.

"Unknown," the secretary replied.

"Unknown? How can that information not be on file?"

"The file is probably incomplete," she said. "We have only become automated in the last fifteen years. Chances are that the information never made it to the computer."

"Convenient," Coles grunted. He shuffled his feet, stood up straight as if to stretch, and glared at Commissioner Burks. "Well?"

Burks offered a knowing nod. "For information not entered into the database, hard copy files go back more than forty years. That information is likely in the storage room for old, obsolete files."

"It's no longer obsolete," Coles hurried. "Let's dig it out."

Agent Coles followed the four of them down a tight corridor past a break room and into a dusty, unkempt room stacked ceiling-high with boxes. Partially wedged behind the boxes was a nail in the door frame, upon which was suspended a key. The receptionist unlocked the door. The room behind the door was crowded and littered, yet oddly accessible. Boxes containing old files were stacked on top of filing cabinets littering all corners of the small room. Such disorganization. They needed someone to clean up the mess. This room probably contained decades-worth of files under Adams County jurisdiction. Coles caught himself smiling at the mess, but not because it was funny. No, it was simply ironic. Years ago, he'd cleaned up the county's mess, but not literally.

The receptionist stopped to stare at a poster on a wall. The poster displayed a map of the room. Again Coles found it peculiar that a room this small required a map to navigate. Instead of smiling, he shook his head and frowned.

After examining the map, the receptionist approached a filing cabinet, upon which was stacked a litany of boxes. She pulled open the bottom drawer, flipped through some folders, and then pulled out a folder with the address to Rassine's old place. She brushed some dust off of its cover and opened it. Inside were more than two dozen sheets, some containing pictures, but mostly legal mumbo-jumbo, which would probably take a whole team of lawyers and a DA to figure out how to litigate.

The fourth page in the mini book was a title of sale from Stedson Construction to Regal Real Estate Services. Regal held the home for less than a year and sold it to Art Rassine, using his legal name.

"The dwelling was occupied for ten years," the receptionist noted. "First Interstate Bank, which had acquired Regal Real Estate went into foreclosure against the owner. The situation was resolved. It appears that the property had already been abandoned."

She flipped through five more pages of garbage before settling on a promising-looking document. She scanned through it before paraphrasing its jargon.

"After abandonment, Adams County filed a suit against it claiming that the unit was to be condemned. First Interstate, which had already merged with a larger bank, agreed to the terms of the condemnation and the property has been owned by the county ever since."

She flipped through a few more pages of junk, and then came across the document that changed the game entirely. She continued to narrate. "Just before the property was condemned, a civil suit was filed against the previous owner claiming that neglect had caused invasive weeds to overcome a nearby rancher's field. Rassine was never served because he had disappeared."

Coles tried to look interested. This was helpful information because it assigned a timeline for when Rassine had gone off the grid and essentially become a shadow.

Also affixed to the file was a bank statement showing that Rassine was the heir to a healthy sum of money. The account was suspended due to inactivity, but the document showed a large sum of cash having been withdrawn. So that was how Rassine managed to come up with enough loot for his heroin addiction. Only it was somewhat sketchy on whether Rassine had actually used the heroin. He remembered that Reginald St. Clair had claimed Rassine was drugging his victims. This evidence seemed to support that claim.

That hurt, because Coles always considered Reggie to be irrational and borderline insane. Of course he could never prove it, but to be wrong against a civilian was downright humiliating.

Coles cleared his throat and insisted it was time to leave. Without thanking any of the four for their time, he signed a legal slip indicating consent that the documents had changed hands. Without accompaniment, he exited the building with the file clutched under his left arm. He managed to make it all the way to his car before his phone began to ring.

After opening the door and sitting down, he answered the phone. Agent Torrance Marks sounded irritated.

The phone line crackled with static before cutting in and out. Their location wasn't the best and a thunderstorm was causing minor satellite disruption. Reggie knew that this would be the best time for this conversation because there would be little cellular coverage in the canyon of the Lochsa River.

"New information," Rebekah said after quickly greeting him. "You want it?"

"Everything you got," he replied.

She cleared her throat and allowed perhaps a second or two to pass before speaking. "Agents Marks and Coles were speaking on the phone a while ago," She said. "Coles has been to the Adams County admin building looking into Rassine's old property."

As Reggie listened to her, a headache began to throb behind his temple. Instinctively, he put his fingers to his forehead as if he could simply wipe the pain away.

"Rassine, a.k.a. James Bullock, purchased the cabin from a now-defunct real estate agency. The property was condemned by Adams County officials years ago, but no demolition has been planned."

"Anything useful?" Reggie asked.

"I thought that sounded innocent enough," she continued. "But here's the interesting part. Rassine inherited a rather large sum of money. He withdrew several thousand in cash from his account more than twenty years ago, but the account was suspended because of inactivity. Coles speculates that Rassine has been using that money for supplies and heroin."

"Good thought," Reggie said. "Never would have come up with that if I didn't tell them as much ten years ago."

"Another thing," Rebekah added, "is that James Bullock was sued because of invasive weeds. They never served him the papers because they couldn't find him. Shortly thereafter the property went into foreclosure. It changed hands between multiple banks until it was officially condemned."

"That's a long time to disappear for," Reggie pondered. "Cash only, and probably in small enough amounts as to not be easily detectible. I bet the only thing he ever bough was drugs."

A sad pause wedged itself into the conversation. He had a feeling he knew what she was thinking but didn't want to say anything.

"Honey, you don't think he'd use..." Her voice trailed away and a short sigh offered finality to the incomplete thought.

Reggie didn't need to hear the remainder of the sentence to get the idea. Its reality struck him like pain from a bulging knot in the pit of his stomach. His heart leapt and his muscles trembled. His lip quivered.

"Please be safe," she said. "I'll try to keep you up to date."

"From here on out there won't be much cellular coverage," Reggie said. "If you don't hear from me in a couple of days, alert the FBI and tell them we're somewhere along the Lochsa River."

"I will," she said.

"Goodnight," Reggie said quietly. "I love you."

"Good luck," Rebekah replied. "Love you too."

The phone went dead just when Reggie was about to hang up. It didn't take him long to realize that Willis was wearing an inquisitive expression laced with thoughtfulness. Reggie shrugged and looked away. He didn't want to share anything about his conversation with Rebekah, but in truth it didn't matter. He came to realize that Willis could hear everything Rebekah said. His body language said it all. A careful folding of his arms, a tilt of his head, and a silent nod indicated that he had been reacting to the conversation as if he were a part of it.

For the moment, Willis was not apt to beg Reggie to share his thoughts. Willis's thoughts alone would probably suffice. Then again, chances were high that their lines of thinking lied somewhere on the same plane.

He was glad Willis was at his side. One didn't always need to speak to be a reliable and valuable confidant. The truth was that in this landscape, Reggie simply had one friend—one ally. He shuddered when he thought of it. Though he always had an independent and even defiant streak in him, he knew that this task relied heavily upon his interaction with Willis. Both mentally and physically he needed Willis. Without him, he'd certainly suffer defeat and would probably not find Taleah at all.

Then again, Willis needed him. Reggie could sense that, as prepared as Willis seemed to be, he was not ready to tackle the swings of emotion that would inevitably batter them from all sides. It wasn't that Reggie was particularly impervious to the influence of the dark, but that his presence was favorable. It lightened the load on both of them.

The pitter-patter of rain on the windshield distracted Reggie. Willis had parked in an abandoned lot of a gas station in Grangeville. He'd already filled up the tank and they were using the time to rest. It had been a long drive and neither of them were exactly in a state to go searching through darkness.

The problem with this reasoning was that Taleah might not have a lot of time left.

A roll of thunder crumbled in the sky above them as the rain began to intensify. The recent wave of heat had caused a swell of big storms to form over the Central Idaho Mountains. The cluster of thunder cells was marching toward the Canadian border.

Reggie rarely put much stock into what the weather did these days, but this time the storms seemed foreboding. The thunder rocked his spine and sent slivers of chills to his heart.

When the rain started and the thunder roared, it painted the landscape with strokes of impenetrable darkness. Reggie's mind had told him to use the darkness—to take advantage and to seek shelter. But Rassine himself was perhaps little more than a resident of the same darkness. It made Reggie want a way out, but for now the pattern was inescapable.

Anger remained entrenched within his heart, but the passion behind it—the force with which he exerted its benefits—transformed into blackened fear. He didn't want to imagine what Rassine could be doing to Taleah, but images forced their way into his brain. He remembered how Mindy Caldwell looked after she'd escaped. She was filthy and sweaty. Terror held as much a spot in her heart as did hope, and as a result, she didn't trust anyone. Weeks in captivity crowded her mind with punishing waves of agony and desperation. And even after she escaped, she remained a slave to their horrifying influences. Rassine did indeed rape, drug and torture Mindy as well as the other prisoners.

Knowing that Rassine still had this capability was harrowing. God only knew what terrors Rassine could be unleashing upon Taleah. With every fiber of his being he wished he could shield her from it. No woman deserved that carnage.

A tear slid down his cheek as he turned to face Willis. Willis nodded silently, as if agreeing with the heartache. "Bad news," he whispered.

"No," Reggie muttered. Just as he said this, his head exploded in a dizzying headache the likes of which he hadn't experienced in years. The madness that engulfed him in misery all those years ago was returning. Without even trying, Rassine was transforming Reggie into nothing more than a monster which he vehemently meant to expunge. But this beast had no master.

Reggie bit his lip and balled his fist so tight that his fingernails began to gouge craters in his palms. He shook from head to toe.

Willis looked horrified at the expression. He recoiled and attempted to massage the pain in Reggie's heart away. "Bottom of the ninth," he said. "But there's only one out."

Reggie exhaled. The void in his lungs inflated with a surge of anger. His heart went from frenzy to frozen. The frown on his face deepened and turned crimson. He slammed his fist into his thigh and then his legs convulsed in pain. The trembling became even more violent. This emotion was too dominant to put into words. No cursing could satisfy its horror. His heart was a mass of terror and guilt. Rage boiled in his veins.

16
Precision

"Reggie St. Clair," a voice growled. The voice was menacing and tinged with unexpected nuances of agony and discord. Its sound altered Taleah's senses and caused her to convulse against the boulder she cowered behind. *Is he here?*

Don't speak, precious.

She shook her head at the random thought. *Dad?* Her heart began to race. If what she felt was true and her father was in the vicinity, possibilities too numerous to categorize sprung to the fore. How would he know where she was? And if she called out for him, would the man who called himself Art make it to her first? Would he kill her dad? It would have been more provocative had she understood where she was. Some kind of cave. But where? Beneath what mountain was she sheltered? She didn't want to think about it. Many years ago she'd realized just how massive the continent was. She'd travelled halfway to the East Coast for a softball retreat. She'd spent countless hours in the car and once every five minutes she'd stared out the window at the plains. The landscape had stretched beyond the extent of her vision. On and on it had gone. She had been less than a dot on the map. But she'd only seen a small fraction of the continent in her lifetime. Now she could be anywhere.

Her mind made little attempt to narrow down her location based on her surroundings. Instead, she silently quivered against the rock—against the cavern's chill. The ropes bound her wrists as tight as ever. It seemed that after her recent escape attempt, he'd secured the rope with a new knot. It proved much more difficult to loosen, but she tried. If she could make it out of here, toward where Art's voice came from, then perhaps it would be easier for her father to find her. With that, her plan was formulated.

Still, she remained motionless and allowed seconds to pass into eternity. Art was near enough to hear. His voice sounded even and gruff, startlingly calm. This meant he was close. He was close enough to hear her shuffling against the underbrush outside the cave. Her plan needed something else. Some kind of diversion.

"You won't get away with it," Art said.

No answer came. Either her father was lost for words or—worse—wasn't even here. Hope sunk into despair.

"What's that they say 'bout revenge?"

Still no response. There was no sound at all. No shuffling dirt and underbrush, no running, no planning. No gunfire.

Tears rolled down her cheeks. The sensation that time was running out somehow concerned her more than any other circumstance. When she was six, she remembered a time just after the divorce that she'd felt desperate and alone. She'd wailed for hours while her mother feebly tried to console her. "I want Daddy," she remembered pleading. That was all she wanted. While valuable, her mother could not offer the steadiness she craved.

Her body shook. She was hungry. And this man had the audacity to offer her food. Even in desperation she had no desire to take it from him. If she died of starvation, it would be a better fate than to die of poison. If he poisoned the food. Something about him was so unfamiliar it was jarring. Even on television, she'd never seen a man whose methods and motives were this strikingly incongruent.

Instead of allowing the thought of poison to dominate her mind, she decided that food would be easily obtainable amongst the vegetation outside the cave. She just needed to make it out undetected. That would prove to be easier said than done.

The clay floor of the chamber was cold and unforgiving. Like revenge. She slowly lay down and wriggled herself away from the rock, further into the cave. She opened her hands to feel for anything she could grasp.

She stopped and slowly inhaled through her nose. Was that water she could smell? She smelled again and remained as motionless as she possibly could. *Drip.* Silence. *Drip.*

"Water!" she whispered. But it sounded distant, probably near the back of the cave, which could turn out to be hundreds of feet away. Such a trek would be dangerous. The threat of getting lost was as real as falling off a huge boulder onto a pile of jagged rocks. That was still a better fate than dying by poisoning or the violent hands of her captor. If she even made a sound, he would come after her. And he was much better equipped to handle the darkness of the underground terrain than she was. If that happened, it would not be a rock that would kill her.

She stopped to weigh her options. She'd heard the babblings of a brook nearby when she was near the mouth of the cave. That was out there. With him. And he'd hear her shuffling. The consequences would be severe.

Instead of pursuing that option, she scooted further away from the boulder along the clay floor. A small stone passed against the flesh of her hand. She grasped it. Instead of sharp, it was smooth and rounded, as if shaped by running water. *How would that get in here?* Instead of keeping it, she slowly rolled it away from her and kept moving. With every inch, her heartbeat turned into a violent kick drum that she feared Art could hear. Her heart began to strike at the inside of her chest with agonizing pulses. If she could find the water, it could sustain her enough to… *clunk.* Her head collided with what felt like a wall. A spasm of pain erupted across her scalp. She couldn't have hit the wall that hard, but then again, it was made of something much harder than the bone and soft flesh that comprised her own cranium.

She rolled away from the wall and almost immediately crashed into another wall. This one felt as though it had more give—as if it were hollow. She pressed her back against it and almost felt it move. Beside it, she could feel numerous other stones of varying sizes. Most of them were jagged, which meant they had at some moment in unrecorded history fallen from the ceiling of the cave. She sifted through them, trying to make as little sound as possible. She needed something big enough to throw and sharp enough to cut rope with.

An idea struck her. Again, the possible outcomes of her plan were numerous. It seemed to be inviting chaos, and even though chaos was discomfort, it could cause enough distraction for her to make her way toward the brook, near where there were surely some edible plants. If that was what she was going for, she needed something that could cause enough commotion for Taleah to lose herself in the fray. And then she could just return to the cave as innocent as a bee.

Then came another idea. It would certainly cause her more agony and trauma. This was a game where everything came with a cost. And with stakes this high, the cost would invariably be steep. She shrugged, grasped one of the larger stones, and made her way slowly to the mouth of the cavern.

Sparse pockets of flame danced above the glowing coals, illuminating a dome-shaped portion of the darkness and the features of his face. Perhaps a campfire was not the smartest idea, as the dry season—the forest fire season—was entrenched over the Northwest. Not only that, but it would be easy to see flames from the highway. And all he needed right now was a ranger to drive by smelling smoke or seeing flames. While true that this spot was mostly out of sight from the road, he could not hide the glow of the flames.

He traded intervals of listening for noise from the cave and paying close attention to the details in his mind. Perhaps this cavern was not such an ingenious hiding place when compared to the chamber at Lance Harrison's ranch, but it would do. The section of land remained isolated and, especially after dark, the road was almost vacant. Once every few minutes he heard the rush of tires on pavement or the clatter of diesel engines churning toward the pass that separated Montana from Idaho.

Using his old well was not a good idea. The FBI had been keeping tabs on that property for years. They knew about the chamber. And if anyone important had half the brains of a pencil eraser, they'd know he'd taken St. Clair's daughter. He had to get away. To disappear into the night. One of the great things about the Northern Rockies was that it offered nooks so numerous that not even he could know more than a fraction of them. It was in his best interest to avoid his old stomping grounds. One misstep could spell doom. Everything had to be done exactly right.

"Reggie St. Clair," he growled. And then he added in a whisper, "Where the hell are you?"

The girl would be good for bait and a little entertainment, but what he wanted Reggie more.

A snapping twig invaded his stream of thought and caused his attention to snap onto his surroundings. She should be awake. In a little while, he'd cook her some dinner and bring it to her. As far as he could tell, she made no sound. The snap didn't repeat. The silence was practically deafening. A knock on a distant tree penetrated the quiet, followed by a chirp from a nocturnal bird or a squirrel.

After the intrusion, he attempted to reassemble his thoughts on the operation and perhaps modify his plan should the need arise. Instead, all he could think of was Reggie St. Clair, holding the gun and moaning in pure agony. It would have been so pathetic he would have laughed hysterically. But Reggie was lucky. Art could not have foreseen Reggie getting involved with Adams County's investigation. After Art caught on and studied him, he realized he had a loose cannon on his hands. That should have been more disastrous to the investigating team than dangerous for Art. But he'd brought this on himself.

Reggie was unpredictable. He was cunning. If his life had not been falling apart and had he not displayed the symptoms of madness, he wouldn't have been a threat at all. Still, Art had chosen Reggie as his target because he didn't deem Willis a worthy opponent. That much proved to be true. Willis was nothing. Easily defeated. St. Clair was already defeated. So all he needed was the catalyst for ultimate destruction.

Then things got out of control. Reggie had become so emotionally invested in the case that it was his inane desire to hunt Art down. A skillful hunter or not, Reggie still pursued him. He needed a safe place and a quick plan. All it took was for the man to break down into nothing but a worthless pile of agony. It provided a wrinkle through which he could attack. And he did. But Reggie had one shot left. He was somehow able to transform despair into just enough hate to pull the trigger. But his shot was not clean. He was not a good marksman. Not good enough to be accurate in darkness while still woozy from getting pummeled with a rock.

Was that lucky for St. Clair or lucky for Art? He'd debated this topic before but it wasn't worth exploring any further. Reggie got off the shot and it connected. Art had nothing to fight back for. The mud and the injury caused him to slide to the bottom of a ravine. Before he would have been able to make it back to the top to finish Reggie off, the FBI would have been landing a helicopter.

Art's veins bulged when he thought about it. His blood pressure skyrocketed. Without closing his eyes and without saying a word, he lifted up his sweater and placed two fingers below the wound where the bullet had penetrated him. That was the game changer.

"Reggie St. Clair," he repeated, louder. He stared into the dying coals. They became a cloak of orange over a black night of ire. Under his sweater, he withdrew his fingers into a fist. He stomped his right foot into the ground hard enough to produce a loud thump. He trembled as his frown etched itself ever deeper into his face. His anger was a fire that swirled around him.

And then he heard a noise. It came from inside the cave. Rocks were moving.

He stared into the puncture of black and considered. Reggie was either too cowardly or too stupid to be coming, but Art still owed him retribution. It was high time for some entertainment.

The rain ceased and settled into puddles across the pocked pavement of the service station in Grangeville. Both Reggie and Willis had grown weary and, after more than thirty minutes during which no conversation took place, Reggie nodded off, blinded by his own tears.

Willis sighed once or twice himself, but Reggie could not be certain whether he too had fallen asleep. Reggie's light sleep was marked with a paralyzing nightmare.

He was running again, in the dark. Cold, echoing voices carved craters in flesh of the dream. Running. Tripping over rocks and branches. Yet there was no one chasing him, unless he considered the static concept of time something more than an inanimate object. Time breathed and moved; it was as alive as anything in this forest. Yes, time was the enemy.

Taleah was still out there, grappling for survival as the ghost of a shadow traced her every step, determined to hunt her down and destroy her. Maybe her fate would be worse than destruction. Finding her seemed more important than anything. It was more important than casting light on the shadow, Willis's companionship, his wife spying on the FBI, and any shred of evidence they'd uncovered.

Blurry strokes of blood flushed the corners of his vision. Boiling scars rose up on his flesh. He moaned, attempting to bat them away, but for one reason or another his limbs would not move. It was as if some unseen force were controlling his muscles. And then the reality that he was indeed nothing sunk in. He was nothing. Only flesh. But on that thought, was Taleah much more? Yes, of course. In contrast to his existence, hers was everything. If she lived, time did not exist. If she died, it would never cease.

Anger pulsed through him while the demons of his own past contorted that rage into desperation. There was nothing else.

Dark, scabbed fingers reached out of the darkness at him, beckoning him to join those who lingered amongst the trees in silence—those poor souls of innocent women put to untimely deaths. A roar penetrated the night. Fire soaked the horizon and then surrounded him in its fury. When the flames parted, one figure stood at the fore: A shadow making more shadows amidst the dancing flames.

Reggie's eyes bolted open. A trickle of sweat coalesced on his brow. As if out of breath, he was panting. His body trembled from terror and cold. His eyes darted back and forth from his own hands to the incandescent lights beneath the eaves of the building. A tear trickled down his face.

Willis stared at him and neither of them spoke. Instead of asking what Willis wanted, Reggie stared back. The last strands of rage floated in front of his eyes. Willis's face, by contrast, remained blank yet exuded concern. He placed both hands on the steering wheel, sighed, and listened.

Reggie didn't speak.

After what seemed to Reggie like ten minutes, Willis broke the silence. "I don't want to know."

"Just a dream," Reggie lied.

Willis shook his head. "Just a dream, in the way God is just a religion, or Taleah is just a girl."

"Shut the hell up."

Willis obeyed the command. He let the moments pass into the furnace of oblivion as if simply the observation of time was enough to whittle the tension thin.

"Bloodshot eyes, tears, irritability..."

"Shut UP!"

Again, he heeded. The tension had worn Reggie to nothing but powder. Willis spent the next ten minutes observing him, watching for signs that the effects of Reggie's dream were about to wander into the dark. The motion of Reggie's body eventually cooled, but the fire in his heart remained. *Find her.*

"Start the car," Reggie demanded.

"What time do you think it is?" Willis asked.

"Just do it. We have to..." *Find her.*

The voice was warm, but firm. Just like the voice that invited Reggie to *'come to me'* eleven years ago.

"Yeah, we do," Willis said. "But let's be careful."

He started the car and eased onto the highway that connected US 95 to Highway 12. After a few minutes of gently winding turns, the road twisted downward in a series of sharp turns with lower speed limits. Willis carefully navigated this road.

"Highway 13," Reggie said. "Kooskia, twenty miles away."

"Kooskia?" Willis uttered a curse word under his breath. "Isn't that where..."

"Stop the car."

Willis obeyed without question. He flipped on the emergency flashers and looked at Reggie for further instruction.

Reggie didn't say anything. He opened the car door, got out, and strolled along a concrete barrier dividing pavement from cliffs. He stopped and looked down toward where the Clearwater River flowed. Only the car's headlights offered a clue as to how far down the embankment went. It had to be at least a hundred vertical feet. The slope appeared to be made up of rockslides and pockets of underbrush with sparse white pines. He looked back toward the car, where Willis was eyeing him with curiosity. The steel back of a mileage marker appeared in the glow of the vehicle's taillights. Reggie quickly walked toward it. This must have been the place where Sandra Coombs plunged toward the river. It was twenty-eight years ago. She would be near fifty today had Art Rassine not collected her and allowed her to die.

Reggie didn't care to read the front side of the sign. Something was written on the back of the sign in permanent marker.

He shook as he read it to himself. A fresh batch of tears exploded in his eyes.

"You were too late."

17
Trauma

"I think he's referring to that Coombs woman," Willis guessed. He momentarily stroked some of the stubble on his chin before refocusing his attention on the highway. Navigating the turns required the usage of both hands and a steady dosage of braking.

Reggie grumbled something inaudible. A stabbing pain slithered through his head. Without thinking, he reached for his temple.

Travelling almost as slowly as Willis, a car appeared at the crest of a sharp bend. The luminance of its headlights struck Reggie's face. He squinted. When the car passed, Reggie glanced into the rearview mirror. The passing car's taillights illuminated his outer shell but seemed to bathe his inner demons in hues of scarlet. What he saw wasn't a man. It was the monster that plagued his nightmares eleven years ago. The scowl was nothing more than an anthropomorphic mask. His reflection deepened his frown.

"It's bad news," Willis said. He was visibly attempting to concoct a scenario where everyone involved came out better. But words failed him. "Well, it could be...if you think about it."

"Story of my life," Reggie said.

"Your timing is impeccable," Willis sneered.

Reggie glared at him. His lip quivered. "I'll pay you anything to stop."

"I'll take a Subaru MKZ turbocharged with a sub in the trunk."

Reggie sensed that Willis wanted to grin, but everything was pain. He balled his fists as if preparing for a fight that would never come.

"Did anyone think to look for Ms. Coombs?" Willis asked.

The pain in Reggie's temples intensified. He bit his lip and stared out the window, where the shadows of passing pines plunged spears into the murky river.

"And he meant to leave a message," Willis continued. "Which no one ever found."

Reggie mumbled. "It would imply she died on the scene."

"Could be."

"No," Reggie said, more subdued. "Sandra Coombs lived at least another eight hours."

"But no one knows that. Not even the FBI. They said themselves that she died too long ago to estimate the actual time of death, or even the exact cause. You know, other than 'complications from injuries.' And what kind of medical help did Rassine try and give her? Something that failed."

Willis was reaching and Reggie wanted no part of it. He turned to voice his displeasure with the one-sided conversation, but only a cold sigh could escape his lips. He shuddered. The thought of losing Taleah crowded him from all sides. It was much more than simple fear; it was unabashed, unquenchable terror. It raked over his bones as if its figurative blades were encrusted with diamonds and imbibed with venom. A fresh tear escaped his eyes, but he attempted to hide it. It was a good thing Willis's attention was elsewhere.

Certainly, Rassine had a plan. He played this game with remarkable precision, always thinking several moves ahead. Always anticipating. Like the events in the clearing eleven years ago, Reggie and Willis were unconditioned newcomers. The turf belonged to Rassine and his advantage was staggering.

"You need me," Willis said flatly.

Reggie did nothing to respond but had a feeling that his inaction spoke much louder than words could ever hope to. Words, after all, were a human invention to categorize everything and fashion it into communication. Emotion was the more primitive form of communication, in which Reggie was fluent.

"You know you do. Where would you be if I weren't here? Huddled up in Rassine's old bungalow searching for more dust and cobwebs. Laying on a rock by the river?"

"Unlike now, I'd be finding my daughter," Reggie said, showing more heat than he'd intended.

"And you would be no closer to finding her than we are right now."

Reggie wanted to react with an insane indictment of everything that Willis represented, but he scarcely had time to open his mouth.

Willis continued. "But it's not just you. Like it or not, I'm on this excursion with you. I'm on your side. I need you, too, man. I wouldn't last out here, and we both know it. I'd be crazy, dead, or both."

"Why, then, are you patronizing me?"

Willis peeled his eyes from a tricky curve on the highway long enough to shoot Reggie and icy glare. "I'll pretend I didn't hear that."

"I can't stand you."

"Feeling's mutual," Willis said. "It isn't you, it's the state you're in. You've been binging on this mood since we passed New Meadows. Easy to notice. I know you're angry. Hell, we're all angry. I am, your wives are, and so is Rassine."

Reggie stopped to appreciate a moment of scorn, but he gaped at Willis instead. "What did you just say?"

"I'm pissed at the way this thing is going down."

Coaxing a snarl to the surface, Reggie bolted into uncharted territory. "You said Rassine's pissed."

"Well, why shouldn't he be?" Willis explained. "You shot him. If you shot me, I'd kill you."

"Not if you were dead."

"Point is, you caused the sonofabitch a lot of grief. You ended his reign of terror. You put the FBI on his tail. You'd think he'd feel free running around on the lam for eleven years, but his number one goal had to become avoiding capture. That figuratively puts him in a prison. You follow?"

Reggie stared out the windshield at the double yellow lines. A rabbit zipped across the highway in front of them and paused to watch them pass by like a spectator of a night game. Reggie imagined it staring in pity, but the blankness in its eyes spoke volumes. It had no idea what had happened in these parts eleven years ago. It was vaguely aware of its own existence.

"So this guy never let go of that. He's probably still got the scar."

"He's got a plan, "Reggie said. "Probably a better one than we've got. And we have no choice but to follow. No one knows where he's going to take us. We need to be alert."

"You, alert?" Willis frowned. "That's a great idea. What is his end game anyway?"

"You want to know?"

Willis lifted his left hand from the steering wheel during a gradual straightaway and shrugged. "Gives us a better Idea what to expect."

"Revenge."

"Yeah, but he's already had that. He kidnapped Taleah. In his book, that's aces. Then what? As they say in Vegas, he's got more up his sleeve than that. If he didn't have a plan for that triumph, Taleah would already be dead. And why would he want to kill her? Doesn't match his MO. He's only killed when he's had no other choice."

Reggie shifted his head gravely, resting his hand upon his forehead, where convulsions of pain were shooting through him like electrified bullets. He stifled a groan. "I know what he wants."

"Money? Some untold millions?"

Both of them knew that wasn't the answer. Rassine had no need for money. He hadn't for years. Such was the coup of a primitive lifestyle. In the wild, there were more important and more dangerous commodities than money.

Reggie looked up. Pale rapture coalesced in his eyes. He knew what Rassine wanted. "Me."

The conversation wavered and then faded away into deep waves of contemplation. The dark was eroding Reggie's soul. Willis, while sincere, didn't know the heart of the matter. There was no doubt that he cared. He'd been a friend to Reggie and Taleah for years. He knew the case, but its dark and ominous undercurrents remained little more than a mystery to him. He frowned as he navigated the sharpest turns the road had yet to unleash. Within minutes, they had reached the canyon floor.

The speed limit dropped just after the highway straightened out. The shadows of conifers ascended to the majesty of starlight. Such a sight could put many men in awe. But tonight, Reggie felt too much worry for any of it to matter. The quiet of this location was striking. After midnight, there wasn't much traffic and this place was remote.

Reggie rested. His eyes watered, became weary, and sealed themselves shut.

Entering Kooskia. For Reggie there was a certain fantasy about this tiny town. It served as Sandra Coombs's destination. Sandra had a friend in Kooskia. The name sounded as if it exuded charm from every possible angle and in any light. He imagined it to be an isolated mountain haven at the confluence of the Clearwater River and its south fork. Reggie had never been here. He saw little reason to traverse these highways when traveling from the Boise Metro Area. This highway stretched from Lewiston to the Montana border towards Missoula, yet Missoula was at least a hundred miles away from Kooskia.

The building that once served as the local tavern was boarded up, its windows shuttered, and its neon extinguished. The concrete sidewalk crumbled into a patch of dust near the side of the highway. A narrow dirt trail traversed through a network of mounds towards the river. The silence of the town was eerie, as if not one soul lingered.

Reggie stumbled towards the doors of the bar. Wondering what secrets it encased, he eyed it. The building, which appeared to be more than a century old, was constructed of pine siding. Its second story contained what basically amounted to a loft apartment. Cozy. But Reggie didn't have time for this diversion. Taleah was still out there, hurt, dirty, and confused. Terrified. She likely faced a litany of emotions she almost didn't know humans were capable of feeling. The only feeling Reggie understood at this moment was intrigue.

Could Art Rassine have used this building at one time? He shook his head as if someone stood next to him asking the questions.

Reggie peered around the left side of the building where the shadow of a large ponderosa crawled up the siding. The second story loft had a window. From this angle, he couldn't see much. Just a step or two would reveal whether the loft was occupied. The window punched a dark hole in the siding. A dog barked somewhere. Reggie looked away. Just as he turned his head, the curtain fluttered. He caught it out the corner of his eye. When he retrained his gaze, it was still.

A mystifying sensation crept over him. Someone was watching him. Luring him. *Come to me, Reggie.* A swath of cold air encircled him. What if...

He didn't have time to think. A pair of headlights appeared around the nearest bend in the highway. The car's motor revved as it approached Reggie. The cover of darkness promised safety. He was tucked away in the building's shadow, but he only had a few seconds to react. What if the door was open? He ran to it but felt as if he were running in slow motion. The driver of the vehicle could see him by now.

He pulled on the handle of the wooden door, and it opened. Reggie slithered through the crack and thought about hiding behind the bar. He scooted across the dusty floor. In here it was so dark he could scarcely see his hand in front of his face. He tripped on a chair, but retained his balance. The sound of the chair scooting across the floor and then settling again sharpened his sense of hearing. From above came the sound of light and cautious footsteps. Whoever was up there was aware of Reggie's presence, yet the mood suggested confidence—even safety. He felt his way to a stairway along a far wall. He grasped the handle as he climbed. Something cold and liquid touched his fingers. Instinctively, he reached his hand to his face. The scent was coppery and forlorn—unmistakable for blood.

Reggie had seen blood on a post before. Someone upstairs...was dying. He abandoned all caution and vaulted up the stairs two at a time. He wanted to signal that he was coming, but no sound could escape his lips. Only a whisper that fluttered in the dead air and then evaporated. Taleah?

He tumbled to the floor atop the steps and writhed in agony. His muscles were somehow expecting one or two more steps. His ankle twisted and his knee slammed into the hardwood floor. Still, he could make no audible sound. Instead of struggling to his feet, he crawled. A faint blue light cut a gap across the bottom of a nearby door, as if the room's occupant were watching television.

When he got there, he reached up, turned the handle, and pushed the door open. The television was on but was displaying only snow. He shuddered. The scene reminded him of an old horror movie, but something about it was different. A musty scent wafted in the air. And there it was again. The smell of blood. Reggie followed it, hoping to find someone to speak to or someone clinging to fraying threads of life. He scooted away from the television and onto a small rug. Footprints in the dust were easily distinguishable as those of a woman or child. *Not Taleah,* he pled.

She was there, behind the couch. Reggie accidentally touched her shoe.

"Please," she whispered.

Her body writhed. He needed to see her face—to witness the light dancing in her eyes, but her image flickered. She was there, but just barely. Something about her seemed wrong. He slid up next to her. In any normal situation, what he saw would have been a relief. Instead, what he saw paralyzed him to the core. He gazed upon the souring face of Sandra Coombs. He'd only seen a picture of her once. He'd seen her bones. She gasped and then wailed in terror. "Please, don't."

Her face was bathed in a blue fury. Her eyes punctuated her face like star garnets. They filtered all of the life in the room into a black sphere that was like a canvas on which he could paint the portrait of a woman. Cold stretched across her skin. She looked oddly translucent, the way a spring fog after a heavy rain seemed to make the plants float on thin air. Her breathing was erratic. Her skin felt as cold as if ice were running in her veins. The fear transformed into a tantalizing comfort that seemed too sweet to be real.

"I knew you'd find me, Reggie."

Reggie let out a dull moan just as he heard the door downstairs open. That would be Art Rassine. There was nowhere to run and nowhere to hide.

Willis was shaking Reggie. Reggie's eyes flung themselves open, only to take in more of the blackness that seemed to perpetually surround him. He shrieked.

Willis had pulled the Subaru up to a stop sign that conjoined the two highways, which seemed to be the only two roads in the town. He stared at Reggie, as calm as could be, yet Reggie could see the storm brewing behind his eyes. An intense pain rocketed into his head, causing him to feel dizzy and disoriented.

"You had a nightmare," Willis said. His voice sounded flat and uninspiring. Too simple to be real. It was like Reggie was trapped in a parallel world where his worst nightmares were coming to fruition before his eyes.

Pain rocked his head. His eyes watered. He hadn't endured a headache this severe since... "Vicodin," he snarled.

"You're alright, pal. It was a nightmare."

"Just a nightmare," Reggie said. "In the way the Holocaust was a murder."

Willis conceded the point and nodded. He slowly looked away from Reggie to where Highway 12 curled into the dark mountains ahead. Somewhere in that wilderness was Taleah. And Rassine. This thought conjured images of burning ropes being flung around him. What surprises did Rassine have in store for them this time?

Instead of pushing the conversation, Reggie leaned back, lowered his eyes, and frowned. The headache seemed to blast the insides of his brain with explosives fit for a bomb range. The pain throbbed, ebbed, and then surged. With any luck it would fade away. But the more Reggie moved, the worse the pain got. What he needed was a deep, dreamless sleep, yet such a prospect seemed impossible.

"Headache again?" Willis said. He already knew. The answer would not be confirmation, only more noise to block out the pain and fear he absorbed from Reggie.

"No," Reggie lied.

"That's good. You got any oceanfront property in Utah you want to sell?"

Reggie didn't answer.

"Utah would be a great place to relocate to. Lots of women. Maybe I could meet my first six wives there."

"Stop with the polygamy jokes," Reggie said. His eyes were narrow and his expression sagged.

"Fine," Willis agreed. "Have they been frequent?"

"Have what been frequent?" Reggie asked.

"You sound innocent, but your pistol's smoking. I can see it from a mile away."

Reggie balled his fist. This wasn't getting them anywhere. He glared at Willis and lowered his face. "Good, then maybe I can drop you off a mile away. We'll test that theory."

"Well, we know it has nothing to do with Anna. Just Taleah," Willis surmised.

"And Rassine."

Willis nodded slowly.

"No," Reggie said, answering Willis's question regarding the frequency of the headaches. "First one in years."

"Eleven years?"

"Maybe not that long, but this is easily the worst since I shot Rassine." Reggie was tempted to relish the thought of shooting the shadow. He pictured the brief horror it flung across Art's face when he staggered and slipped. It almost made Reggie smile. It was cathartic, yet unfulfilling.

"Well, just try to keep that head straight," Willis prompted. He eyed Reggie for a moment before leaning back in his seat, gripping the steering wheel, and peering into the dark corridor of the ravine.

"Let's move," Reggie said. His voice seemed to intone finality when played back in his brain, but this was little but the tip of the proverbial iceberg. What dangers lurked ahead he could only imagine. And if he should fail, what would be Taleah's fate? Her fate was more important than his.

Willis turned right on Highway 12. He gently accelerated to the speed limit and then let the car's momentum keep them near the proper speed.

"This dream," Willis said. "You think it's important?"

"I don't know."

"What happened?"

Reggie rolled his eyes but decided to humor Willis. He told him every detail he could remember, though the details were already becoming sparse. One image, he would never be able to forget. He would carry it to his grave.

"I saw the building," Willis said gravely.

Reggie shook his head and almost continued to speak. The remainder of Willis's words still travelled through Reggie's brain. "You…"

"I know. I hope you don't think this whole scenario could be real."

"Who knows?" Reggie said. "Art Rassine seems to have a full deck up his sleeve."

"That's a lot of tricks," Willis said. His expression was grim. His eyes seemed glossed over, yet no matter his body language, he communicated volumes.

"Maybe we should get the women to look into this. A little fodder for the FBI."

"No. If we drop that nugget, they'll be on our tail by morning."

Willis shrugged and leaned into a gentle curve. The moonlight sparkled and danced on the waters of the Clearwater. "Is that such a bad thing?"

"They will alert Rassine. They'll insert chaos into an already uncertain chain of events. It could spell disaster."

"Well, yeah," Willis said. "When you put it like that. We may very well need them to know something. We could all end up dead. As you were saying, Rassine's playing with more cards than we are."

"I doubt it's real," Reggie said. "Just a little something the devil likes to put in my way from time to time. Reminds me how frail I really am."

"But how will they find us?"

"They've got resources we don't. If they want to find us, they're going to have to try. If we give it away, it will make it too easy. If they have to work for it, that would buy us some time."

"Time," Willis said. "It's ironic. Something we don't have, yet something we need."

"Shut your trap and drive."

Willis nodded and leaned into another turn.

"Besides," Reggie said. "We don't have any evidence. They can't take the contents of a dream seriously. It isn't their job."

18
Display

Apervasive chill invaded the cave. Taleah clutched her elbows to fight off the cold, but her own embrace could not provide the comfort she craved. "I love you, Dad," she whispered. She considered extending her comment, but decided the words were only for herself. They did her as much good trapped in her skull than echoing and dying in a cave.

What was it that happened eleven years ago? She'd heard some of the stories, but the deepest and cruelest secrets remained hidden. Did she have the right to know now? Because of those stories, she knew the name Art. The stories painted him as cold and savage—'composed entirely of nature.' She never understood what that meant. Not until now.

Eleven years ago marked the changing of an era in her family. Mom and Dad divorced for reasons not divulged to Taleah. And then the big event happened. The details were hazy by now, but she still clung to the tales like they were popular urban legends that somehow meant something more to her. They meant far less to her than to Dad. He'd lived through it. Survived. But he still marked it as a failure because Art escaped. The FBI had hunted Art by helicopter for at least a week and had come up empty.

Art took pride in his ability to remain concealed. It proved one of many great strengths he possessed. Instead of giving him credit for devising such a scheme, however, she passed him off as simply possessed.

Thoughts hammered the tissue in her brains into a soupy mush. Time seemed to stand still. She flitted her eyes in all directions, hoping to see something that could give her hope. Only darkness prevailed. She attempted to scoot toward the mouth of the cavern, wherever it was, but met a large boulder she'd hit her head on earlier.

Taleah believed that, based upon the passage of time, her brain contained some sort of a natural clock. Time was often measured in accordance with light, yet the darkness had disoriented and estranged her from the world at large. She tried to ignore the pain in her scalp. Instead of crawling headfirst into the black, she reached out her hands and surveyed a tight arc in front of her. Only after assessing her next few inches clear would she proceed. At this rate it could take an hour to reach the mouth of the cave, but she didn't remember traveling that far. Then again, she had been either barely conscious or vaguely interested in her surroundings.

Rocks shuffled as she moved. After several minutes of searching, she reached a crease between boulders. A dull patch of blue filtered through the air. It exuded an air of serenity laced with poison. Starlight. She stared up at it from between the boulders for several minutes. The freedom the sky proposed tantalized her senses. She wanted to reach for it. To run for it. Instead, she simply adored the spectacle.

Moments passed. Water dripped from overhead rocks somewhere distant. A breeze shuffled through the vegetation outside. The noise, while eerie beyond the veil of dusk, presented itself as a fond neighbor. The girls' camps she'd ventured on ages ago painted a broader portrait of what she imagined nature to be. Then, it welcomed her into its midst for recreation and enjoyment; now nature was a hiding place.

The breeze continued, then ebbed. A trail of dull thumps penetrated the night. Art approached. The underbrush shuffled in his wake. Not much stealth, she thought. But in this location, he hardly needed it.

She waited, hoping he could not see her. His shadow stood black against the canopy of stars. He surveyed the entry way for a few moments, thinking and planning. She shrunk behind the boulders. A click echoed and then yellow light flooded the interior of the cavern. This shouldn't have been unexpected, but she recoiled just the same.

She peaked around the corner. His posture was domineering. The light colored portions of his silhouette with the earth tones of his clothes and skin.

"Where are you?" he growled.

She remained silent. He didn't need to speak at all, for he'd seen her peeking from behind the rock.

"A little too clever for your own good, sweetheart." His breathing was heavy and bestial. "Aren't you going to come out and play?"

"No," she whispered.

"It's okay. You can be the good guy."

His words sounded like a snarl but gleaned playful intrigue. She cowered further. She didn't want to know what playing entailed, but a feeling that it meant no good persevered.

"Come on," he begged. "You can do better than this."

Tears overcame frustration. "You'll never win."

"Your family. Always about winning and losing. Sometimes life's just shit."

Taleah clawed at the flesh on her left arm. Her lip trembled. Ice swept over her nerves. "Yours is," she responded.

He supplied an indifferent *humph* and strode further into the den. Guessing his distance provided her nothing of importance. The light penetrated nooks between boulders and large formations of granite, shale, and limestone. His footsteps continued until he halted on the other side of the boulder behind which she cowered.

Relying upon sound when the supply of light was limited was never Taleah's strong suit. Before, everything real she could touch, taste, or feel. Darkness often coaxed her demons out of the shadows. Though her peers almost always referred to her as strong, some unseen vulnerable side to her personality blossomed in the dark.

Art kicked a jumble of loose rocks. They scattered across the clay and rock floor and echoed through the den. His footsteps ceased. He was breathing easy, toiled from neither adrenaline nor mood. Silence. The light flashed across a massive pile of rocks that provided a narrow pass to another room further into the tunnel.

Behind her, a dull slapping sounded like flesh on flat rock. After another silence, this one shorter and more pronounced, more rocks scattered amidst heavy footsteps. The pass between the rocks narrowed the trail. With proper light, Taleah could have navigated the hazard unimpeded. She'd seen enough of Art to know that he was much bigger than the average man, so she doubted he could make it through the gap with as much ease.

Immediately, fabric brushed against stone. Loose rocks rolled. He did not speak. Taleah scooted further away from the opening but could not get far before she reached yet another blockade of stone. Trapped.

A moment from a softball game replayed in her mind. Recalling the visual helped her to cope with the dark. A simple ground ball through the gap between shortstop and second was enough to get her to first base. She led off, baiting the pitcher into throwing to first. She made it back with ease. The first pitch sailed wide. The batter offered a subtle, but sly nod to Taleah. She took a few casual practice swings, then tapped the bat on home plate. The pitcher wound up and lobbed what looked like a perfect strike. Her form was breathtaking, but the delivery was off-speed. Taleah sprinted to second. The catcher's throw arrived late. Safe.

The batter had only watched the ball slide right in front of her. But Sara was great at getting into the pitcher's mind. After Sara watched another ball float past, Taleah got the sense that the pitcher believed this girl was going to go down easy. On the next pitch, she swung. She smashed the ball in the sweet spot and took off down the baseline. Taleah followed suit. The ball bounced in deep center field, but Taleah did not see it. She rounded third just before the ball arrived. When the girl at third threw to the catcher, Taleah stopped and headed back for third. It was the rare, but often successful squeeze play. Taleah played it gracefully, but the two defensive players cornered her. The girl at third base tossed the ball back to the catcher. Taleah ran when the girl released the ball. Instead of stopping, she plowed straight into the catcher. They both landed in a heap on the dusty baseline. She was out, but she went down with dignity.

Taleah gripped a heavy rock. The light shone into her crevice long enough that she could see a huge hand reaching for her. She lobbed the rock and recoiled against the barrier.

Art growled. "Nice try."

She turned her head. Art was close enough that she could hear him breathing. His hand fell on her shoulder and a blast of steely cold jolted her veins. When he moved his fingers, he touched her hair. He calmly combed his fingers through it like a lover. She kicked against him in vain.

"Nice and cozy."

"Drop dead." Her voice wavered and she trembled.

He stroked her hair again. "You know, fear makes some people do things. Questionable, maybe. Sometimes outright crazy. Try anything you want, you just can't outlast cowardice."

"You're the coward. My dad's going to kill you. Bastard."

"Such strong language for a pretty little princess."

She wanted to spew more verbal venom at him but found herself at a loss for words. He reached to the top of her head to comb his fingers through her hair one more time. He paused at her ear. When the strands reached the end of his fingers, he held them. He pulled to draw her nearer.

The hell with this. She grasped another rock, this one heavier than the first. She flung her bound hands toward his scalp but did not release. The stone crashed down on his cranium. He staggered and fell over. The light illuminated a scurrying cone that fluttered through the den at random. Taleah felt her way with her hands. Her fingers fell upon his beard. With all of the energy she could muster, she frenzied through his grasp. She stood to climb over him, stumbled, and hit her head on a rock. She clawed her way through the rubble. He kicked her. The force of impact launched her at another boulder.

She shielded the impending blow with open palms and pushed herself away from the stone. The light allowed her to find her bearings quicker. She hurried toward the gap between the boulders, but an unseen force was holding her back.

A fresh jolt of pain seared across her scalp. Art had a fistful of her hair. Flailing her arms in a vain attempt to free herself, she ran in place. He held on, staggered to his feet, and then thrust her through the opening without letting go.

"Resistance is...what's the word?" He grumbled.

She let out a scream that only seemed to pierce her own eardrums.

"...Futile? That's not it. Dangerous? Disastrous. That's the one."

"No!"

"Run, little girl. You're never going to make it."

She ran. Art let her hair slacken but retained his grip. She stumbled as she made her way toward the cave's mouth. Art kept up and pulled to keep her from running headfirst into a tree. She fought her way through the underbrush, pitching her voice in a cold, garbled whimper. The sky, once an opaque blue encrusted with shimmering stars, was beginning to morph into a paler, cooler hazel. It signaled the coming of dawn. Another day. To her dismay, she was awake throughout the ordeal.

A column of smoke wafted toward the sky just ahead of her. On instinct, she turned right toward a steep downslope. The way was treacherous and obstructed by dark, fallen pines.

"Nope, that's a good way to die."

Art kept her hair taut as the camp appeared amidst a thicket of pines. She batted her arms around as if attempting to swim in a rip current. She scurried her feet about until they collided with a splintery pine stump. The unmistakable feel of blood warmed a spot on her ankle. She attempted to plant her feet once again, but Art was dragging her. The pain in her ankle and her scalp swelled. She moaned.

"That's the spirit."

The coals illuminated in orange and red hues a world so exasperatingly different from any she'd ever witnessed. He had no tent—just a pile of unkempt blankets and a burlap sack full of she-didn't-want-to-know-what.

"Help!"

"There's no one here," he said. "Sit down." With his free hand, he clutched her shoulder and forced her down onto a sawed-off log that seemed in danger of rolling down the slope. He released her hair and reached toward his bag. After opening it, he withdrew a rope.

She struggled in his grasp but could not get away. He loosed the binds on her wrists, turned her, and forced both hands behind her back. Again, he secured the rope around both wrists. Behind her, he worked the rope into a loop between her arms and then hitched the slack end to the nearest tree.

"We're good and alone. Just like you and that shaggy mop top in the park. Wasn't that a good night? Remember him? Think about his face. His greasy hair. Think real good. You're never going to see it again."

She shivered. Now that the adrenaline was wearing thin, she was beginning to notice feelings that intensity obscured. Cold. It could have been in the thirties or low forties. Had she been planning this trip, she might have thought to bring a jacket.

"Nothing to say? Must not have meant that much to you." He walked around the tree to inspect his work, then perched on a log next to her and studied her. He fished for something in his vest pocket.

Taleah started to say something, but all she could get out was "wha…"

"He's dead." Art withdrew a carving knife and eyed it carefully. "Just like that Willis and your father will be soon."

"You will."

His eyes narrowed and he let out a calm chuckle. "You got spirit."

For the next two minutes or so, she said nothing. The morning dark was dimming into a blue haze. Cold air persisted and settled. For the moment, no breeze pushed through the conifers. She stared at her ankle. Pain and cold seemed to be scabbing over the wound quickly.

"You're wondering how I know so much," he said.

"No, I'm not."

He picked up a narrow pine stick from the ground and gouged off a sliver of its bark with the knife. "Not that it matters much to you now."

A grunt escaped her abdomen. Pretending like she didn't care was getting her nowhere. The truth that she did care meant that Art needed only push the right buttons to get her talking. Being played like this was never part of her plan, but she quickly discovered that when circumstances turned dire, plans went out the window.

"Explained. Bad things happen to good people. What's that mean for bad people? They get to be the cause of the good person's misery. If bad things happen to good people, then truly horrific things happen to bad people."

"Like you," she whispered.

"Like you, me, your boyfriend, and Willis. Your father. Bad people. Despicable."

She bit her lip, glaring at her ankle and the litter of brown pine needles beneath her feet.

"Yeah. I know more than you could possibly imagine. I know about your stepmother. About Mop Top. Already kissing other girls. And here you are, unaware of it 'till now, bleeding, thinking I'm making all this up."

Taleah groaned, leaned backward, and kicked a pinecone towards the dying coals.

"Willis Ralston. In the end, what could have been said about a man who has such a hard-on for your mom?"

"You..." Her lip quivered. Tears trickled down her face. "...Don't know shit."

"And such strong language from a girl who's about to lose everything, if she ever had anything to begin with."

"Go to hell."

"Don't even get me started about St. Clair. The drug addict. A danger to everyone that was ever around him."

"My father's going to kill you."

"I believe he will. But he's already tried. Did he never tell you that he shot a man with a stolen gun? Let me see if I can remember that night."

Taleah glanced up at him, her vision blurred with tears.

"After I'd gotten that old-timer sheriff into a corner and I knew Willis was tied up, I discovered St. Clair stole the gun. And he ran. Coward. I had everyone right where I wanted. Then he shot me. Probably had only one bullet left."

"No," she stammered.

"I got the scar to prove it." He lifted his sweater and untucked a tan undershirt that had probably once been white.

Avoiding looking was difficult, but she managed. A cruel string of curse words boiled up in her subconscious.

"So you see, some people need retribution."

"Why take it out on me?"

He sighed. "Collateral. Something to give Reggie a good reason to come find me. He won't, as you say, 'win' this time. I'll destroy him. I'll finish what I started a decade ago."

"You are the coward. You're going to die!" She thrashed against the ropes. The pain in her ankle and her scalp ratcheted up a notch, taking the tension to another level. "You pathetic bastard!"

"Ah, high school."

She consciously swished saliva in her mouth and then expelled it in a fevered blow. Some of it landed on his beard and sparkled under the rising sun.

Without warning, he backhanded her. A sharp pain whipped across her skin like poisoned fire. "We're getting nowhere." He gripped the knife, stood up, and walked away. The coals dimmed. His back arched into an enormous mound as he reached toward the ashes. He withdrew something from the bag, placed it on his knee, and then stabbed something in the ashes with the knife.

Instead of watching, Taleah looked away. Her moans became sobs that flooded her brain with a million different emotions. It was too much. She wriggled her wrists and kicked a pile of dust and pine needles away.

Art remained calm. Her peripheral vision alerted her to the fact that he was slicing something with the knife. More food. She wouldn't eat it, no matter how hungry she was. It was likely poisoned anyway.

Her tears shed a different light on everything around her. Instead of sharpness, the world gleaned with molten shadows and hazy, reflecting light. The ache in her scalp bore a hallucinatory sensation that the world was progressing without her. Somewhere out there, beyond the tears and the pain, a pair of men sped along a narrow highway with no particular destination.

Everything was happening on emotion's wings. On instinct. The wild had a peculiar way of showing the true humanity of people—or the lack thereof. Being in this setting was like entering a hell where each of her nightmares unfurled before her eyes. The cataclysmic cycle of another morning cast a veil that separated memory from the present. It isolated the future until the future was all that remained. But in this setting, the future offered neither hope nor happiness. In the now, despair lingered like the dew after a cold, stormy night. What was coming was only worse.

Art stomped back to her, glaring at the foot he'd laid out on a hand-made cutting board. He placed it on the ground next to her, forced her off the log, and then untied one of her hands. "Eat. You'll feel better when you wake up."

Without thinking, she overturned the cutting board. She tried to growl, but all that escaped was a rasp that sounded as if crying had eroded her voice to nothing but a caustic whisper.

He turned his back once again and disappeared behind a thicket of trees upslope where cliffs vaulted toward the sky.

More tears flushed down her face. When she wiped them away, she glanced to the underside of the cutting board. Something was scrawled in black near the corner of the wood, as if it had been burnt. A chill vibrated in her bones as she read the bleakness of the message: *La era sinistra—finale.*

19

Innocence

As if an unseen veil separated her from the reality that constructed her world, Anna wore an expression that exuded dismay. Lines ran deeper into her face. Tugged upon by the unrelenting force of gravity, her eyelids sagged. She stared into an artificial sea of nothingness somehow trapped beyond the computer screen. Rebekah considered her carefully while avoiding eye contact.

The morning was wearing into afternoon. Outside, the heat of the day was bubbling. The forecast called for heat in the valley with thunderstorms in the mountains, particularly up north, where Reggie and Willis roamed.

Swallowing slowly, Rebekah reached over and placed a coddling hand on Anna's fist. No explanation was necessary. She saw enough in Anna's eyes to know that she was staring at a woman in pain—a woman who blamed herself no matter the circumstances and no matter the trials stacking up around her only child.

Instead of speaking, Anna bowed as if to hide the shame—or the tears, which had run dry during the last few days.

"I know it doesn't feel like we're doing anything," Rebekah offered, "but we're providing the men with invaluable information."

"Staring at a computer screen." Anna droned.

"We're doing our part. We can't be out there hunting with them. We'd slow them down, and if we do that, our chances of finding her become thinner by the minute. "

"It will be too late."

"They'll find her."

"At what cost?" Anna suddenly looked up. Her eyebrows were raised in high arches, as if pleading. "I've been callous with Reggie in the past. He was at the edge of sanity eleven years ago, but this will push him over the edge."

"Reg is stronger now."

"He's learned to deal with his surroundings more efficiently. That doesn't mean he's cured."

"There is nothing to cure."

"I know him as well as anyone." Anna frowned and shook her head.

Rebekah nodded. "And I know that when Reggie starts something important to him, he won't stop until he's accomplished his goals, for better or worse."

A lone tear, which had hung precariously at the corner of her eye, trickled down Anna's face. She didn't attempt to hide it or wipe it away. Instead, she let it linger as if it were a shiny badge of endured pain.

Rather than work the conversation to the figurative bone, Rebekah sat back and thought about changing course. A strong rap pounded the front door. Rebekah swallowed again and strode to the door to answer it. The glass revealed the visitor's identity.

"Close the computer and put it away," Rebekah said quietly. She waited for Anna to act before opening the door. She frowned when she greeted him.

He withdrew his badge and displayed it. "Agent Bill Coles, FBI."

"What can I help you with?"

"May I come in?"

Moving slowly, Rebekah swung the door open and led him across the hardwood floor to the dining room table where Anna was seated.

"Good, you're both here."

"Can I get you anything?"

"Have you heard from your husband?"

Anna looked away. Rebekah nodded gracefully, taking a half second too long to think about her answer. "I talked to him last night."

"Where is he?"

"I should tell you because..."

"You're in hot water," Coles finished for her. "But we'll get to that after we discuss Reggie's location."

"Last I heard he was wandering around up north," she said, careful to leave out specifics.

Watching her carefully for nonverbal clues, Anna squinted and laid eyes upon Coles. "You don't want Reggie. You don't want my daughter, either."

Coles flushed. "Listen here, Miss St. Clair. Our first task is bringing your daughter to safety."

"If it was, you'd have a manhunt going on." Anna argued.

"Anna, please cooperate," Rebekah said. She tried not to appear agitated, but Coles had a special knack for getting under her skin.

"Good advice," Coles sneered.

"You're not saying you've lost him," Rebekah jabbed. "Are you?"

"Where is he?"

Frowning, she leaned closer to the table, her heart pounding against the inside of her chest. "Tell you what," she started. "If the FBI is worth its salt, they'd be out doing their own investigation, not trying to track down a man who only means to help."

"Mr. St. Clair is in a dangerous position. To ensure everyone's safety, it's best that he stays out of the way. We've got the recourses to find Rassine in short order."

"Then use them," Anna snorted. Rebekah watched her curl her fingers into a fist. Her face burned crimson.

Studying her with caution, Rebekah shook her head. It was an obvious nonverbal clue not meant for Coles. They were dealing with a professional, and professionals proved more and more adept at getting people with intense problems to unintentionally spill their secrets. She didn't need television to know that.

"You ever hear about the case of Leon Buttars up in—where was it—Ketchum? Guy witnessed a pretty bad crime but hid some obvious ulterior motive when the cops went to question him. Meanwhile, he's under investigation for credit card fraud. Contrary to his knowledge of course.

"Well, they got us feds involved. Had no other choice, really. Normally they play it pretty casually when people lie about what they know. See, people lie all the time. We start knocking them silly every time that happened, we wouldn't get any work done. Not to mention our jails would be crowded while the violent criminals walk the streets, or in Art Rassine's case, the wild. Are you following me?"

"I see you're making vain threats already," Rebekah said.

"Buttars was up to no good. We didn't have to arrest him, but we had him on fraud anyway. You see it in movies, where the bad guy does something not central to the case and the cops deal with him and make the charges go away in exchange for information?"

"No," Anna said.

"It doesn't happen like that. In the end, the guy talked. And we caught the bad guy. To this day, Buttars is still behind bars. And you think you can indict this country's legal system by playing mind games with the FBI. It's a dangerous slope, Mrs. St. Clair."

Rebekah raised her eyes and thought about Taleah. "I'm not saying you guys aren't good. You're really good at what you do. So why don't you do what you do and leave us out of it? Go do your police work. I trust it won't be hard to track Reggie and Willis down if you work at it. Meanwhile, I'm going to let my husband search for his daughter."

Looking up with her deep, pleading eyes still sunken deep into her face, Anna stared at Agent Coles. "Please tell me you're doing everything you can to find her."

"No matter what it takes, we're going to get to the bottom of this. We'll do it professionally because, as you said, that is what we do. I can't say the same for Reggie. If he gets in our way, we can't be held responsible for what happens to him."

A little too forcefully, Rebekah slapped her palms on the table. "Don't you dare threaten my husband."

"No matter what it takes," Coles repeated for emphasis.

"You won't do it," Rebekah scoffed.

"Arrest him? Hell, he and Mr. Ralston are second and third on our short list at this point. We can charge him with obstruction to a federal investigation along with a half dozen other infractions."

"You said yourself that you don't waste time with obstruction," Anna said.

"Oh, but that's where the other part of Buttars' story comes in. Buttars had another arrest warrant in another county on burglary charges. He didn't know that, either. When they booked him for the fraud charge, they slapped that on, too. When you already have a record, these charges start to pile up real fast."

"Reggie doesn't have a record," Rebekah said.

"Trespassing. Carrying an unlicensed firearm. Eluding federal officials, disturbing the peace, etc. There's a laundry list of stuff we can hit him with."

Rebekah looked away. Her heart sunk. Her talents were insufficient to match wits with a trained federal agent who was probably an ace interrogator. In addition, she had nothing to bargain with. "Go find him," she said calmly, but with anger bubbling under the surface.

Coles reacted by relaxing his pace. "It seems we have more pressing matters to attend to, and time is pretty limited. We're going to get your daughter back." He glanced to Anna. "And we'll get Rassine, too. We don't want to be forced to arrest Reggie and Mr. Ralston."

A flurry of emotions tattered Anna's face. They passed over her expression like ravens in the night, searching for a means to an end and for something new to feed on. The tear that had leaked from her eyes left behind a narrow wash on her cheek that zigzagged like forked lighting around her minute features. The lines dug deeper into her chin. What Rebekah witnessed was the gradual breaking of a woman's spirit. The only thing she had to live for was Taleah. The hell with Reggie. She cared about him, but his importance would never approach Taleah's.

A careful shrug and a well-timed sigh indicated that Coles was ready to change the subject. Anna glared at him.

"I went through your daughter's phone. Pictures, calls—everything."

"What were you hoping to find?" Rebekah asked.

"More than we did, I'm afraid. We also did a field analysis for prints. Art Rassine had touched it, but it didn't look like he touched the screen at all. And nothing seems to tie her boyfriend in with Rassine."

Rebekah wanted to laugh. "Jacked that one up from behind the arc."

"Ever heard the phrase 'devils in the details', Mrs. St. Clair?"

"Now you're talking about clichés. Agent Coles, you are on *fire* today."

Coles continued as if she hadn't interrupted him. A coy smirk blemished his face momentarily, but then faded away to stony confidence. "The point is that thoroughness is the key. We look at everything. One of those little devils pops up and it changes the whole game. Without fail, it's happened on every case I've ever worked."

"So you naturally want to know more about the boy," Anna said. "Why wouldn't you go to him instead of us?"

"Just want to know if you've noticed anything out of the ordinary. Has he showed up late at night, wanted to take her to a place she'd never been before?"

"I don't really like him," Anna said. A look of shame dawned upon her face and spread to other parts of her body. "But he's a good kid."

"Skater," Coles said.

"Should that mean anything?"

"I doubt it. But like I said, details."

Rebekah covered for Anna. She leaned forward as if to ease the tension, but only seemed to invite more. "There never was anything suspicious about him. The kid is bright, but as far as I can tell, guileless."

"Have you questioned him?" Anna aksed.

"Done," Coles said. "And his background is flawless."

"Doesn't surprise me," Rebekah said.

"Sometimes surprises are hard to come by," Coles admitted. "That's a good thing. We like no surprises. A lack of surprises makes my job easy.

A batch of rage boiled under Anna's facial expression. She peered to her lap as she spoke. "Why the hell aren't you out finding this Rassine?"

"I've got a whole team of agents working on just that. I've set up base here, but if things get interesting up north, I'll be on the first flight."

"What are they doing?"

"You probably know the answer to that," Coles shot. "We've got Lance Harrison's old ranch locked down and a pair of agents are watching Rassine's old residence around the clock. I seriously doubt Rassine would be stupid enough to return to the area, but you can't be too careful.

"What about helicopters, drones, or satellite pictures?" Anna searched. "You have many tools at your disposal, so why don't you use them?

"Rassine is good at hiding. He's managed to evade our grip for eleven years. We've got satellites. Drones, easy. Hell, we can make thermal imaging of areas. The thing is, Idaho has more isolated public land than any other state by a pretty wide margin. That doesn't mean we're not trying. We just haven't had much luck yet. And chances are some regular lead will surface soon that will help us out immensely."

Rebekah studied his expression. Coles was as skilled as any tenured FBI agent. Chances were that what he'd told them was absolutely true, but Rebekah wasn't willing to exert total trust in him yet. The way she saw it, the smarter they were, the more deceitful they tended to be. She leaned back to cool the emotions, but the flames spread.

A stray tear lingered at the corner of Anna's eye and imbibed gloss form the kitchen lights. The scene lent itself to an aura of dour expression further stoked by Agent Coles' decisive edge. In the end, the need that fueled him tethered closely to the desire that burned within Anna. Rebekah had sensed these opposing, yet equally positive forces more than once, which should have been good news. Still, she couldn't help but feel that Reggie and Willis were closer to Rassine than the FBI.

Anna closed her eyes briefly and turned her head. When she opened them again, she was left staring into the backyard.

Coles eyed her carefully. Rebekah attempted to break his gaze, but no subtlety could influence him. It was time to mount an offensive.

"I don't suppose any of your agents has any profiling experience," Rebekah said. "You feds sure do have a nasty reputation to uphold."

"Of course we do, Mrs. St. Clair. You gotta kiss the right rings to get in this position." He turned to face her as he started speaking. Success.

"And from what I've heard," he added, "so do you."

"I beg your pardon?"

"You've been busy. Real busy."

"Unlike some of us," Rebekah snorted.

Coles took a moment to appear fazed by this comment, but it was clear that he was playing games. He stared at her long enough to draw her in. Rebekah imagined it as if he believed he were baiting a hook. Rebekah was going to fall into the trap, but not because she didn't know he'd set the trap. She wanted answers. If she played her cards right, Coles would paint himself into a corner by talking too much.

"Don't think your little hacking and eavesdropping activity hasn't raised a few eyebrows at the Bureau," he said. "It's an interesting tactic, but highly unreliable and just as unlikely to hold up in a court of law, if you get my drift. Maybe your motives are admirable, but that will be up to the judge. A little leverage goes a long way. But tampering with the FBI…That's a federal offense."

"You'd better arrest us, then," Rebekah said, holding out her wrists so he could slap the cuffs on them.

"Not in the mood," Coles said.

"Then what are you still doing here?"

"Pursuing justice. Help your husband all you want, but if you try hacking the FBI again, we'll send a swat team in here."

"That's like swatting a fly with a hand grenade," Rebekah said. This comment was enough to get Agent Coles to his feet. He glanced at her one last time before striding to the door.

"Thank you for all of your help," he said. He opened the door and walked out.

Anna stared, then brushed the back of her hand across her eyelid. Her eyes were bloodshot. Not enough rest and too much emotion.

"Help?" Anna said flatly. "He can't be serious."

"He was playing us," Rebekah said. "And I've just given him enough ammunition to bring down the Taliban. By not helping, we've helped him more than we imagine. Coles will be on to Reggie and Willis by morning. We have to warn them."

"It had to be done, eventually," Anna said. "After all, we need the FBI to find them, don't we?

Rebekah nodded. A sour expression crept across her face. Coles was graceful, charming, and menacing all at once. The deck was stacked in his favor. All he had to do was deal and he'd come out on top no matter what skill Rebekah applied. She frowned and stared at the table. Now she was the downtrodden one. With one cool sentence, Coles had brought her to her knees. This time, the task of rebuilding a soul would fall on Anna's shoulders. Whether she was strong enough to withstand the burden remained to be seen. Then again, Anna's brushstrokes were a welcome tangent. With only a simple gaze, she painted the world around her with such fluidity and grace that no man or woman could emerge untouched.

20
Residence

The hyphenated yellow lines in the center of the highway were darting across Reggie's field of vision like flaming arrows in a dark battle. He watched as if hoping the energy of the motion could somehow dull the nightmares and squelch the headache.

Willis remained silent, focusing his attention on the road as a whole. Reggie didn't like watching people drive. Instead, he always looked out the window and, as a result, appeared cut off from any and all conversation that was taking place. The haze of last night's migraine lingered and fluttered.

Vibration in his pocket snapped his focus back to what any sane individual would have construed as reality. "Pull over," he said, struggling to withdraw his phone. "So I can keep a clean signal."

Willis did as instructed, without regard for highway signs and narrow lanes. For good measure, he flipped on his hazard signals.

"What's up, babe?" Reggie said.

Rebekah cut to the chase. "We have a problem." She paused, almost as if waiting for Reggie to invite her to continue. "Agent Coles showed up this morning. He's looking for you."

"Convenient," Reggie said. "And Taleah?"

"He says she's his number one priority."

"Let him try to find us," Reggie said.

"It's a matter of time, dear. He knows an awful lot more than he's telling us and, apparently Anna and I have not covered our tracks well enough. I'd say you have about a day before they track you down."

Reggie considered the news. "Hopefully, that's all we need. How did he find out?"

"Can't say I'm surprised," she said thoughtfully. "After all, they are good at what they do. We didn't tell him much, but we tipped him off anyway."

"Damnit," Reggie grunted. "I told you to be careful."

"I'm sorry. But I think I was too careful. They caught onto us pretty fast, I think. He warned us to stop trying to eavesdrop or he'll send us to jail."

"It's a vain threat."

"I know, but if we don't deal, he's going to get really sour on us. You and Willis, too."

"All because he wants Rassine?" Reggie raised his voice inadvertently.

She paused long enough for the stark reality to encircle her. Breathing slowly, Reggie waited.

"He aims to find Taleah. He wants all of us out of the way."

"The FBI is too slow. We're close. I can feel it."

"We have to hang up now, Reg," she interrupted. "I have a feeling they're listening to us now. I don't want them locking onto your signal and finding you too fast, because if they arrive before you do, Rassine will get spooked. Your chances are better if we end all communication from here on out."

"Goodbye," Reggie said. He tossed the phone over his shoulder, glared and cursed.

"Bad news again," Willis said. "Seems that's about all we're good for lately."

Reggie stared at him, burying his fingers in the cloth upholstery. "Floor it."

"Copy." They regained highway speed quickly. The day was wearing on. Scraping across the blue over the gorge was an innocent-looking line of pale cumulous clouds. Knowing that weather had either nothing to do with the task at hand or everything to do with it, Reggie watched the sparkling waters of the Lochsa randomly intersperse with pockets of pine. This was beautiful country, but it kept an ugly secret.

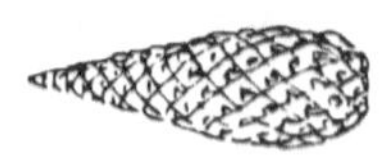

"Need more manpower," Coles barked into his phone. He was speaking with an operator, who on a last-minute effort had decided to feign immediacy. Such a persona irked Coles so much that he had no tolerance left.

"Well, Sir," the operator said. "The United States Forest Service was obviously interested enough to phone it in…"

"Talk faster."

A pause brief enough to register as an annoyance but not long enough to elicit sincere anger sliced a gap in the dialogue. "A survey man found an illegal campsite. They further investigated the scene and found some uneaten food, a powdery substance and lock of hair. They heard we had a missing person case and made a few calls. While you have agents in the vicinity, it is worthwhile to check it out."

"Probably nothing," Coles said impatiently. "A few youngsters having too much fun, probably didn't know camping wasn't allowed."

"Are you saying that you don't want more evidence?"

"I'm saying I've got a manhunt to conduct. Every agent I got, I got in important spots, and they can't run off chasing unicorn tails every time someone sees some ashes. Jesus!"

"The director's office's orders specify that…"

"Dispatch a couple more agents. I got DeLaren and Clark staking out New Meadows. Johnson and Killburne are watching Rassine's old property. I don't expect the man to be stupid enough to return, but you never know."

"Evidence would suggest he's heading north," the operator explained.

"Isn't evidence at all unless an agent says it is. Riggins, you say. Where is that?

"Fifty or sixty miles north of New Meadows," he said. "It seems that if the agents you demand decide that there is evidence there, then that would render New Meadows obsolete."

"Not exactly," Coles said. "Just because he's north of his old home base doesn't mean he isn't going back. We're dealing with a criminal smart enough to figure that out."

"And when the agents you demand are finished investigating?"

"They'll join our manhunt," Coles said. "Send them. Now."

"Devine and Murdoch will be on the first flight."

"Devine," Coles yelled. Isn't that the guy that took a job in forensics last year?"

"The same. He's ready to do some more field work. We figure that his experience in forensics will be of some use to you."

Shaking his head, Coles tapped his feet on the floor of the car. "Whatever they find, if they find anything they can use, will still have to be transported back to the lab. Getting to that spot is a bear—don't mind the figure of speech. They won't find anything for days. Even then, what does it mean for us? We know the girl's missing, we know who's got the girl. Only thing we don't know is where to find him. Once we have a good location, I join all four of my men and scour the area. I think lab results will be a little late."

"Do you want both of them to aid the search?"

"I want the ashes, the food, the hair, the heroin or whatever the powdery substance was, shipped to Salt Lake ASAP. If Devine can still shoot, I want him and Murdoch on my team. Agent Coles over and out."

He hung up the phone and tossed it a little too forcefully into the cup holder. Glaring at the traffic, he revved the engine hard and took off. "More work," he muttered. Not a shred of it was helping to find the girl, or Art Rassine. Rassine was currently America's most-wanted criminal. The hell if Coles was going to let him get away this time.

A somber shadow drifted in front of the mouth of the cave. Taleah watched the sky for a moment, anything to keep herself from focusing on the black inside. Resting against the rock she'd hidden behind last night and trying to remind herself that her father was coming did little to no good. Instead of inviting hope, it wrought a sense of urgency careening toward despair. She'd pled silently for more than an hour that Dad would find her today. A touch of blue crested near the ceiling of the cave and wandered out of sight. Cloudy skies were coming. It could possibly rain, she thought. Good thing she had shelter, but it probably didn't mean an advantage.

In addition to dimming the sun and turning a soulful situation to rust, the clouds converging meant a gradual cooling. It might have been a comfortable seventy-five outside today, but it didn't matter.

Taleah's ropes were double-knotted around her wrists and tethered behind her in yet another secure knot. She'd been able to fray the rope loose with a sharp stone before, but not this time. Rock or no rock, she wouldn't be breaking this bind. Her next chance had to be the next time Art decided to try feeding her.

At this point, food was a necessary evil. Her stomach had been warning her to eat for days. Malnourishment, while not the least of her concerns, would certainly have dastardly consequences in the near future. Then again, what if the near future never came? What if all she had was a day, a few hours, or even twenty minutes? She shuddered.

She didn't really want to eat in the first place. She didn't know whether or not he was trying to drug her, poison her, or neither. Still, her brain could simply not reconcile the notion that filling up would cure what ailed her. It wouldn't help her at all. If she admitted to Art that she was hungry now, he'd beat her into oblivion. The man did not possess kind hands, but rather the unforgiving hands of an animal. Those brutal tree trunks he had for forearms doubled as weapons of unbelievable violence.

Taleah had seen a lot in the last few days, but she'd seen very little. Details were sketchy at best and probably little more than deeply sub-conscious notions of reality. Some things she remembered were probably false and somethings she didn't remember had come to pass. What that meant was anyone's guess. Again, Taleah shuddered. Tears welled in her eyes and faded away.

Where exactly was Art? It had been hours since she'd heard any sound from him. He could have been out hunting or God knew what else. If so, he would not be watching her and guarding the entrance to the cave. If she escaped it would come as a great surprise. That commu-nicated to her that Art was confident in the bindings.

Unfortunately, that confidence ripped whatever hope she clung to out of her grasp like instinct ripped the bat out of her hands after a home run. Being tied up like this made her want to run. Fight or flight. The sad thing was that this time, her body had no choice but to accept what was coming—to wage the war with scalded hands and aching legs.

"Art," she said.

There came no answer.

She repeated, louder. Still, only silence resonated.

Alone again, she began to build a scenario where she could free herself from the ropes, which were currently pinned against the rock. Making plans required a surprising amount of strength. Although thinking usually came naturally, she found her mind somewhat hazy and slow to react. Without the fuel to keep her going, she ran the risk of shutting down completely. Passing out again became a very real possibility and one that was accompanied by the jolting realization that her danger might have been even greater unconscious.

It was in that subconscious zone of her mind that fantasies were forged into terrifying realities, where water trickled like the blood oozing from the scab on her ankle. There, what was left was an inverted tapestry of a million different emotions and fears. Furthermore, Art could perform harrowing acts on her body if she didn't have anything with which to defend herself.

If Art came, she would eat quickly. The risk painted itself worth the reward this time. Her strength would reassert itself. And while she was untied, she'd find a way to run—a fleeing that would certainly lend itself to further agony. She stifled the will to scream, to let loose of every conviction within her. She didn't care that Art wasn't around to hear her.

Unquenchable terror was the state of the game and, whether present or not, Art delivered in spades. Hope was nothing but a four-letter word. Fear reigned supreme.

21
Assisted

As far as the eye could see, towering cumulous and nimbus clouds flanked the gorge. Reggie silently referred to the phenomenon as 'tunnel syndrome' as if the words alone could describe the emotions it enhanced. Truthfully, the weather could never bring about emotion or feeling. Those traits already existed in Reggie, in one form or another. The weather simply had a way of intensifying the emotions and casting a dominant shadow over all else.

Before the day was out, it was going to rain. It was easy to see and easy to predict. Bad weather marred the previous showdown with Art Rassine. The location had been isolated—more than a mile from any road, paved or not.

Willis didn't focus on the weather, but he had noticed it, Reggie thought. How could he not notice? The darkness beneath coming storm cells was always more pervasive from the outside. It was a threat, but it wasn't so bad when he was living it.

The only problem with this line of reasoning was that 'tunnel syndrome' preempted a total emotional collapse. When the threats closed in from all sides like a bloodthirsty army bent on destruction, the simplicities of fear and sorrow shrouded everything else. These...tempests raged on. They were viscous orbs of energy that brewed nothing but darkness.

Reggie needed the darkness. *Come to me, Reggie.* It was his one true advantage in dealing with Art Rassine. The shadow roamed the woods almost constantly; his eyes were accustomed to adjusting to the scant light. Reggie, on the other hand, was rarely surrounded by total darkness. He could always see something.

Then again, the darkness his mind alluded to was mental rather than the physical lack of light. The dark his mind provided was a match for Rassine's motives of pure black. Conjuring and dwelling on that abstract was like fighting fire with fire.

Fire. Another thing Rasine was skilled at. Reggie had never really worked out how it had happened in that little valley all those years ago. It was raining. Everything was wet. Yet somehow, fire seemed to shoot in all directions. His best guess suggested that Rassine had poured kerosene in a circle and drenched the rope with it. This logic was riddled with holes, however. In the end, Reggie never cared to further explore the possibilities.

Willis glanced from the road and eyed Reggie for a moment. When he returned his gaze to where it should have been the whole time, he swerved to miss some forest rodent with a death wish.

"How are we going to do it?" Reggie asked, knowing that Willis wanted to start a conversation, but couldn't manage to issue a first remark.

"What?"

"We're getting closer. I don't know why, but it seems like something is drawing us up here, like destiny or something."

"Maybe it's God trying to tell you something," Willis said. "You speak God fluently, so why don't you politely ask him in what basically amounts to English where we're going?"

Reggie didn't even smile. He looked down and clenched his fingers on his lap. "I can tell you aren't up to the task."

"I am, believe me. Can't a guy joke around now and then?"

"We don't have time for jokes."

"Right," Willis said. "I seem to forget that time is our perpetual enemy."

"Shut up and pay attention. We need a plan."

Wasting no time in forming a blistering retort, Willis fired back. "A plan usually includes some event or something to set it in motion. What are we going to find?"

"No idea."

"You're expecting some sign? 'God, if you want me go crazy, say not hing.'"

"You already are crazy," Reggie said.

Willis nodded. "Yeah, and you are the kindling."

"Get with it!" Reggie shouted.

With another pathetic little nod, Willis managed to keep up the pace by speeding through a turn. "Okay, then what are you planning? I just don't understand how you're going to conjure the faith to lead you to stop in the right place, that's all."

"I don't know. But let's look past that."

"A glaring omission," Willis said. "Logic is supposed to be your strong suit, but here I am coming up with all of the daggers."

"You're not making any sense."

"Sense? You won't find any in this car."

"How are we going to outsmart him?" Reggie said, staring out the window. A blur crossed in front of his eyes. He shifted his focus to the road in front of him. It was nothing but the long shadow of a barren tree. Allowing a bleakness to drift over him, he succumbed to the dark and invited tunnel syndrome to take effect.

"I don't think we'll be doing any of that," Willis said. "Doesn't seem like we fared too well in that department last decade, either."

"But we didn't know what to expect then. Now we know what he's capable of."

Willis parted the conversation with a pause that was more like an incision meant to inflict minimal amounts of pain. He was calculating—a sign that things were about to start unraveling quickly. "Eleven years is plenty of time to learn a few new tricks."

"Where's he going to learn them, the internet?"

"Hands on. It's his style. You know that as well as anyone."

"I'm thinking we have to take a route he doesn't expect us to take," Reggie explained. "When we were fighting for our lives in that little valley, Rassine knew exactly which way we would be coming."

"Because he knew we'd already been there," Willis interrupted.

"Partially. But it was also the shortest distance and the least work to get there. He'll expect us to take the easy route."

"The easy route is the safest route," Willis said. "If we get hurt along the way, we'll just chalk him up another advantage. Then what do we do?"

"We climb. We go the wrong way on purpose. If we're supposed to turn right, we'll go left."

Willis' eyes bolted open wider. He navigated a tight bend and gently accelerated past a fallen rock on the road's shoulder. "A few lefts make a right."

"Exactly. We go over rocks, though dense pockets of trees. Places no one would think to set a trap in a million years."

"But we gotta be careful," Willis cautioned. "Or we might end up trapped anyway. It's a good way to end up dead."

"If it rains, this tactic will present serious issues," Reggie admitted. "It might be dark by the time we make it anywhere close. You figure a day of hiking or so, maybe a little more, we're looking at travelling by night"

"He won't see us coming."

"But we won't know we're there, either."

"It isn't foolproof," Willis said. "But it's the best we've got. You ready to cause mayhem?"

"As ever," Reggie answered. "Let's go get her."

A wisp of high clouds floated over the ridge north of the city. Beyond that, somewhere in the mountains, bubbled lower, darker clouds. Anna sat with her elbows on her knees, which was a contemplative gesture, to say the least. Rebekah considered it a signal that Anna was tired, but that the horror she felt prevented her from sleep. If that were the case, Anna's actions were merely a product of insomnia. Rebekah coolly stared toward the butte north of the city as if to completely ignore Anna.

Further worrying Rebekah, Anna buried her face in her hands and yawned. Rebekah took a sip of her water, shifted her focus to the street, and watched a pair of cars roll by. Without smiling, she waved at one of them. The gesture caused Anna to look up.

"You should get some rest," Rebekah said.

"Can't."

Rebekah paused and waited for a warm breeze to pass. "I know. I can't completely understand how you feel, but I'm here for you."

Anna peered through a crack between her fingers.

"I know it doesn't seem like we should be friends at all, given our histories with Reggie. The way I see it, we're in this together, so we might as well at least act as if we tolerate each other."

"I don't hate you," Anna said.

"No, but before this you were understandably apathetic to my existence." Another car slowly eased down the drive as if the driver were watching for a specific address. "We both were."

"Friends," Anna said. "It should be more awkward than this."

Rather than say anything, Rebekah sipped her water and watched the car roll to a stop in front of the house.

Anna looked up.

The car's door opened and a woman stepped out. She was wearing blue jeans, a tee shirt that looked as though she'd used it for painting, and a clean pair of running shoes. The woman stepped across the strip of grass separating the street from the sidewalk, paused, and looked at the house. She made eye contact with Anna first, then Rebekah. A smile flashed across her face, and then she made her way up the walkway to the porch where Rebekah and Anna were sitting.

"Is this the St. Clair residence?" the woman asked.

Rebekah nodded. She wished she were as fit as this woman, but instead of dwelling on it, she warmly welcomed her to have a seat on the small wooden bench by the door. Simultaneously, Anna and Rebekah stood and rearranged the patio furniture so as to face the visitor.

"I know I shouldn't have come by unannounced like this."

"Don't worry about it," Rebekah said. "Do I know you?"

She shook her head and looked down to her feet. "I guess you could say I'm a friend of your husband's. We met ten or eleven years ago."

A knowing expression carved a dark crater in Anna's expression. Rebekah glanced at her and then continued to focus on the visitor. "You're Mandy?"

"Mindy. Mindy Caldwell."

"I've heard about you. What can I help you with?"

"I saw on the news that your daughter...Reggie's daughter...was..." She couldn't continue.

"Yes," Anna said. She scanned Mindy's somehow vacant expression.

Whatever emotion that lurked beneath her outer shell was hidden, as if trained into a dark cavern meant to keep it hostage. Rebekah spoke carefully, so as to not upset either of them. "You're the one that got away. I know how awful that must have been."

In truth Rebekah had no idea what Mindy Caldwell had been through. Instead of attempting to establish a common ground, Rebekah meant to console. It didn't appear to be working.

"It was a long time ago," Mindy admitted. "Most of it I've forgotten."

To say that she was lying would be an omission of the truth—the real truth. You don't just forget things like that. Instead, it probably felt to Mindy as though the events of that ordeal concluded only yesterday. Mindy's portrayal of the act was not convincing. She stared at her feet, folded her hands, stared at a house across the street, and generally avoided eye contact.

"Tell me about yourself," Rebekah said. "Where do you live? Any kids?"

Mindy shook her head. "I live on the north side of Nampa, about ten miles from here. After my grandmother died, I couldn't bring myself to live in her house anymore. She was just about the only family I had. So I looked around at renting, and then just decided to buy."

"Are you seeing anyone?"

"I can't deal with men. I dated a few six or seven years ago. Didn't work out. They were just...men. And I'm..."

Rebekah thought she understood what this meant. "Whatever your taste is."

"I have no taste," she said. "I guess I'm supposed to be alone."

Anna stared at her. Once again, reminders of tears made her eyelids sag. "I know what that's like."

Rebekah glanced back and forth between them, and then focused on Mindy. "No one is supposed to be alone. We find people when we are ready, or when the other person is ready."

"Maybe what happened to me is preventing it. Maybe I need closure."

"Closure involves..." Rebekah stopped abruptly. She knew what Mindy was insinuating and she didn't like it. She frowned, leaned back to gather he thoughts, and then attempted to continue.

Anna cut her off. She spoke as though a fresh batch of adrenaline transformed her soul into some radiant gem sparkling in the sun. "My daughter is like you. Athletic, attractive. But she's strong. And Reggie won't stop before he finds her."

"You can't," Rebekah said. She wrinkled her forehead and watched a neighbor water the flowers. "It's not a good idea."

"Rebekah," Anna said. "Let's hear her out."

Instead of talking, Mindy glanced at Anna, and then fixed her gaze on some potted flowers hanging from the eave to her right. She gulped and stammered. "I...I don't...think you...under-stand. I want to help."

"What can you do?" Anna asked.

"No," Rebekah said. "I'm not going to allow it."

"Took me...years to cope," Mindy admitted. "He killed one of my friends—a girl he had trapped in that cave with me. And he...got away with it."

Tears formed in the corner of her eye. She wiped them away hastily and continued. "You can't even imagine what it was like. Daily torture. He drugged us and raped us and kept us chained in that filthy hole. Filthy just like him.

"I got away somehow and ran, and then hid, because he would find me. Then I found Reggie. It was like a weight had been lifted from my shoulders. I didn't trust him at first. Being in the presence of someone good was...was something unexpected and I didn't know how to react. He said I was captive for two weeks or so. It felt like a year.

"After that, I went back to live with my Grandma Caldwell. Vera. She tried to help, but I needed professional counseling. I went to a psychiatrist every week for four years. Still I can't...get the horrors..." She sniffed, looked down, and trembled. Tears began to pour from her eyes.

"I still have to go see this woman every so often to remind myself that I'm still real and can walk away with purpose, thinking I still matter to someone for something."

"You had it rough," Anna said, leaning closer to her.

"I wanted to...kill myself sometimes. The abuse, the shame, the outright neglect. Everything bottled up and ready to pour out like a poison that could send a person to hell and back. There's just too much bitterness and anguish."

"They say captives sometimes begin to relate to their captors..."Anna started. This unleashed another realm of provocative energy. Her face sunk into her hands and her shoulders lurched.

Again, Rebekah found herself having to be the strong one in the setting. She meant to retrain the topic. She stared at Mindy, waiting for more.

"I've heard about that syndrome. Named for the capital of one of those Nordic countries. But that didn't set in. Maybe it did for Teresa. I don't know that much about her."

"Rassine is a horrible man," Rebekah said, still staring.

"Worse," Anna sobbed.

Mindy's shoulders fluttered. "I used to think that. But he's just a beast. In more ways than one, he's just nature at its darkest and most untamed. It's something my psychiatrist told me. I've heard so many people say that to find peace, you have to forgive. It's hard to forgive when you know that things like this are still going on.

"I know I have a purpose now." Mindy paused and allowed the momentum of what she was about to say settle. "It's my duty to help. When I heard about your daughter, I knew right away that I had to do whatever I could. When we get her back and put...him behind bars, we can let go of the past."

"Closure," Anna said, drying her tears.

Mindy nodded.

"What do you plan to do?" Rebekah said.

"I'll help find her," Mindy said.

"My husband has already gone to look for her and I can't help but think he's on the right track."

"Tell me where he went," Mindy said.

"No." Rebekah stood up, walked past the front door, and then back before standing in front of her chair with her hand over her mouth.

"I have to. I think it's what God wants."

"He doesn't want you to get killed. You don't think this Rassine will recognize you? From what it sounds like, I don't think he'll hesitate to kill you. If I let you do that, your blood will be on my hands."

"It's my choice," she said. "I don't know if we'll be successful, but I believe past experiences and circumstances help shape destiny. The choices we make always have meaning. What I had for breakfast can have a big impact on someone else somehow."

"Rebekah, she has a point," Anna said.

"I can't let this happen."

"If I find her daughter, I'll help her to safety."

"No," Rebekah said.

Anna lurched in her seat. The tears were still fresh on her cheeks. "Damnit, Rebekah! You're saying we don't want this woman's help. I want my Taleah back. I can't live..."

More tears spilled from her eyes.

"I'm afraid you have to go," Rebekah said. "I'm sorry, but this isn't going to happen. We all have choices. I believe in my husband. And I can't let you go die for this cause."

Understanding, Mindy rose to her feet, glanced back and forth between Anna and Rebekah, and then walked briskly to her car.

Rebekah's cheeks flushed. Anna sobbed. Scooting closer to her but not wanting to wage the war that would certainly come, she refrained from touching her or saying anything. She glanced behind her. Mindy slid a yellow piece of paper out the narrow slot of her window and then pulled away.

Watching the neighbor water her plants was like letting time pass for the sake of ushering in a new era or sensation. Time was withering in the sun, and somewhere beyond the horizon, was folding in on itself, collapsing to became a singularity so dominant that the night could not discover relief from the heat of emotion. Anna continued to sob.

After a few moments of reflection, she stood and quietly made her way to the strip of grass between the sidewalk and the street. The neighbor waved. It was funny how this old woman was pretending to not understand or care about the conversation that had just taken place next door. It had certainly been a dramatic one, and probably very entertaining. Rebekah always felt as though watching drama unfold was a sorrow that she simply could not look away from. She was always filled with caring, but not in a position to help—only to watch. Yet, everything that happened in front of her or in the stories she'd listened to was somehow more real than television.

On television, people made questionable moral choices. Rebekah was strong in her convictions, but what if her convictions were wrong? Taleah's life certainly meant a lot to her. Over the years, she'd come to love the girl. Still, her faith in Reggie was unwavering. He was the rock that she clung to when all life seemed to be on the brink of converging into a bleak storm of oblivion. Her choices always had merit and she often wondered whether they were the correct choices at all. She'd learned to contend with the consequences of her choices. The outcome more than her beliefs would tell her whether it was right or wrong. But sometimes, circumstances were so complex that consequences seemed to come in many shapes and disguises. Some paraded as a sea of light and grandiose music. Some inundated her with sorrow. Still, the constant always remained. When the events unraveled and sorted themselves out as they always did, the answer was displayed right in front of her.

Rebekah reached down to pick up the paper Mindy had left. She held it before her and her hands began to tremble. It read: The 'era' is not over. How many must suffer? Call me if you change your mind.

The phone number was scrawled on the bottom of the paper.

Slowly, Rebekah carried the note to the porch and sat down next to Anna. She still leaked with tears, but her expression began to transform into something resembling interest.

"I don't know what you think you're doing," Anna said, wiping more tears from her face. "I thought we were friends."

Rather than saying anything, Rebekah sighed and drew her phone from her pocket. She tapped a few times and scrolled on the screen. Anna watched her.

"What are you doing?"

"I'm calling her back," Rebekah said. "Please, God, give me the strength to accept the consequences."

The phone rang four times and seemed as though her call was going to be sent to voice mail. Instead, a weak voice answered. Mindy sounded as though her voice were tattered with emotions Rebekah did now know the extent of.

"Mindy," this is Rebekah. "Reggie and Willis are in the Lochsa Gorge near Kooskia, heading east."

"Towards Montana?"

"US Route 12. They are in a blue Subaru with bumper stickers on the back. Please be careful."

"Thank you, Rebekah," Mindy said gracefully. "This is all going to be over soon. You'll see your daughter again, I promise."

Rebekah hung up the phone, scooted nearer to Anna, and wrapped an arm around her. Anna's tears were beginning to dry. Guilt and hope were dripping in her mind and in her heart. The two conflicting emotions oozed together to form a concoction of mystery. She didn't know where this was going to lead. She hoped against hope that the consequences would not prove disastrous. The results of this decision were bound to be a mixed bag, and Taleah's fate somehow rested in the hands of the choice Rebekah made. Her decision weighed upon her like lead, yet felt oddly empowering.

Anna looked up and said "thank you" quietly. Rebekah frowned, furrowed her eyebrows, and clenched Anna like a best friend.

22
Callous

Black and white clouded her peripheral vision. The stone structure of the cavern, temporarily visible with the angle of the afternoon sun, seemed to exude an otherworldly charm. Taleah wondered if this cave contained bats. If bats lived in this cave, she'd surely have seen a few by now. Then again, wildlife wasn't her first interest.

Today was a different day. She'd been planning and thinking, which led to both mental and physical exhaustion. She leaned back against the rock to which she'd been tied for the majority of the day and wriggled her fists behind her back. The cold moisture of the stone and clay floor spilt a musty scent across the heels of her palms. She didn't know long she'd been trying to get loose; starting the task was a subconscious and unplanned event.

The rope was tight, but she thought she could feel it loosening. Every few minutes she spread her hands as far apart as the bindings would allow. At first the distance was nearly nothing—perhaps a gap large enough to wedge of fragment of paperboard into. Hours ago, she thought she could have grabbed a stick or clutched a rock. Still, the rope would not release her wrists enough for her to pull them out and put her hands to use.

A pervasive cold leaked from the back of the cave. Again, she wondered how far into the mountain the passage would take her before finding a way to seal her in. The risk certainly wasn't worth the reward and the darkness that prowled those unexplored territories offered far more dread than hope. She shivered, wriggled her hands again, and stared at the rock in front of her. Her shadow constructed a pyramid-shaped mountain of bleakness.

Allowing moments for the scene to filter into her subconscious mind was doing her more harm than good. When it was all said and done, Art would come. And with him would arrive further torture.

Hollow chopping sounds emanated from outside, signaling that Art was near. It seemed that he wielded some sort of axe he used to extract firewood from the forest. She listened for a moment. The chopping came nearer. The sound changed into that of a log being struck against stone. She shifted her hands and crouched low for reasons she didn't quite understand. He was near—too near. A stain of black eroded the rock in front of her as he silently approached. She waited, quiet as she could until he was close enough to hear his footsteps.

"Dinnertime, sweetheart," he growled.

A pang in her stomach leapt toward her throat and a wash of saliva spread across the roof of her mouth.

"In your favorite hiding place," he reasoned. This time, he didn't bother trying to ignite the insides of the cave with a flashlight. He used the sunlight and altered his own shadow to maximize the light.

She stayed frozen to her spot. Even if she wanted to move, she wouldn't get far.

"Don't make me drag you out of here."

Forgetfulness? Was there more on Art's mind than she'd expected? She didn't let the thought magnify or latch onto the insides of her skull. Whatever his perceived weakness, he remained much more dangerous than all of nature combined.

"I can't," she whispered.

With a sudden lurch, he appeared beside her, wedged in the gap between the boulders. He grasped strands of her hair. "That's right. Don't forget that. Because you're mine."

"Bastard," she spit.

"Clever." He forced his hand down to her collar and yanked with enough force to shoot a jabbing, stinging sensation across her throat.

She gulped but succumbed to his will.

Without speaking, he released her shirt and ran his hand down her back. His huge hands felt as though he was caressing her. She shuddered and shrunk away from him, which provided him more a gap through which to work. He carefully lifted a heavy stone, untwisted the rope, and pulled her free. Her hands remained bound. He pulled on the rope as though he were merely out walking his dog on a hopeful morning.

"Hungry," he muttered.

"No," she said quietly, looking down to the scar on her ankle. When she applied pressure by standing, deeper pain swelled. That wasn't a good sign, but the way she'd struck the ankle on the splintered tree trunk suggested that no bones were broken.

"Wasn't a question."

"I know what it was."

"A fact?" He shook the rope briskly, stepped behind her, and shoved her forward. She tripped, but the rope caught her and helped her retain balance. "A funny thing about what you teenagers will believe. They teach you all kinds of 'facts'. About life, love...but you still don't know the half of it. After this is over, I imagine you'll 'know' things you never imagined. Everything's how we take it in."

He was waxing philosophical, which made her uneasy. She didn't listen—only passed his words off as the ramblings of a madman. Still, truth rang in his words. His explanation about her future seemed to communicate that she did have one. Then again, Art was eloquent when he needed to be and brash when the circumstances warranted. His speech, figuratively, was like a work of art both wild and tasteful.

Another stiff shove sent her tumbling forward between the two boulders. A patch of sunlight tore through the canopy of the trees and sparked discomfort in her corneas. She stumbled, regained her balance, then tripped again, landing haphazardly on her bad ankle. Her mouth emitted a muffled groan as another spike of pain shredded her ankle. Grimacing, she limped forward to where strewn pinecones and dry grass met stone.

Rather than attempting to fight him, she stepped forward. Ten feet beyond the mouth of the cave, the landscape sloped downward in a rugged incline studded with dense forest, fallen trees, and enormous rocks. She knew where she was headed—where art wanted her to go. The stump on which she cut her ankle loomed at the edge of a miniature cliff that dove into ragged underbrush five feet below. It would have been a hell of a fall had Art allowed her to run unimpeded. That probably would have hurt more than the little stump did. But even this pain was something she was not accustomed to.

When she reached the makeshift camp and stumbled toward the log he'd perched her on before, she sat down without being forced. Art lopped some fresh plants and what looked like rabbit meat on the same slab of wood he'd used to serve her earlier. She scowled at it but decided that eating was in her best interest.

More slowly than she wanted, Art reached behind her and loosened the ropes enough for her to slip her hands out. She allowed herself a moment to enjoy the freedom but was careful to observe Art's every move. Watching him from her peripheral vision, she hurried down a dozen or so gulps of food so fast she could barely taste it. It wasn't home cooking and didn't compare to the wonderful meals Rebekah had prepared for her on occasion. It seemed like a silly thought at a time like this, but she missed her stepmother almost as much as her father.

Swallowing, she looked around as if hoping to see a sign of Dad's arrival. Instead, she only saw trees. The mountain loomed to her left, its rocky face somehow glistening against the penetrating sun, which was currently protruding through a gap in the clouds.

Art cleared his throat, stared at her for several moments longer than was comfortable, and then abruptly turned away. He began pacing, glancing back and forth between her and some invisible point deep in the forest. He wrung his hands together. Fidgeting?

It wasn't that he was nervous. What did he have to be nervous about? More likely, he was anxious, but his mood probably veered more towards impatience. The look in his eyes somehow communicated more than his body language. His expression was all fury.

Art circled a tree beyond his makeshift fire pit. He glanced up and paced back to her. Taleah gripped the wooden cutting board as if she were preparing for a fastball.

In an explosion of movement that surprised even her, she leaped from her spot, vaulted the fire pit, and launched herself in his direction. Adrenaline surged. A fervent patch of venom boiled in her veins. Without allowing a split second to balance or cease her sprint, she cocked her hands and whopped him in the face with the cutting board. He staggered backwards, lost his balance, and fell into a tree.

Without looking back, Taleah intensified her sprint. Ignoring the pain seemed more and more difficult. She darted between a pair of tall junipers and then zigzagged through a rugged section of terrain littered with underbrush and rock. Leaping tree stumps, she continued along what seemed like a narrow ledge. Unaware that she was beginning to travel away from the road and deeper into the wilderness, she quickly calculated a steady descent down a steep slope.

She was about two hundred feet above the floor of the notch between two mountains. Falling seemed a real danger, but some unknown force would not allow her to slow.

A tempest of noises crashed through the forest behind her. A bird skimmed past her as a gust of wind whipped the swaying pines into a frenzy. The gale altered her direction of travel ever so slightly. Precision wasn't her first priority but remained important. Underbrush shuffled under the weight of the massive man that chased her. Rocks scattered and tumbled down the slope, colliding with trees and other boulders.

Incoherent grunts suggested that Art was frustrated, but also somewhat amused. Teleah aimed for a narrow gap between a pine tree and a large boulder. The path was risky. With a steady skip, she jumped. She was off the mark. Her leg grazed the coarse bark on the juniper and her toes caught on a jutted portion of stone she hadn't seen before. Panic sent a spasm of disbelief down her back.

After a graceful midair adjustment, she landed awkwardly on her feet. Her bad ankle buckled as it struck the uneven ground. She splayed her hands out straight in front of her. Her dive resulted in an uncontrolled somersault down a steep slope. She screamed something that sounded like a combination between a curse word and a nonsensical exclamation. Pain erupted in her back as she tumbled down the slope. Her world inverted, righted itself, twisted sideways, and spun in a dizzying series of tumbles.

With terror coursing through her, she willed her body to straighten in the middle of a roll. For a split second, she observed that she was aimed directly at a large tree. Her momentum forced her into a painful back flip. Her tumble became a slide. Her back arched as her rear end rammed into a rock at the base of the tree. Gravity did not allow the motion to stop. A deep crease created a gap between the rock and the tree. From the top of the rock to the bottom of the tree trunk was about a foot, maybe two. Her feet twisted and collided with the tree, launching her upright.

She clumsily slumped against the tree. Fear rocked her senses. Pain scorched her leg, her back, her ankle, her neck, and her scalp.

Her eyes darted in all directions. She wasn't really looking for anything at all. Her surroundings had become a confusion of green and grey. The brushstrokes her motion created appeared as streaks across the field of her vision. Her heart pounded at the inside of her chest like a bass drum.

"Taleah!"

Art. She managed to scoot to the side of the tree. Her tumble seemed to have taken her near the bottom of the slope where a tiny stream carved a narrow gash through an endless jumble of rocks.

Run. She limped away from the tree and carelessly cast herself over a steep drop in elevation. One foot landed firmly. The other buckled. Horrified, she attempted to maneuver so that she could remain upright. Instead, she tipped sideways and fell onto a sharp rock. Another jolt of pain crossed her spine.

"Taleah St. Clair!" The voice was a grumbled fury that echoed across the steep valley. She looked up. Between what seemed like a long corridor of tree trunks, she saw him emerge from behind a dense pocket of underbrush. He towered over her dominantly.

She stifled a moan, shuffled against the rock, and then rolled sideways. The slope of the ground allowed her to slide about ten feet. She was wounded and the pain would not allow her to move much more. If she could somehow further disorient him, she could gain the advantage and buy enough time to follow the stream to the highway.

Art was beginning to descend the slope. He stepped carefully. His long legs allowed him to erase about four feet of distance with every step. "Careful, you bastard," she said quietly.

Taleah lay sideways with her head on the ground and her ear resting against a pinecone. A quick survey of the valley revealed large piles of rocks, running water, dense stands of pine, thickets of undergrowth, and pine needles littered everywhere. She needed something she could defend herself with. Desperation led her to scan the area once again. Before she realized what she was looking at, a quaint air of hope drifted over her. Perched in a slot between two rocks and buried in dust and pine needles was a heavy stick. She hoped it wasn't attached to a tree.

Slowly, she made her way to it, inching across the ground like a worm. Art played the part of a bird surveying its prey from above. He quickly descended the slope. He sidestepped a boulder and then carefully maneuvered around something she couldn't see. His distance seemed like two hundred feet, but he was closing quickly. She willed enough strength to pull herself up on a rock. She limped in place helplessly for a moment.

Art disappeared behind a deep thicket of brush. Taleah limped toward the stick, grasped it, and swung it through the air. If she could load enough force into her swing, she thought she could knock him unconscious.

When she looked up, Art had already reached her. He reached out his hands. A terrifying expression of rage and want contorted into a ragged smile. *Come one step closer.*

All of the adrenaline she could muster flooded into her shoulders and her arms. He momentarily looked dazed. Teleah flung the stick with as much power as her muscles could possibly wield, which somehow seemed like more than enough to blast a home run over the center field fence. He attempted to dodge the arc of the swing by moving his head to the right.

With a heavy thump, the stick smashed into a point at the base of his skull behind his ear. She lobbed her makeshift bat some ten feet and sprinted. Art staggered and collided with a tree. She didn't see whether he'd lost his balance or if he remained conscious. All she could do now was run.

Spasms of pain eroded the stream of adrenaline. Her joints and her muscles became tired and started to lock up. She didn't know how far she was from the highway or even if there would be a car nearby to pick her up. Terror was like a potent gasoline that ignited everything around her into a pungent aroma of smoke. Her vision faded, reasserted itself, and then dulled again. Her leg muscles cramped and shut down like pistons starved for oil. For a moment, she swayed, unsure whether she'd fall face first into water or rock.

A loud roar indicated that Art was still conscious. She peered back at him. He vaulted toward her with huge steps and a broad expression of hate perched on his face.

She could not escape. Hope dwindled to nothing. Still, she struggled forward, fighting against reality and the very potent thought that these could be her last moments alive. Tears sprung from her eyes. "No," she whispered.

Art was barking a storm of obscenities. Taleah limped onward, dragged her aching ankle over a sharp stump, and collapsed. Her breathing was erratic, and her heart was on the precipice of escape. She rolled toward the stream, grasped a rock, and launched it at Art. He reached out. Her legs kicked as if moving of their own accord. Her heart seemed to melt into oblivion and her vision faded to a cacophony of black and vibrant color erupting in a kaleidoscope of pain.

"No," She said again. "No!"

Her eyes blinked open for a split second. Art's hands folded around her throat. He was going to strangle her. "No," she rasped.

"No," Art said. "No more trying to run."

A faint squeal erupted from her lips. Art lifted her to her feet by the neck, flinging her around like a rag doll. Her muscles had no fight left. Pain scoured her entire body. Flailing her arms, she attempted to scratch his face or yank on his greasy hair. It was in vain. She felt a momentary sensation of being airborne. Art flung her against a thick tree. The back of her scalp collided with its trunk. A new wave of agony poured over her. The light drifted in shades of grey and morphing colors. Darkness crowded her from all sides, and then simply vanished to nothing.

23
Wounded

Dusk approached over the uniform peaks of the Central Idaho mountains as Reggie and Willis wound their way along the banks of the Lochsa River. Some time ago, what felt like hours, they had passed the confluence of the Lochsa and Selway Rivers, which joined into the Clearwater River. US Route 12's bends proved easy to navigate. The turns provided enough motion for the drive to remain interesting without obstacles such as sharp curves or narrow shoulders. Reggie alternated his focus between the river and the yellow lines on the pavement.

The one major thing Willis had to look out for, especially in the late evening hours, was wildlife. Because the turns were fairly wide and the grade relatively even, the speed limits remained higher. This always led to greater hazards when darkness descended and wildlife came out.

"It must have been hard on your wives to have the FBI snooping around like that." Willis didn't remove his eyes from the road. His expression remained glum, while his body language suggested a certain need for accompaniment. "You don't imagine Agent Coles was fishing, do you?"

"He was fishing," Reggie said. "But Rebekah can be strong-willed when she wants to be."

"Ever been fishing?"

"Why are we talking about fishing?" Reggie asked, certain that the conversation would lead them into a node of unproductivity.

"Hey, when in Rome..."

Reggie rolled his eyes and lightly slammed his head against the headrest. "There you go again."

"Where?"

"Imagining we're off on some adventure. We're on a mission."

"A few remarks about the state of affairs in this neck of the woods never hurt anyone," Willis said. "Besides, when driving there's only so much you can do. Plus, it's your job to keep me awake."

"I'd say wake me when we get there, but we don't really know where 'there' is yet."

"That's like saying a Salmon is a fish."

Reggie gritted his teeth, but gave in. "I've been a time or two. Takes a lot of skill. The most experienced fishermen get the most and biggest fish. Right now, I'd guess no one is a bigger fish than Rassine."

"Is that true?"

Letting his gaze relax, Reggie spoke cautiously and slowly. "You gotta know all the right gear for the right conditions. If you use the wrong lures, go at poor times of day, wear the wrong clothing...talk too much...you won't catch much. The pros know how it's done."

"Only problem is, Coles isn't catching anything," Wills said, tilting his head. He raised one eyebrow but didn't flash a smile.

Reggie's knees instinctively started to pulse up and down like a pneumatic jackhammer blasting away at the Subaru's floorboards. "You have to account for the fact that Rassine isn't the only fish. He's just the big prize. To use fishing lingo, the one that got away."

"So you think The FBI is out fighting drugs and picking up shoplifters?"

"More like tracking a couple of rogues," Reggie said. "No matter what we do, we'll be easier to catch than Rassine. Then he can use us to get him."

"Makes for a neat little game," Willis said. "I don't think it's a good sign that he's using us and the women for leverage."

Reggie nodded. "It smacks of desperation. A guy like that looks for advantages anywhere he can find them. And he knows where to look. You could say he knows where all the best holes are."

"On the golf course," Willis joked. "The 18th at Banbury is a classic."

"Let's not meander to golf," Reggie warned.

Willis lowered his voice. "Ralston's got an uphill putt, a little left to right, but it straightens out at the end. He should make it in two."

Reggie's knees bucked hard against the dashboard. He fidgeted and gnashed his teeth while trying to maintain an even edge. Willis wasn't making it easy.

"So what do you think Coles..." He trailed off when he realized that Reggie wasn't listening.

Watching the shoulders of the road proved therapeutic. It allowed him to relax and to think more clearly. Willis, while good at getting the job done via his own methods was not particularly adept at the Reggie St. Clair method of analysis and reflection. As such, his mind wandered just enough to find the right avenue to travel. Reggie always paid careful attention to the details before rushing into conclusions that might have been wrong.

A deer appeared down a short, rocky slope, but disappeared before Reggie could set eyes on it. He decided they were making good time, but without a destination, time almost seemed meaningless. This line of reason presented obvious problems. Rather than consisting of meaningless seconds ticking away into oblivion, time was of the essence. It controlled everything, even life. Taleah's life.

A fresh jolt of pain rocked his forehead. His vision momentarily became fuzzy. Focusing became a torture he didn't want to endure.

The roadside blurred before his eyes. Rather than looking laterally out the window, Reggie focused on the landscape ahead. A break in the trees and a brown and yellow sign signaled a road ahead. The sign was barely readable in the glare of the headlights. Instead, something else caught his eye. Something was hanging from the sign as if had been nailed to it. Reggie's heart leaped as he made out its shape. Its fins and deceptively dark eyes were like a beacon—a sign that they had at last arrived.

"The hell?" Willis said.

Reggie shouted, part victorious and part scorned. "Stop the car."

"A fish? Doesn't make any sense." The tires squealed on the pavement as Willis slammed on the brakes. They skidded to a halt in the roadside gravel about fifty yards beyond the sign.

"It makes perfect sense," Reggie said.

"To a person as deranged as you."

"Or Art Rassine. Think about it. You remember what we found at Rassine's old house?

Whispering an obscenity, Willis shook his head. "I don't believe it. You found your sign. It's a miracle."

"It's bait." Reggie shook his head, unbuckled his seatbelt, and propelled himself into the fire he knew was coming.

As if instinct guided and accelerated his intensity, Reggie forced his fingers to his forehead. Exactly how he knew this was the right place was a matter for another day. He could *feel* it. Some unknown darkness washed over the distant shores of a river running to nowhere. The sting of its waves altered the energy of Reggie's mood. Where darkness had crept along the perimeter of Reggie's thoughts throughout the day, the shadow was now emerging into the mainstream.

A venomous wisp of steam blurred his vision and burned his eyes. He balled his fists, trembled, and frowned. His insides turned to rubble. Rassine was here. Somewhere.

"What do we do now?" Willis asked.

"I'm going to kill him." Reggie's voice broke and rasped in his throat as he whispered.

Willis said nothing and only waited for a proper reply.

"Park the car in the campground."

"I don't know about this. Doesn't that fall right into his plan? I mean, if it looks that obvious..."

"Do it."

Willis cursed and lightly tapped his fist on the steering wheel. He spun the steering wheel hard to the left, paused to scan for headlights, and then proceeded through a U-turn. He crept along slowly until they reached the entrance to the campground. This campground appeared mostly deserted. One stray car was stationed in one of eight stalls, but Reggie saw no sign of a camp. Rassine's vehicle?

Reggie's breathing became labored as Willis backed into a narrow stall framed with a concourse of barren pines. A fire pit and a picnic table loomed unused and forgotten behind the trees.

"No one camps anymore," Willis commented. "It's weird. You see people with motor homes and boats and trailers and ATVs, sometimes even fishing gear. They just park their trailer and go have fun. Tents, barbecues, hot dogs, smores—it's all gone the way of the dodo."

"You don't say."

Willis turned the car off, spun his keys around his finger, and opened his door. He stood up and looked around as if all at once cautious of every danger that lurked in these woods. Peering towards the other car with a look of mistrust spanning his face, he spoke quietly. "Who do you think it is?

"Don't care."

A shadow sprung from behind a tree to Reggie's right. His heart leapt, but instead of launching himself at the intruder, Reggie stayed frozen. Wills strode quickly to Reggie's side as if preparing for a fight.

"Can't say I'm surprised to find you here, Reggie," the man said. Dusk enveloped him in a shroud of murky tan and gray. He seemed much older now that when Reggie had last seen him.

"Smith?" Reggie stammered. "How did you..."

"The FBI."

"Deputy Monaghan, how times have changed," Willis said.

"And yet stayed exactly the same." The deputy eyed him suspicion but feigned friendliness.

"Coles sent you?"

Smith shook his head. "The guy's smart, but not that smart. He forgot that Rassine has been at the top of Adams County's wanted list for a decade. Why shouldn't he be? Bastard murdered a senior deputy and a friend. 'Sides, not all is quiet in Idaho these days. We heard the news. After you called us, we knew we had to take action somehow. An informant tells me that the feds are en route right now. You must have tipped someone off."

"Coles has been suspicious from day one," Reggie said. "After telling him how frustrated I am, we just left. He figures he's going to follow us to find Rassine. Then he figured out that my wife has been listening to their phone calls..."

"I'm not even going to ask."

"So he turns the tables and somehow figures out where we're headed."

Smith stared at the sparkling river, a section of which was visible through a notch in the trees. "How long till they get here?"

"Maybe twelve to twenty-four hours."

"You shouldn't park here," Deputy Monaghan said. "This is the place they'll look if they're after you."

"They're not after me. We just need a little more time before they come in and screw everything up. Stall them for us."

"You asked for my help," Smith said.

"Then help us."

"By staying out of your way?"

Reggie was already walking away when the deputy opened his mouth. Willis lagged, looking dumbstruck. He offered Smith a warm smile and nodded. "You look good."

"Where are you going?"

Willis whistled to keep Reggie nearby. From the trunk he withdrew the necessary supplies. He was careful to grab the flashlights, the rope, the canteens, food items, and a small first aid kit. The last item he loaded into the pillowcase they brought was the gun. Attempting to hide the weapon from Smith proved a challenge, but the deputy didn't say anything. With a healthy lurch, he slammed the trunk shut and half-jogged to catch up with Reggie.

Reggie and Willis didn't speak for a long time. With caution and stealth, they crossed the highway without truly knowing what horrors were about to unfold. It was a dread they had to deal with sooner or later. It loomed on the horizon like an emotional storm billowing with untold quantities of energy. The day had expired. Dark now ruled the landscape, imperious, yet powerless.

Whispers invaded Reggie's mind as he paused at the edge of a ditch that paralleled the north side of the highway as it followed the river to its headwaters. *Come to me.*

Willis gulped. Together, they stepped into the wild.

The first obstacle to navigate was a sharp, grassy incline. The tree line painted an opaque stripe about twenty feet above the road. He lost his footing and almost slid back down to the ditch, but Willis helped him regain his balance. The going would be easier when they reached the trees.

Entering the forest was like succumbing to a shadow that lurked in his nightmares for years. The pain was beginning to return. He rubbed his scalp as he grasped at tree limbs to help him up. They hadn't eaten in too long.

"We need a rest," Willis said.

"Already?"

Willis sighed. "Reg. We've spent all day driving, stopping, driving some more. It seems like we need to recover some energy."

"Fine, Reggie said. "When we're nice and secluded, we'll find a spot, build a fire, eat, and sleep a couple of hours. You first, then me."

"Why separate?"

"Someone's gotta be on the lookout. Rassine knows the area and he might seek to make our trip really short and not worth the effort."

"I think that's probably his plan."

They shared no more conversation for more than an hour. The night seemed to trudge on forever. An uneasy feeling swept over him again, but he curtailed it. Focus was, at this moment, his deadliest weapon. It helped him fight off the demons that attempted to hijack his thoughts and torment his mind with delusions wrought from hell itself. The rubble in his heart shifted and settled.

Reggie's breathing became more and more labored with each passing minute. The fact that they were traversing up the side of a mountain was not subconscious—it was part of the plan. The higher the ground, he reasoned, the better. The idea was that the raised elevation would provide better, more advanced warning if Rassine discovered their position and decided to come after them by starlight. This was the very reason some ancient civilizations preferred cities constructed on natural overlook positions. The advantages of elevation proved numerous and, in many cases unmatchable.

From this vantage point, Reggie believed he would have a wider view of the area. Although starlight illuminated relatively little, the advantage still belonged to him. Most of Reggie's perception during the night would have to be audial. He silently encouraged Willis to remain quiet through the use of subtle hand movements and avoiding making abrupt noises when he stumbled. The use of the flashlights had to be limited since Reggie had little idea how thick the tree cover was on this mountain.

"You don't think we'll find them by morning? Willis asked.

Reggie didn't answer.

"And what about the FBI? What happens when they start landing helicopters?"

After a low grunt, Reggie answered. "Look around. You see any advantageous places to park a helicopter?"

"I don't see anything," Willis complained.

"They'll have to drive it. Turns out Smith is camped out at a strategic position. He won't stop them, but he'll stall them."

"How long?"

"Long enough." Reggie's voice dripped with false hope, as if a doctor were telling him that terminal cancer would mostly feel painless. The simple fact was that the FBI's presence did more than warned of danger. Reggie feared that Coles and his agents would be the catalyst for Taleah's destruction.

"What happens if we find Rassine first?" Willis asked. "Would you kill him first, then go look for Taleah?"

Reggie pondered silently on that question for the next twenty minutes. With each step, the pain in his forehead grew stronger and the proverbial stones in his gut denser. Reggie felt as though he could wither from the pain, the expectation, and the agony all rolled into one simple disaster. There was no good answer for a valid question. Through the turmoil, all that remained was consequence steeped in despair.

The waiting proved to be too much for Willis. Instead of posing his question again, he chose to change the subject. "Good weather tomorrow, I think. Plenty good for the fish to start biting early."

Reggie felt the need to force a coy smile, but the notion passed. What little Willis knew about fishing showed. Then again, Reggie sensed that Willis wasn't simply talking about snaring a big rainbow trout. "Don't say things like that," Reggie said.

"Okay," Willis agreed. "But you never answered my question."

"I don't have a plan for that." He mulled it over some more. A few minutes later, he finished his thought. "I think we'll have to let chaos take its course."

Willis stopped walking and frowned. "A dangerous proposition."

"But probably our only choice," Reggie amended for him.

The finality of that statement tore a crater in the conversation that lasted the remainder of the hike. Reggie stopped about forty-five minutes later to survey what appeared to be a thick blanket of pines shrouding this position when viewed from below. This spot seemed to be a narrow ledge overlooking an offshoot to the gorge through which a smaller feeder stream flowed. He scanned the area below, hoping to see movement, but decided nothing would present itself. Weariness had been taking its toll on him for much of the evening.

Last night, sleep seemed spotty and chaotic. The waiting for coming events was like a cliff. A false breath or two would send him cascading into a flurry of thoughts that could only bring him to the edge of his own demise. Yet, thought was unceasing and, at times, thoroughly enlightening. No good could come of the lack of sleep.

Willis offered a long sigh when Reggie cleared a spot beneath the canopy of a pocket of conifers. He shrugged and sat down. Both of them knew that tomorrow could offer nothing but more walking. Doubts abounded that they would find any clues to Taleah's whereabouts.

For ten minutes, Reggie let the tumult in his heart subside into little more than waves that brushed against the jagged rocks in his mind. He welcomed sleep—begged for it. His eyelids drooped as the pain in his forehead sagged just enough.

Two minutes later a shrill echo shredded the gorge below. On instinct he flung himself forward as if danger awaited. His heart hammered against his chest. Confused, he looked around him. With his palms at his side, Willis leaned forward. His eyes were wide open, and his scalp erupted in sweat. For the moment, Reggie didn't want to ask what had made the sound. But the answer on Willis' face played out in vivid detail the unrest that was taking place below.

24
Pursuit

Faces etched against a snowy background glared back at Agent Bill Coles. Their expressions ranged from bleak to torrid. It seemed as if the photographs were engineered to elicit a certain emotional response from trained federal agents. Coles' muscles twitched and his eyebrows sank lower into his face. Atop the list, of course, towered the dark image of James Bullock, also known as Art Rassine. His photo stood as cold as the white flickering screen on Coles' phone. It was almost as if Coles could hear him growling half sentences in what basically constituted his native tongue. *You got nowhere to go, fed.*

After studying the photo for a moment too long, he closed the picture and nestled the phone in one of the center cup holders. Waiting was like watching seconds float by into memory while events somewhere beyond the realm of his imagination played out and faded. An uneasy feeling crept over him but did not set up dominance before his phone rang.

He picked it up without glancing at the caller ID on the screen. The ringtone gave him all the information he needed. "Coles."

"Agent Clark here. We got a problem at the residence of Art Rassine."

"Say again?"

Clark paused. "The place has been broken into. We suspect Reggie St. Clair."

Coles shook his head, considered the news, and then trudged on. "Not altogether unexpected. What did he find?"

"Nothing of significance." Her voice remained smooth and level, yet cold as ice. There was a good reason Coles believed her to be an impeccable agent. She continued. "Wasn't much to find in the first place. Footprints and fingerprints suggest more than one intruder."

"That would be St. Clair's cohort, Willis Ralston," Coles said without thinking. "What do you think they were after?"

"You know the answer to that," she scoffed.

"Based on what little evidence remained, where would you go next if you were Reggie St. Clair?" Coles spoke slowly, as if attempting to warm Clark into Reggie's point of view.

"Fishing."

"What? Where, specifically?"

"Going on what the fish tells us, somewhere along the Lochsa River, wherever that is."

Coles subconsciously looked it up in his mind. "Up north. Why?"

"Because he believes that's where Rassine went."

Stroking his chin, Coles shifted his head and rested against the headrest. He was growing impatient already. A subtle sigh indicated that this was already old news to him. "Do you believe it?"

She spoke firmly and confidently. "Absolutely. Rassine had a fish mounted on a wall, like one of those trophies people clutter their living rooms with. Caught this one along the Lochsa River. It's like Rassine is luring us there."

"Luring Reggie," Coles corrected. "But there's no proof it worked yet. Hold at that location until further notice, over."

"Ten-four," Clark said.

"Coles out."

Just as he replaced the phone in the cup holder, it began to ring again. This time it was an operator from the Salt Lake field office. He thought he knew what it was about.

"Agent Coles," the operator said. His voice sounded gruff but exuded the faint remnant of victory. "We have a location on Reggie St. Clair and Willis Ralston."

"Good work," Coles said.

"On your orders, we tapped Rebekah St. Clair's phone."

"Give it to me."

"St. Clair was calling a Mindy Caldwell. The conversation was short, but she told Caldwell where her husband was headed."

"The Lochsa River," Coles said. It wasn't in the form of a question. He wasn't sure whether Reggie would believe the evidence sturdy enough to follow, but he sensed that was what the operator was about to tell him.

"How did you know?"

"Thank you," Coles barked.

"Who is Mindy Caldwell?"

Coles groaned, balled his fist and placed it on his forehead. His knees bounced up and down. He offered two words before hanging up the phone and bursting into action. "A victim."

When he hung up the phone, a vile feeling of disgust crept up in his stomach. Though the information paved a path to Reggie and, by extension, Rassine, this wasn't a good development. He quietly considered the news and wondered whether Mindy Caldwell would try to track Reggie down.

The possibility seemed wrong from every angle, yet Rebekah had to have given Caldwell the information for two reasons. Rebekah wouldn't have called Caldwell unsolicited, which meant that Caldwell had volunteered. But why would a woman that Rassine beat, raped, drugged, and tortured want to have anything to do with finding him? Such a quest would have been extremely dangerous and bordering on suicidal. Then again, that could have been what Mindy Caldwell wanted. But eleven years later? It didn't make any sense.

This news made Coles consider arresting Rebekah for reckless endangerment. He could send agents to nab her, but that mission required time he could ill afford. He meant to save a life. This gave him something else to worry about.

Rebekah proved good at causing confusion and disorder—obviously what Reggie had enlisted her for. Before now, Coles hadn't taken her seriously. Her attempts to sidetrack the investigation had seemed sophomoric and inane, but had he understood her true value, he would have recognized that she was exceedingly smart. Smarter than Reggie, and maybe even Rassine himself.

She had given Reggie advice. The consideration of sharing information with Caldwell would have heavily burdened her mind. This suggested that the moral responsibility was inexorably steep on both sides. Whatever her motive, she had invited more danger than necessary.

This time, Coles didn't bother to put the phone down. He immediately dialed back agent Clark.

She sounded surprised. "Wasn't expecting to hear from you for over five minutes."

"I want you and Agent DeLaren waiting at the service station in New Meadows at 2200. Redezvous with Miller and Thurmond and wait for me. We're going fishing."

The living room was dark, yet warm and inviting. A lamp perched on the corner of an end table filtered dim light through the living room, leaving long shadows in the corners. The light reflected off the screen of the laptop Rebekah was using. The glow seemed to induce weariness, but she was too entrenched to simply turn it off. A subconscious sensation that darkness crept along the outer fringes of the room was a notion paralleled in her own mind. The research she was doing was like the glow of the lamp, yet dark skirted the corners of her subconscious.

She glanced up from the screen. Anna lay partially covered by a thick woven blanket. She had fallen asleep from the weight of the day. The embers of an unknown future likely burned bright in her dreams. The stain of old tears painted splotches of smeared makeup on her cheeks. If Rebekah were in a place where thinking about Anna seemed appropriate, she would have pitied her.

The two women were like opposites tethered to a common goal. Too often Rebekah exerted her own strength to erase the chasm between them. But Anna was sometimes like ice and sometimes like simply glass. She gave off a certain cold at times, yet at others, she was so transparent that Rebekah didn't even need to look at her to understand the way she felt. It would have been easy to say—though admittedly true—that Rebekah had no idea what Anna was going through. Sometimes, however, life itself was a tool of comparison. A woman need not experience such tragedies in her own life to understand the sorrow associated with them.

The topic of research was more a matter of casual interest at first, but the resulting findings drove her to further realms of discoveries. She mostly wasn't interested in statistics. She could find those anywhere. Often they presented themselves like advertisements designed to induce panic. She shuffled through them carelessly until stumbling upon a page built with stunning facts.

Contrary to some beliefs, the FBI regularly investigated missing person reports, especially when they became too large and too complex for local law enforcement agencies to effectively deal with. Also contrary to beliefs, the FBI frequently solved these cases. This was an interesting ray of hope shrouded by the bleak revelation that many of the missing turned up dead.

Rebekah covered her mouth. Her heart leapt, but she uttered not a sound. Instead of dwelling on that revelation, she continued to sift through pages of reports in an effort to find a case similar to Taleah's. There seemed to be nothing remotely close. She mentally noted that each time the kidnapper demanded considerable ransom, the victim remained relatively safe. But ransom was the primary motivation for a vast minority of cases. Most often the kidnapper had no demands at all. Children lured by sex predators often didn't survive. Children taken by relatives survived a majority of the time, but the results rent countless families in shreds.

Considering this, Rebekah moved to close the page. She almost clicked when she saw a tiny image floating above a 'help-wanted' link. The face looked eerily familiar. Not sure what to expect, she followed the link. It led her to a current FBI most-wanted list. The first and largest picture on the page was that of Art Rassine. She'd only seen his photograph once, but his face was unforgettable. The grizzly nature of his cheeks and his think mane of greasy hair remained perpetually entrenched in her mind.

Art Rassine was simply a madman with no concrete motive and no demand. This realization torpedoed her heart. In disgust, she turned off the computer and closed the screen. Waiting for news while inactive was torture, but a cruelty she was forced to endure. The cascade of facts would come. Whether or not these facts would be pleasant remained to be seen. Yet an inescapable consequence underpinned the whole state of affairs. Whether or not Taleah survived—or Reggie for that matter—her life would undergo a massive change. For good or bad, that change would mark Rebekah, Reggie, and Anna for life.

25
Orientation

A faint orange light flickered somewhere beyond her eyelids, in the world outside. She'd become increasingly aware of her world, where her own thoughts and feelings dominated. It remained a starkly different place from the real world, where countless people scurried about their everyday lives. Taleah groaned when she gained consciousness. The ropes bound her to a tree. Cold air leaked from the cave to bathe her back in a piercing chill.

For a moment, she struggled against the ropes, but it was no use. Her bonds were tighter than they'd ever been. It seemed that Art had taken extra precaution by applying double or triple knots as a sort of fail-safe system. Fear rattled her bones.

He was near. She could almost feel the heat of his fire teasing at her extremities and her exposed flesh. She tried not to move. Best not to draw attention to herself. All at once, motion seemed like a natural grace afforded to all human beings. For perhaps the first time in her life, she noticed that motion was much less a luxury than a necessity. The 'fight or flight' response was installed in our nervous systems for a reason. This time, however, she had little choice.

The sounds of the forest awakened. A pair of birds chirped and cawed in nearby trees. Small rodents scurried through the grass and brush at random intervals. Taleah looked around. The night was beginning to wear into dawn. For so long, dawn meant only hope. Today, it promised further agony.

She was alone. She couldn't even remember how long it had been since he took her. Four or five days, maybe? No one was here to help her.

Becoming aware of her circumstances and surroundings wrought a sense of despair and torture. She recalled getting loose and running from

Art. She remembered falling and tumbling and taking a swing at him. The remainder of the previous day's events were hazy.

Now that the scant light of the morning was beginning to penetrate the alpine canopy, her vision sharpened. Silently, she looked around. Observing her surroundings would be important. If the opportunity to escape presented itself again, she'd need to have a plan. Still, she wondered if such a chance would arise at all. Art would likely have learned from his mistake and would be hand-feeding her with a spoon.

Not only were her hands securely fastened to the tree, but her feet were ensnared in rope as well. She could move them across the ground together, as Art had little reason to tie her feet to the tree. The fact that Art had tied her outside the cave intrigued her. Her position seemed to indicate that Art was using her as a signal or something. She remembered what Art had said about believing her father would kill him. This fact flashed across her mind like wildfire tearing through a wood shop. It meant that Dad was coming, but it also meant that Art was luring him. He had unfinished business with him. The bullet wound in his side proved that. This time he aimed to finish her father off. And Taleah would only be a spectator to the horror.

Somewhere, Art moved. Fifty yards away through the dense trees, it proved impossible to see him, but she could hear him. His footsteps thundered nearer, then faded away. He issued a grunt to the nature surrounding him, almost as if communicating with it. Footsteps returned and then subsided once again. Was he pacing? What did that mean?

Motion somewhere to her right snapped her out of staring toward Art's camp. When she brought herself to focus on the eerie blue and green landscape to her right, nothing caught her attention. Fearful of making a sound, she stared. It was her imagination.

Taleah shook her head and tried not to think about anything. Instead, she turned her focus to herself. Her clothes were torn. Her shirt hung in tatters, dangling from her shoulders by mere threads of fabric. Dirt and scars from the fall and the fight marred her skin. Scabs were forming across the wounds. The jeans she'd been wearing for days had loosened. Long cuts slashed up the sides of the legs and frayed holes open at both knees and her hips. The top button had come undone somehow...

More noise issued from her right. She quickly turned her head to look, but she could see nothing. If she had company, her visitor made some conscious attempt not to be seen.

This time, she almost had to force herself to look at her clothes. Wondering what it meant—this kind of damage didn't result from falling—she swept her gaze up and down. A horror unlike any she'd ever endured washed over her. Art was a madman. He'd won the fight in brutal fashion with his bare hands. He was like a shadow of nature. He'd won because he was bigger and stronger. He knew the territory well. She'd hit him twice, but neither strike had done so much as disorient him.

Still, there was more to this horror than she'd realized. His brutal attack had rendered her unconscious. What dastardly things he'd done to her body in the meantime could only be guessed at. The gruesome nature of this revelation was something she didn't want to think about. Her thoughts scattered like beasts from a forest fire and cast a bleak shadow across her mind.

The dark soaked through her soul until she believed nothing but black could exist therein. Fear stoked the waves of anger, but she could do nothing about it. Rage spit into her vocal cords. At last, she couldn't hold back from screaming every curse word that came to mind. "You son of a bitch. I'll kill you. I'll watch you die screaming, you bastard!"

A roar bellowed from her left. She didn't immediately look in that direction. Instead, she looked forward and then right. Someone lurked there. Her venom had inspired a new batch of motion and a calming whisper, which barely even reached her ears. Her nerves settled slightly. Art would be coming at any time. She waited, holding her breath. He'd brutalize her some more, maybe even take advantage of her again.

He didn't come. She looked back toward the camp. The orange glow of the fire seemed to be fading away. Only the stray popping of pinecones sounded from that direction. There were no footsteps. He could have gone away. It seemed possible, but...

A warm hand rested on her shoulder. With a sudden lurch, her back erupted in a spasm. Ice poured through her veins and she issued a cold shriek.

A woman appeared, pressed her index finger to her lips, and carefully eyed her. "I'll get you loose if you promise not to run."

"Who...who are you?"

The woman whispered back. "A friend."

"A friend or Art. Get away, bitch."

She shushed her. "A friend of your father's."

Taleah felt uneasy about this. It didn't make any sense until she remembered her father recounting the tale from ten or eleven years ago. "Mindy? How did you, um, find me?"

"Your stepmom told me where to find Reggie." Mindy rested her hand on Taleah's shoulder. Instead of chills, it offered her warmth and a sense of comfort. Taleah struggled against the ropes for a moment, but once again fell silent.

She looked into Mindy's eyes. They sparked with some untold energy and reflected all of the torture Taleah had endured back at her. This evoked a sense of commonality. Mindy had been Art's captor all those years ago. She'd endured horrors unimagined, maybe even worse than Taleah's experiences. That kind of fear could have crushed any woman into a fine powder, yet here she was, staring Taleah in the face and at last facing her captor once again.

"How do you feel?" Mindy asked.

"Um...I don't know. It hurts, but it's like it should feel more painful."

Mindy shook her head and moved her hand from Taleah's shoulder to the back of her head. "You've got a scar here. You should be nearly unconscious."

"I was. I tried to get away, but I fell. He hit me."

"Plenty of times. All of these bruises. And your clothes. I'll get you another shirt out of my pack."

Taleah summoned a nod but didn't say anything.

"The madman...Art...probably gave you something for the pain," she said. "Don't worry about it. It's pretty powerful. I'd say you were lucky to be unconscious."

"What are you...what?"

Mindy closed her eyes as if to think about something deeply. She shook her head as she spoke. "Never mind."

Without adding to her comment, she walked away slowly. Taleah thought she knew where Mindy was going. She trod carefully and quietly. In the distance a slow zipping sound followed a little bit of shuffling.

As carefully as she'd walked away, Mindy returned with a fresh tee shirt that might have been a bit too big for Taleah. She didn't care; she was grateful for the woman's kindness.

"It's not a perfect fit and maybe not your style, either," Mindy admitted. "But it's the best I've got."

"Thank you."

Mindy tucked the shirt under her arm and began working at untying the knots. It took perhaps a bit longer than Taleah found comfortable. "It's really tight. For obvious reasons."

A cool sigh indicated that she'd given up. She reached into her front jeans pocket and withdrew a knife sheaved in leather to keep it from cutting into her as she walked. The knife had a serrated portion that made it look military grade. Bending over carefully, she easily cut through the ropes that bound her feet. She didn't bother discarding the rope.

Taleah's ankles were red from the rope. She looked down and remembered her collision with the tree trunk. The wound oddly didn't produce pain at this moment. She wondered what Art had given her and how long ago.

"What do you do for fun?" Mindy asked. Taleah thought it an interesting way to break whatever tension that existed between them. A hint of mistrust had spread through her, but Taleah was careful not to let it take hold.

Cutting through the rope that bound her wrists to the tree proved more difficult. Mindy severed the portion tied to the tree first so that she could work at a better and safer angle. After at least thirty seconds of slicing and sawing, Taleah was free. As if instinct guided her every move, she stepped away from the tree.

"I play softball. Shortstop."

"Sounds fun. I dabbled in sports a little bit in high school, mostly track."

"You still run?"

"When I can and when I have to. I'm not winning any marathons, but it's good exercise. My shrink always tells me to get plenty of exercise. Solid advice for anyone, I think."

Taleah only stared at her.

"It's from my past experience with Art. You understand."

Nodding and turning her head, Talah shuffled her feet. She knew the story about how her father had found her and didn't feel the need or the desire to bring up any of the nightmare she'd suffered through eleven years ago. "How did you find me?"

"Your stepmom told me where your dad went. I came to help."

"Why?"

"I consider Reggie a friend. Even though we haven't spoken for many years. He probably saved my life. I owe him, but the biggest part is that closure comes from helping someone in need." She paused, swallowed, and then continued. Most of it was dumb luck. I found Reggie's car, talked to some deputy and started to hike. After a while I saw his footprints in mud, so I followed where they pointed."

Taleah didn't respond. Mindy seemed as though she were reflecting on some bit of history as dark and layered as what Taleah endured. She studied her carefully while fighting off the urge to run. Depending on how far away Art was, they could make it back to Mindy's car. Then again, Taleah could tell that Mindy had a secondary motive at heart.

"Your father is here, somewhere."

That simple sentence spread a comfort across her nerves that seemed to warm both her skin and her soul. At this point, hope was a drug she craved more of.

"We have to stay safe somewhere he can still find us. I think he'd be grateful for my help."

"In what?"

"Art is a bad person," Mindy said. "You already know that. My guess is that the cops will be here soon, also. But if your dad and Art run into each other before then, I fear he might lose the fight."

"You intend to face him again? What would make..." She didn't finish her question. Mindy was looking up at the canopy as if in search of something.

When she leveled her gaze again, Taleah studied her eyes. A glimmer of hope tainted a concoction of fear and anguish in her expression. She wedged her hands in her pockets. Taleah thought she understood the emotion that drove Mindy. Instead of further questioning her motives, she relaxed her brain and turned toward the cave.

Mindy watched her.

"It's a good place to hide, but it might be a little dangerous. He had me tied up in there earlier."

Mindy shook her head. "It's going to be too hard to find. But if Art comes back before your father gets here it won't be any good elsewhere."

"So you hide," Taleah said. "If he comes back he won't see you. I'll just hold onto the rope and pretend I'm still tied up."

"But what if he tries to untie you?"

"He won't."

Mindy nodded slowly. "What if he does?"

"Then I'll run. He won't expect you to be there. And maybe if we make enough noise, my dad will hear it and come help us."

"And Willis," Mindy said.

Taleah stared. A faint smile parted her lips.

"Yes, I think he's here too. Based on the way they interacted when we first met, I assumed they were inseparable. Plus, I don't think your dad's foolish enough to come himself. Not after what Art put him through.

"You know about that?"

Mindy closed her eyes. When she opened them, a faint gleam of sunlight reflected back at her like a piercing ray shot into a chasm of darkness. It signaled a new direction and a different adventure. Danger lurked in every corner. All Taleah had to do was leap and leave the rest to faith.

26
Baited

Little sleep interrupted a painful night for Reggie. Taleah's scream had ensured that whatever sleep Reggie did achieve was tattered by increasingly horrid dreams. At some moments, he did nothing but stare up at the stars pretending he wasn't even tired. Sometimes, sleep won anyway. This ground didn't provide much comfort, nor did the air. The aroma of rain and the distinct feel of humidity prevented rest. The air also carried the unanticipated sensation of cold. Throughout the evening they had been lucky enough not to get rained on. Over the night, the thunderstorms gradually scooted off to the northeast and dissipated. The clearing exposed expanses of stars Reggie could not see from the city.

After realizing this, sleep had won him over. He dreamt about a star garnet and the eroded, ghostly flesh of Sandra Coombs. Though he'd never met her personally, it was as if he could still hear and feel her sullen voice resonating within his brain. *I knew you would come for me, Reggie.* When he awoke from that dream, fear paralyzed him. Every node of the wild conspired into treating Reggie to one of the worst nights he'd ever had.

When sleep prevailed again, Reggie's dreams turned to his daughter and Art Rassine. He awoke from images of Rassine stabbing her and then sleep blasted him with nightmares about Rassine sexually abusing her. The horror and the anger pummeled him from every angle. Reggie awakened with a shriek and didn't sleep the rest of the night.

Instead of offering hope, the dawn revealed that this could be the final day of his journey. He would either kill Art Rassine or die trying. Whether or not he succeeded, life would never be the same.

Reggie didn't have to wake Willis. He woke on his own with the sun. For a moment, he didn't even move. Reggie noticed his eyes open. He was staring at him like a similar dream had just punished him. They didn't talk. Reggie didn't dare start a fire. Chills burst forth across his skin. He felt as though hypothermia could kick in, but with each shiver, the thought of his daughter ignited passion. This passion sent artificial heat surging through his veins.

Willis dug a bag of simple trail food from the pack and tossed it to Reggie. He wasn't in the mood for raisins, nuts, and granola, but he didn't really have a choice. When he stood, his bones and muscles ached. He could do without another day of walking, but it seemed like a requirement.

After at least forty minutes, Willis cleared his throat. "What's the plan?"

"We find Rassine."

Willis didn't respond for several minutes. "How? Where do we start?"

Looking around, Reggie opened his mouth to speak, but didn't say anything. They were in a small clearing amidst a patch of dry grass. Above them stood perhaps another thousand feet of mountain. Below them, the landscape seemed to drop off toward the stream. The highway cut a narrow ribbon through the trees, while the blue of the river painted strokes against the canvas of green. "We need to get a better view of the gorge. So we either climb higher or find another viewpoint close by."

The ledge they camped on narrowed and entirely disappeared two hundred feet away from them along the same elevation. Reggie looked up. The trees appeared thinner, but the landscape was too steep to climb. A few rocks would aid such a climb, but they were scattered too sparsely.

Willis stepped toward the trees and looked down the slope. He observed the quiet forest, possibly pondering on where the day would take them. After a few moments, he spoke. "Looks like there is a little clearing down there."

"How far?"

"Three hundred feet or so, straight down."

Reggie stood next to him. He eyed the treacherous slope and decided to give it a try. "Let's see what it gives us."

He turned around to pack up, but Willis beat him to it.

"I got this," Willis said. "You just be careful."

Reggie ignored him, but gave in. Dramatic shifts in the soil and rock impeded the climb down. If the slope were wet, they certainly would have slid until colliding with trees at full speed. Five minutes later they stood shoulder to shoulder staring into a gap in the trees. They were perched on a large boulder, which produced a cliff. It was a natural overlook position.

They could not see much. No smoke, no fire, no Rassine, and no Taleah. A half mile away, further into the side ravine, an old gravel road snaked through the trees. It loomed below them. Reggie eyed it carefully and then looked away. A glimmer of light danced across his peripheral vision. He stopped and stared at the road again. The reflection indicated the presence of a parked vehicle.

He said nothing and pointed at it.

"Hunters," Willis said. "We should probably leave them alone."

"Dammit, what if it isn't hunters? What if..."

"I know what you're saying pal. But if they think we're deer, they'll get visions of taxidermy and shoot us without a second thought."

"Okay," Reggie said. "Let's start by getting closer. Maybe a better view will yield better information."

Willis sighed and gave in. They climbed down interspersing steep and shallow sections of mountainside. A hodgepodge of clearings and dry grass gouged the side of the mountain. As far as they could see, more mountains and more trees spread across the landscape. This location was as isolated as a person could get.

It would take the FBI another twelve hours to get anywhere close to finding them. Assuming they hopped a flight from Boise to Lewiston and drove the rest of the way, they could be reaching the campground where Smith was stationed sometime around noon. After that, map or no map, it would take them the rest of the day searching through the woods.

At least an hour later, a horizontal clearing appeared in the trees. With renewed vigor, they walked in that direction. The sunlight gleamed bright at first, but a few passing clouds painted grey shadows across the landscape.

"Careful," Reggie warned. "Rassine could be anywhere."

"He's not here."

"Shut up."

Willis lowered his eyes and frowned. "Why would the guy hide out in plain sight? A drone could have picked him up hours ago."

"I don't think the FBI has sent any drones out." He scratched his neck, wiped a bead of sweat from his forehead, and considered slapping some sense into Willis. Such an action would have been counterproductive. If anything were to happen, it would happen with Willis at his side.

They emerged from the tree line a few minutes later. Reggie scanned the trees, looked up and down the gravel road, and then stepped quietly along the grass fringe. Narrow ditches paralleled the road on both sides. At certain intervals, one or both ditches deviated from the course of the road where a metal culvert passed under to alleviate possible flooding from strong storms. Even so, the road was heavily eroded and washboard. If one wanted to navigate this area for any reason, a four-wheel-drive vehicle would be necessary. He doubted whether the FBI employed suitable vehicles, which would prove advantageous.

The road doglegged hard to the left in front of them. As they approached, they saw the vehicle clinging to the rim of the ditch beneath an overhanging section of ponderosa. The trees provided shade, which would have been a useful commodity if the owner of the truck intended on returning to his or her vehicle soon.

"Definitely a hunter," Willis said.

"That's Rassine's truck."

Willis nodded, but it was clear that he didn't believe this to be true. "How do you know that?"

"I'm telling you..." He didn't finish his sentence. Cautiously stepping across the center of the road to the shaded side, he pictured a dark scene where Rassine was holding Taleah's throat. The boulders rolled in his stomach. His heart pounded into his ribcage.

Another hundred steps brought them to the side doors of the vehicle. Reggie peered into the cabin of the Chevrolet almost expecting to find a gun. He almost turned to walk away in frustration when something caught his eye. Examining it further, it appeared to be some sort of photograph.

The doors were locked. Willis sighed unexpectedly, but this didn't deter Reggie. He squared his elbow by cupping his fist in his free hand. With a swift, upward stroke, he smashed the window. He considered acting with care so as to not leave his fingerprints on anything, but it didn't matter.

Willis watched him carefully. He paced back and forth in tight arcs with his fist up to his chin. His eyes wandered.

The photograph was wedged into a crack in the dashboard near the ignition, but within eyesight of the driver. Reggie pulled it out. His heart fell to his knees. Pain roared through his forehead. The photo depicted Taleah dressed in her softball uniform. Reggie remembered the occasion.

The sun beat down strong that day, allowing temperatures to soar into the nineties before the April showers ceased. Reggie clung to her. Both of them donned huge smiles. Celebrating a win was always important, but during this game, Taleah had smashed a monster home run over the centerfield fence to snatch victory from the charging opponent. It had been Taleah's first round-tripper of the season—of her entire softball career.

And now the commemoration of the event belonged to Rassine. How did Rassine get the picture? Reggie sent the question through his mind over and over again, mulching it to bits before he found his answer. Taleah had her wallet. Reggie searched the interior of the truck until he found it stuffed under the passenger's seat. It contained her student ID, a picture of Reggie and Rebekah, one of Anna, and about fifteen dollars in cash.

He stuffed the wallet in his pocket and knelt on the seat. The picture was worn and faded, as though it had been stowed away in a wallet for three months. But Rassine had taken particular interest. Why?

When he flipped the picture over, he found his answer. In blue pen, Rassine had illustrated what clearly resembled a diamond. Beneath it was scrawled the words Reggie didn't even need to read.

"What's that?" Willis asked.

This breakage of the silence seemed to provide an edge that he hadn't displayed since the other night when they met Deputy Monaghan. It gave him a reason and a motive to lash out verbally. He bit his lip, attempting to hold it back.

"What the hell? You were right again." Willis looked at the picture as a deep frown stained his face in bleakness.

"Son of a bitch!"

"That's strike two," Willis said.

He patted Reggie on the shoulder, an act which did little to calm the storm flashing through Reggie's heart.

"Don't worry. We'll get him."

They didn't need to plan their next course of action. The position of the truck seemed to indicate that Rassine and Taleah were on the same side of the road. Instead of following that logic, Reggie and Willis haphazardly retraced their steps up the side of the mountain they'd just come from. Jagged boulders littered the way, adding further danger to the trek. They followed a different route up the mountain subconsciously, which led them further into the forest.

The highway meandered at least a mile behind them—far enough that only a forest fire or aerial fireworks could attract a passerby's attention. Reggie was intuitive enough to recognize this fact, but he didn't care. More and more, he sensed that he was wandering around a dark world in search of a doorway through which he could escape. Clearly only one action could provide the opening he was looking for. He sensed they were trekking away from the opportunity—from the conflict—but wasn't sure why.

Hours passed as they climbed the ridge. Afternoon progressed to evening, which served to level the playing field. Darkness crept up the walls of his heart, crowding his mind with wicked images where Art Rassine burned while Reggie threw daggers into his chest.

They paused in a tiny clearing at the edge of a steep portion of the mountain. Storms were beginning to swell overhead, bathing the valley in murky shades of effervescent grey and green. Willis stared into the valley, scanning for anything. His gaze stopped.

"What?" Reggie said.

Instead of answering, Willis pointed. Reggie stared at the mouth of a cave across the ravine. This structure was closer to the road than they were. It marked the edge of a rocky section of the first major mountain north of the highway. Reggie gasped and thought about the trek.

"I'd bet money that's where he's keeping her," Willis said.

Without speaking, Reggie negotiated a gap in the rocks and descended the slope. "I'm going to go get her. Coming?"

"I don't feel good about this."

"Neither do I, but I'm going anyway."

Willis cursed just loud enough for Reggie to hear and then began to climb down the slope. "Let's just be careful, okay?"

This time, the descent went faster, or at least it seemed so. Willis offered clipped statements about the weather at key intervals. Reggie purposefully ignored them. Storm or no storm, he would get his daughter back.

Almost running due to the force of gravity, Reggie successfully navigated through a series of sharp rocks and a steep decline without losing his balance. Willis was not so lucky. Carefully, he leaped from one rock to another, but misjudged the next obstacle, which sent him reeling face first into a bush.

Hours of this would certainly get the better of them, Reggie thought. It had already been a long day and injury would certainly prolong the agony.

This was going to be the end of it all, he told himself. Even if he succeeded, he would be a different man—nothing but a bleak shadow of his former self. While true that, for better or worse, everyone involved would change, perhaps no one would be altered as much as Taleah. What she'd gone through so far was a dark admission of trauma. He didn't want to think about it, but the dark fueled him.

"Rassine," he grunted.

"What?" Willis asked, once again accelerating faster than his body could adjust.

"Never mind."

The half-hour descent to where the road should have been seemed to take less than fifteen minutes. The grey from the building storms slowly erased all sense of nature while black invaded seemingly from every direction.

They traversed a relatively flat stretch of forest for nearly five more minutes. When they finally reached the roadside, Reggie looked in all directions. From down here, the landscape hardly even resembled the one he'd observed from the mountainside. He shuddered. If not for the road, they would be lost. Still, Reggie hadn't completely lost his feel for direction. Generally, the next task would be to find whatever creek emptied into the Lochsa and then climb the next mountain.

As problematic as the lack of light would prove to be, Reggie felt such determination that he believed he would find Rassine and Taleah soon. Just ten more minutes or so...

"This has got trap written all over it," Willis warned.

"I know," Reggie answered without slowing down.

True to logic, the sound of a meandering mountain stream interrupted the sounds of ambiance. When the world fell asleep, the forest came alive. Reggie swore he nearly stepped on a snake just moments after a rodent crossed his path. Crows cawed overhead, but resigned to silently observe the determined travelers.

Crossing the stream was not difficult. Large, rounded stones studded the rocky bottom of the creek, sending white swells of water around them. Graceful pines lined both sides as far as Reggie could see.

When he reached the other side, he stretched out his hand to aid Willis. Willis safely stepped to the shore and looked upstream and downstream for signs of life. The land to the right seemed to climb at a slower rate than straight ahead. Reggie had no idea how much closer to the road they'd traversed, but his general idea indicated that they'd need to cut diagonally across the valley to approach the slope at the desired angle.

This adjustment seemed positive. The climb came abruptly, leading them up the leeward side of the mountain that contained the cave. A few boulders marred the journey. The going proved slow, but Reggie was convinced he'd headed in the right direction.

Ten minutes passed, and then twenty. The dark outline of the mountain they'd descended loomed behind them. The world was awash in a humid darkness that foretold of rain. Reggie shuddered at the thought of once again fighting Rassine in the rain.

A large boulder seemed to split the mountainside in two halves just ahead. Reggie accelerated and quickly scaled the edifice while Willis lagged.

"Reggie..."

"Come on, damnit."

Willis hardly had a chance to open his mouth before the scene unraveled.

Reggie didn't stop his climb, but he heard Willis grunt from the labor of the climb. Brush rattled in the darkness as if some unknown beast meandered through the undergrowth. Reggie gasped.

Willis's hand slipped from the rock he clutched, and he began to slide away faster than it seemed possible.

"Reggie!" The invisible force dragged him away. Reggie relinquished his grip on the rock he clutched and sprinted after him, all at once careless to the perils that surrounded him. A rope appeared in the underbrush. This was one of Art Rassine's famed traps, so cleverly designed that even a careful hiker could not notice. The sound of rope slashing through the brush intensified. The rope cracked taut all at once. A sudden thud sounded from below, followed by a hollow grunt.

"Willis." He didn't think. Willis's shadow hunched against a large ponderosa just ahead. The slope turned steeper just before the tree and continued downward on that angle for at least a hundred feet.

Coming to Willis's side, Reggie panted.

"Go," he said.

"I don't think so." Working quickly, Reggie used the knife to carve the knot into shreds while his heartbeat thudded inside his chest. He guessed that Willis had sustained at least a sprained ankle from the trap but saw no use in leaving him for dead.

"I'm a danger to you."

"I'm not leaving you here as bait,"

"It was never me," Willis said. Panting, he reached into the bag and removed the pistol, which he promptly placed in Reggie's hands. "Create mayhem for me."

Reggie shrugged. He looked upward, somewhere beyond the rocks he'd just scaled. A faint silhouette painted a slim shadow against a group of pines. A flash from lightning illuminated blonde locks that were frayed and dirty.

"Taleah."

She didn't move. Slowly, her image froze into Reggie's memory. Again he attempted to scale the rocks. After struggling for longer than he'd anticipated, he looked upward. She had disappeared. "Taleah," he whispered.

The cliffs spanned what seemed like a hundred yards in either direction. He leaned over and placed his hands on his knees to catch his breath.

After the rest, he trudged onward. Little warning could have prepared him from what came next.

Somewhere deep in the canopy, a spark ignited against rock. Flame vaulted toward him, illuminating the trees. Reggie sidestepped it but felt the heat of the passing projectile warping his flesh in a blister.

Ahead flashed another spark. Reggie dove beneath the cover of the tree. The flame fully engulfed a dry tree behind him. It would certainly ignite a forest fire if it hadn't started to rain. Reggie returned to his feet and climbed some more.

Further blasts of fire erupted all around him in a flurry of bullets intended to destroy any comers. One such burst narrowly missed his head. The smell of singeing hair added peril to the journey.

"Reggie!" A call came from below as a warning. Reggie turned around, stepped sideways to avoid hitting a tree, and felt something coil around his ankle.

Without precious time to react, Reggie attempted to step free from the snare, but it only tightened its grip. A thundering snap echoed through the trees, followed by a long swoosh. Before he knew what was going on, Reggie was airborne. A flash of lightning bathed the forest in an eerie yellow succeeded by more blackness.

The height disintegrated before a single thought could form. Long branches of pines broke his fall. Screaming, he tumbled to the earth. The slope remained steep. He clung to a nearby root to retain his grip on the mountainside. His momentum flipped him backward, violently twisting his wrist. On instinct, he let go of the root. His tumble sent him cascading back toward the cliffs. His back collided with a rock and his knee twisted.

Attempting to sit himself upright was a daunting task. His fall had ceased, yet danger lurked in every shadow. He groaned as spasms of pain shot through his wrist, his back, and his ankle. If he hadn't managed to grasp the tree root, the tumble would have spelled death.

Rage boiled in his veins. As if swallowing his heart in a murky brine, anger scoured him. He quivered, gripped the gun, and steadied himself in preparation for battle. Another bolt of lightning flashed. A spark ignited and a stiff wind pelted the mountainside. The rain intensified as Reggie shivered and struggled to his feet.

The last blast of fire soared over his head. Reggie ducked but continued his climb. He hoped Willis would somehow make it, but doubt crowded his mind from all sides.

Another flash of lighting revealed a ghastly scene around him. Carcasses of small animals littered the mountainside amidst the trees. Sharp streaks carved chunks of bark and wood from several trees. Ashes and dead coals indicated there had been a fire. Thunder roared just as the light faded. Rassine had been here, signaling that fate had arrived.

27
Annihilation

The last embers from the fireballs faded quickly with the rain. The rock became slippery. Struggling to retain his grip, Reggie gasped from the pain. A scorching batch of hatred stirred up in his heart. If it was the only thing he did tonight, he was going to destroy Art Rassine.

"You son of a bitch," he muttered.

The storm answered with a grumble, followed by an intensifying cascade of rain. Reggie pulled on a root to lift himself up and began to climb once again. Rassine lurked somewhere in the pines, a predator awaiting attack. Wherever he was, the darkness could not penetrate him. Rassine bled shadow. It oozed from his every pore.

Somewhere below him, a muffled grunt died in space. More thunder bellowed. The muddy slope made the climb treacherous. Grabbing at trees, rocks, roots, and underbrush to steady himself, Reggie carefully placed his steps to gain traction.

Another bolt of lightning illuminated the scene. Amidst the trees loomed a steady, round shadow as domineering as the night. It beckoned him. *Come to me, Reggie.* A harrowing cold filtered through his veins. This proved the result of the tunnel syndrome he'd thought about the other day.

A vapid whisper hushed the rain. Reggie didn't understand the words and wondered whether they were real.

"Taleah."

The whisper repeated, but it meant nothing.

With each step the mountain seemed to become steeper. Reggie avoided a stream of mud that cut a miniature canyon into the slope. He launched himself forward with as much force as he could muster, grabbed a tree to keep from slipping, and used his arms to pull himself around the tree.

The dark yielded only more trees. A sharp inhale revealed only the scent of pine and rain. Another stream sliced through the dirt and underbrush. Reggie jumped over it and dove into a bush.

Lighting. Reggie counted just two seconds to the clap of thunder.

A jumble of rocks presented an obstacle in front of him. He dashed through them without caution. A tiny slip could send him tumbling down the slope to meet Willis, but he didn't care.

The cascade of rain ebbed. Reggie looked straight ahead. No shadow prowled. Certain that this was where he'd seen the shadow, Reggie blinked. Somewhere to his left and up the hill lurked a forlorn presence that plunged his heart into an abyss. He spotted her hair, dirty, wet and knotted amidst the stands of ponderosa. Scars and bruises covered her face. Her jeans were torn, revealing scabs and blood. She appeared as though death had taken her, but she remained alive.

Reggie abandoned all caution and ran for her.

"Not so fast, my friend." The growl was instantly recognizable.

Stumbling, Reggie cut off his run. After falling to the mud, he looked up, frowned, and narrowed his eyes. "Rassine."

"St. Clair. Knew you'd find me when no one else could. Counted on that from day one."

Struggling to his feet, Reggie kept his focus on Rassine. He could lurch at any moment. Rassine hardly waited for Reggie to gain balance. He swung his wide arms and missed.

Reggie sidestepped the blow and suddenly started to think about strategy. He withdrew the gun from his pocket, aimed it at Rassine's head and pulled the trigger. Nothing happened. Surprised, Reggie looked down.

Rassine lunged, grabbing Reggie by the hair. The sudden movement caused a shift in the mud. Together they slid until Reggie's scalp collided with a tree. Two wild punches swept past Rassine's neck.

The shadow recovered by grasping the tree with one arm and scooting up. Again he pounced before Reggie had a chance to react. The mud seemed greasy. In the fray, the firearm slipped from his grasp, slid down the mountain and stopped on a jutting shard of granite.

Rassine slammed his fist into Reggie's chest. Reggie howled in pain, rolled away, grasped at a root, and steadied himself. He looked away down the slope, where Willis was hunched against a tree. "Willis!"

A splashing stomp echoed, fell silent, and then continued. Lightning flashed. Just in time, Reggie witnessed Rassine's approach. He swung his legs into a spiraling kick as he held tight to the root. Momentarily, his legs tangled with Rassine's. Rassine stumbled and slid about a foot but remained standing. Uttering a hurried grunt, he pushed his foot deeper into the mud, which somehow strengthened his stance.

This time, Reggie spun to attack. He flipped himself upright by swinging his hips downhill, loosening his grip on the root, and letting gravity do the rest. Feet away, Rassine recovered his step, balled a fist and swung wildly at Reggie's face.

The punch wasn't close enough to dodge. Hurriedly, he landed a flurry of hits on Rassine's midsection. He pounded him with fervor and rolled on top of him. The drumming of his heart scorched his bloodstream with a violent lust for destruction.

The shadow gathered him in a bear hug, rolled downward, and smacked Reggie's back. The strength of the jab sent Reggie recoiling. He bounded downward, rolling instead of sliding. His side slammed into a tree. A stabbing pain erupted in his skin and the warmth of blood sent a spiraling sense of terror through his mind.

Rassine took but a moment to stand. Two careful steps and he towered over Reggie. "You fight like desperation."

With a careless scurry, Reggie sat himself up. Rassine reached for him as if to help an old friend recover from a fall. If this fight was going to be to the death, Reggie feigned confidence he'd win. He'd have to, but not for his own strength. He didn't have to do it himself.

Ducking, Reggie crawled toward Rassine in an attempt to take out his legs. The action was too slow to catch Rassine by surprise. He reacted by grabbing a fistful of Reggie's hair and pulling him up like a doll.

Reggie grabbed the madman's arm and dug his fingernails in. Applying pressure was not difficult, but Rassine didn't wince. He opened his right palm and violently slapped Reggie across the face. His head flung backward and twisted from the blow. He formed a fist in his left hand and pestered

Rassine's shoulder with a series of blows. Rassine shrugged it off, flung his shoulders, and released Reggie's hair. The toss sent Reggie stumbling, but his foot caught a rock. He remained upright but pretended to teeter. The madman lunged at him, but Reggie was ready. He ducked his head and pushed off against the rock with his feet.

His body acted like a javelin, pummeling Rassine in the chest. In surprise, Rassine groped Reggie's neck. He twisted his waist and spun Reggie into an uphill trip. Splashing in the mud, he watched Rassine lose his balance. He tumbled back-first into the rock Reggie had sprung himself from. Reggie scooted uphill toward where Taleah observed.

The whisper he'd heard before issued once again. Rassine began to peel himself from the granite protrusion. His motion was slow as if marred by pain. This suggested that Reggie was winning.

Wrong. A sudden jolt of lightning and thunder alarmed Reggie. He flailed and slipped in the mud. A clink of metal on rock sounded. The rain had scoured the gun from the rock and sent it sliding straight toward Rassine.

Reggie looked and lunged for the pistol but missed. Rassine raised himself against the rock and grabbed at the gun. Sliding feet first into a tree, Reggie managed to spin himself face down. He pushed against the mud and summoned the strength to stand. Just as Rassine gripped the gun, Reggie swiped at his face. The swat caused a moment of surprise. Grabbing the gun, Reggie spun to face the madman.

He spit into Rassine's face and launched an assault that should have left Rassine unconscious. The shadow was just warming up. With his free hand, he hooked one of Reggie's jabs and twisted his wrist violently away from him.

Wincing in pain, Reggie recoiled to hit again just as Rassine took aim. Reggie closed his eyes, but no shots echoed.

Rassine appeared bewildered. He looked to his right and up the hill. Taleah should have been standing there, but for the moment, Reggie saw no one. He kicked Rassine's legs with as much force as he could muster.

Rassine slid down but stayed facing up the slope.

Without thinking, Reggie looked in that direction. A mysterious shadow stepped from behind a pair of ponderosas. A flash of lighting illuminated a pale face and blonde hair. She moved slowly away, backing steadily up the mountain.

Reggie recognized the face just a split second too late.

The madman tread away from him, following the woman, for he'd also recognized her. This time, he aimed to kill her. His steady gait communicated his intent with frightening clarity.

Clumsily, Reggie shouted at him. He limped up the slope without bothering to carefully plant his feet. Two painful lunges placed him right behind Rassine. Slipping from a rock, Reggie reached out for Rassine's legs. Rassine turned and slipped. The force of gravity sent him tumbling on top of Reggie. Reggie pushed off and buried his fist in Rassine's midsection. Hell seemed to blaze a trail through Reggie's mind, as dark fire and blood dominated the visual aspect of his imagination.

Art steadied himself with a tree trunk and rose into a crouching position. He aimed the gun at Reggie's heart. A harrowing sickness played out in his eyes and he squeezed the trigger.

Reggie attempted to duck a half-second before the boom shattered the ambiance of the falling rain. The shot would have been close, but due to the motion of ducking, his feet slipped from beneath him. Rassine didn't hesitate to unleash three more shots.

A scream bathed the commotion in blood. Taleah thrashed against a tree somewhere up the hill, but her motion was all wrong.

All three of the subsequent shots missed, or at least Reggie thought they did. A piercing sting in his side told him otherwise seconds later. Rather than missing entirely, one bullet had scorched across Reggie's waist. He grasped at it in horror as he slid in the mud. He kicked at the gun just before Rassine attempted to pull the trigger again. This time, Rassine flailed against the tree. He slipped and flung his arms around the tree. The gun wedged free from his hand and disappeared from sight.

Again, Reggie mounted an attack. Rassine countered with a heavy strike to Reggie's stomach, followed by a double dose of pain on the scalp. Rassine backed up the hill quickly. Pursuing, Reggie reached for a bush to retain balance. He missed and slid backward. His crotch slammed into another bush, stopping him from sliding to his death.

Pain rocked his entire body, but enough adrenaline pumped through his veins that it didn't matter.

The new visitor became a cause for concern with every second. Reggie feared for her life, while Rassine walked away to pursue her. Not about to give up the fight so easily, Reggie rose to his feet with the aid of the bush and a nearby tree. He stumbled diagonally upward.

Rassine veered to his left so that his ascent was more defined. A stretch of grass provided Reggie the traction he needed to chase Rassine down.

Art screamed something Reggie did not understand.

Agony scoured Reggie as he quickened his pace. A virtual stairway of granite appeared and he bounded up the steps. Via this route, their paths would intersect. He attempted to alter his stride so he could counter Rassine's attack.

The moment of hesitation proved a terrible mistake. On the last step, Reggie's foot slipped on the granite. His momentum carried him into the next stride, but his toes struck the top rock. Reggie slid to a halt face-first just as Rassine reached him.

A violent kick to Reggie's midsection sent him rolling away. Reggie corrected his route by placing both hands in the mud and pushing himself up. Two monster steps were enough to place Rassine within striking distance again. He landed another kick to Reggie's stomach and aimed a third directly at his head. As Reggie flipped to his back, he witnessed Rassine's boot skimming by his face. He blinked, acting confused.

The woman had stopped running before Reggie thought it prudent. Art Rassine approached her. His yells became garbled grunts that were somehow more distinguishable as human speech.

"Little lady in the forest. Meet the big, bad wolf."

Reggie groaned. The fact that Rassine had turned his back was not lost on Reggie. The opportunity was striking. He rolled, pushed against the rock, and stood up.

"No," Mindy pled.

"You were always going to die."

As Reggie quietly limped toward them, his foot collided with a rock. The rock moved, indicating it was loose. Lifting the stone with a muffled, labored grunt, Reggie narrowed his eyes. A batch of ferocious venom pulsed through his veins.

Rassine lunged for Mindy. Though his first strike erred slightly left, his assault did not cease. Rather than aim another punch at her face, he charged. His considerable mass toppled Mindy with ease. She fought back by pulling his hair and clawing at his skin. He bore down upon her with fury. She could scarcely counter his ensuing blows.

Determined to intervene, Reggie stepped behind Rassine. The madman pinned her to the ground, both hands forcefully clamping her fists into the earth. She screamed something Reggie did not understand. Lifting the heavy stone over his head, he remembered the events of eleven years ago.

Reggie and Rassine had been alone atop a ridge. While he was busy contemplating something severe, Rassine incapacitated him by lobbing a huge boulder straight into his back.

This time around things played out opposite. Rage boiled within him. Releasing the stone, he screamed as loudly as he could. The chunk of granite landed on Rassine's back with a heavy thump and rolled to a stop next to Mindy's leg.

Rassine remained mobile enough to fight back. Reggie kicked his leg. "Run, Mindy."

"She's not going anywhere." Rassine groped her leg as he stood up. Reggie pummeled his shoulders with a series of solid hits. The last strike collided with his collarbone, which likely proved painful to both of them.

Mindy didn't look surprised that Rassine could lift her so easily. He hoisted her onto his shoulders and launched her straight into the air. Reggie recoiled as Rassine turned to him.

The woman landed on an embedded chunk of granite in an awkward, painful fashion. She moaned but fell motionless. Witnessing her agony stoked the fire of aggression in Reggie once more. He lowered his shoulder and slammed it into Rassine's chest.

Rassine stepped backward, grabbed a nearby tree, and spun into a vicious charge on Reggie. Agony bolted Reggie's chest. The full weight of the madman's strike hindered his breathing. Reggie collapsed but continued to kick at Rassine's legs.

The assault was unceasing. Rassine landed strike after strike on Reggie's unprotected face. He hunkered down and beat him into oblivion.

"No!"

Taleah's scream shredded the cacophony and left its tatters in a discarded heap somewhere amidst the trees. She approached at a full run from behind.

Art saw her coming but did not react quickly enough. To the right, Mindy moaned in agony.

A huge jolt forced Rassine down on Reggie as he pummeled him with another punch. All Reggie could do was watch. Rassine rolled to face her.

Taleah wielded an impressively large stick that must have weighed at least three times that of her bats in softball. She pounded Rassine's scalp with two swats, turned her shoulders, and repeatedly hammered at his chest. A rage that Reggie had never before seen in her blossomed in her eyes like an explosion of will. Rassine attempted to parry her blows, but she beat him repeatedly without ceasing.

With one last lurch, the stick fell on Rassine's skull with a thud. She released it. With tears in her eyes, she knelt down and gathered Reggie's hand in hers.

Rassine moved quickly and efficiently. He grasped something. Its shadow in the dark looked like a serpentine rope. With one fluid motion, he flung the rope over his head, hunched down for a new attack, and dragged the rope across Taleah's face.

She whimpered and attempted to elbow him in the gut. Her attack missed entirely. Art tightened to rope around her neck. Reggie swung his legs to kick Rassine in the shin, but his motion lacked the force to do any damage. A hearty smile appeared on his face.

"Not the way you pictured her dying, is it Reggie?"

"Let her go," Reggie said with more pleading than he intended.

Rassine chuckled and dragged her backward. "I'll kill her."

A pair of thumps pounded the earth behind Reggie. He rolled his eyes backward. Willis appeared from behind a tree.

"Not before I put a bullet in your brain," Willis said.

By Reggie's estimate, the gun's chamber contained two shots. If Willis was accurate, he'd only need one.

Rassine violently released Taleah, flinging her to rest near where Mindy writhed in agony. Taleah screamed as she landed. Her legs buckled beneath her and her hip collided with granite. With one motion, Rassine lowered his shoulder and vaulted at Willis from upslope with blinding speed.

Willis was too fast. Without blinking, he squeezed the trigger. The shot roared and then produced a shadow of silence that scattered through the forest like a shock wave. The bullet punctured Rassine's skull above his left eye.

He staggered in surprise, teetered, and then fell face-first into the mud. The agonizing moans of four defeated survivors filled the air until nothing but darkness enveloped them.

28

Invitation

"Don't die on me, pal," Willis panted in a desperate attempt to keep Reggie awake. Agony coursed through Reggie's side as Willis bore his weight down on a ragged tee shirt against his wound. He believed the pain could shatter him if the weight of all his emotions hadn't conspired to crumble his spirit.

Reggie opened his eyes and momentarily stared at him. He imagined that his look was blank, but it must have been filled with a volatile compound of anguish and finality. Rassine dead, the madman finally conquered, and the 'era' at last over—could it all be real?

"You're not dying."

He continued to stare. Willis' expression stained dire. His eyebrows shifted upward in the middle and a paralyzing frown stretched across his face.

How long it had been since the conclusion of the fight Reggie could not be sure. It felt like it had been hours, but for the litany of aches that pulverized him at every tender spot. He opened his mouth to speak but thought better of it. From behind Willis came a groan and a whisper. Taleah and Mindy were involved in sparse and clipped conversation. Lifting his head, Reggie stared in that direction.

The whispering stopped. Taleah turned her head and stared but said nothing at first. Why didn't she move?

"T-Taleah. You hurt?"

Her response was brutally short and eerily quiet. "Yes."

"Rassine got her pretty good," Willis said. "She won't be playing softball 'till next year."

"Mindy?"

"I'm here, Reggie." Her voice softly wavered as if inexplicable pain shattered her words, leaving merely piles of dust sullen and still. "My leg...broken, I think."

"Thank you," Reggie whispered. He eyed the huge lump of Art Rassine's body, careful not to observe his cranial area or the blood that stained the mud crimson. "How long?"

Without speaking, Willis stared at Rassine, glanced at the gun, and then peered down to his own hands. His expression drooped further. "I did this."

"He deserved it."

"Not my place to judge. Who am I but a man? And what value have I destroyed?"

"Stop it," Reggie snapped. "You saved my life. I think you made the right moral choice and you didn't deliberate about it. You still have a conscience, it appears.

He shook his head as concern drifted back over him. The time passed was treading further into a memory but remained real. Though Rassine lay dead, the event wasn't over. Conclusions rarely came swiftly or distinctly separated recent memories. When they became filed away in the vast banks of memory, events separated into neat images marked by neither congruency nor cause to others. In history, events stood on their own. Closer to the present, everything blurred together like an oil painting splashed with rain.

The rain had ceased, but slow rivers of mud oozed down the mountainside. The night was crisp and humid with the scent of rain cooling the atmosphere with a calming, hallucinogenic effect. A few stars twinkled overhead. Most remained obscured above the shroud of cloud cover. For a long time, Reggie stared at nature.

Nature wasn't the villain, as it so often seemed. Nature was just there, simply a backdrop to the horrors. He wondered whether his mind would ever cease to associate the two. It seemed doubtful, but this moment and fragment of the scene showed relentless faith. Taleah was like a heavenly light that searched through the forest and filtered through the trees in stunning white rays. For a moment, Reggie didn't care how much time had passed. His own prophecy seemed to be coming to fruition. Time scarcely existed.

Closing his eyes, Reggie squeezed a tear out. He felt it trickle down his stubbly face as it cooled in the mountain air. Letting all of the emotion loose would have been an easy solution, yet too much remained at stake. Too many tangled strands were left to separate into a portrait of reality.

What seemed like hours later, Reggie's eyes sprung open. He glanced up at where Willis had crouched. He was no longer there. Somewhere in the distance, muffled by scores of pines, the sounds of stacking wood came. Reggie looked around. A white shroud covered Rassine's face. Splotches of blood tinged its corners as the blood dried. None of them could tolerate staying here, but with broken bones, lack of consciousness and a series of other injuries, they couldn't risk moving. One wrong step and death could suddenly swoop down out of the night and pick any of them off.

"Taleah?"

A whisper came from her direction. Reggie rolled to his side facing Rassine's body. He stared at her. She buried her face in her hands. The scant light of the flickering stars sparkled against her cheeks, which were wet with tears. She was on her side facing Reggie. Her body was broken and scarred almost beyond recognition. Reggie reached for her, scooted gingerly up the slope, and attempted to console her. She was too far away to reach before Willis returned.

Reggie's heart sunk. Agony took on a new name. He writhed as a gentle wash of tears spread across his face. Such tenderness was a feeling that rarely shook him this fully. Since her birth he'd never felt this way, not even once. But now that she lay broken like a pile of refuse spit out by a furnace of hate, the despair invaded. He hadn't been there to protect her. This was, to some extent, his fault. "I'm...sorry," he sobbed.

Taleah sniffed. "Dad."

"It's okay," Reggie said, clearing his sinuses enough to speak. "Your friends aren't here."

Her hands parted. Her shoulders vibrated, and a chilling smile parted her lips. A giggle, interrupted by sniffs and lurches of her shoulders resounded.

Reggie tried to smile but couldn't coax his muscles into forming the expression.

"Good one, Reg." Willis dropped an armful of wood to a relatively dry area beneath a particularly large ponderosa.

Reggie stared at him as he reached for the bag he'd used to carry their supplies. Withdrawing a few sheets of paper, he sighed. He quickly crumpled the pages and assembled a pile next to the wood.

There would be a lot of smoke, which would not be easily detected in the night. What Willis aimed to attract attention with was the glow of flames. He clicked the barbecue lighter several times as he held it next to the paper. The paper caught but struggled to ignite the wood.

"Everything's too wet," Willis said. "This is the driest stuff I could find." Frustrated, he lit more paper and wedged it further beneath the stack of wood.

After four sheets of newspaper fluttered into ash, Willis scanned the sky. Reggie watched him carefully. It appeared that Willis had a plan and that he knew how to achieve his goal. Unfortunately nature wasn't helping him out. He hunched over the wood and tried to ignite smaller pieces of tinder. One emitted a huge ribbon of smoke as a flame appeared. Excited, Willis pursed his lips and gently blew on it. "That's it baby, burn."

"I don't know whether they're going to come by helicopter," Reggie said.

"The FBI has drones. I thought I spotted one a while ago."

Where were they? Truthfully, Reggie had expected them earlier. He feared they'd arrive just before he confronted Rassine, but at least an hour had passed since the fight.

More tears scoured his face, but they drained away with time. Reggie's thoughts became increasingly scattered, and then another round of darkness ensued.

At least a half hour later by Reggie's estimate, he awakened to thundering footsteps in the distance. Several people were approaching, drawn to the light of Willis's fire. Reggie waited.

The first agent to appear was Agent Clark. Carrying a large automatic weapon, she stepped from behind a tree and aimed at Willis. "FBI. Put your hands over your heads."

Willis dropped whatever he was doing and obeyed. Reggie remembered their last interaction with her. As a highly trained and intelligent federal agent, she also displayed traits of industriousness. Her personality at first glance didn't seem to have changed much. Willis eyed her. His glance indicated an evocative air of apprehension, at least as far as Reggie saw it. The enamor remained intact.

"Agent Engaged. Almost didn't recognize you with the night vision."

"Ralston." Clark scanned Willis's expression momentarily, then shifted her gaze to Reggie. "St. Clair."

He pointed to the enormous lump—what remained of James Bullock. Calling him Art Rassine now was a pointless endeavor. Reggie sensed in that name distaste for rules and order. Art Rassine consisted of more than simply shadow—or even nature. The name was built on chaos. He'd analyze it more later, but for now, he had a team of federal agents to deal with.

Agent Clark removed her radio from her belt and spoke precisely. "Four injured survivors, one deceased, over."

The crackling voice of Agent Bill Coles responded. "Ten-four. Put up your flare."

She fished an orange gun from her belt, pointed it straight up, and fired. The sky ignited in a streak of red like the Fourth of July. Independence never felt so sweet. He meant to move toward Taleah, to grab her and never let go, but his body would not allow it.

Clark's partner appeared, carefully aiming his weapon at each of them. He didn't speak. Willis shifted his focus from Clark to the tall, slender black man.

"Stand down, DeLaren."

She first approached Reggie. Crouching next to him, she spoke. "You shot him?"

Willis cleared his throat. "I did."

"I'll have to place you under arrest." She nodded at DeLaren. "Cuff him."

"He saved some lives," Reggie said. His voice sounded raspy from dehydration. Still, he pressed on. "Put a medal on him."

"I believe you," she said. Her tone indicated cool intellect rather than a sense of warmth or even friendliness. If sound waves could shatter into a million pieces like ice, her voice would have. "We'll have a series of questions. For both of you. Agent Coles should be here any minute."

Reggie glared at her.

She noticed. "Injuries?"

"Between the three of us," Reggie rasped. "Broken bones. Broken hearts. Broken souls. Bruises, possible head trauma, joint dislocation. Gunshot wound."

Placing his hand over where the bullet had grazed him, he winced. He stared at Bullock's body. Eleven years later and the final scene came down just like it had before, only this time the proverbial shoe was on the other foot. Perhaps Reggie deserved it. Eleven years ago, Bullock had immobilized Reggie by crushing his back with a huge boulder just before Reggie shot him. The bullet had grazed his waist.

"EMT is en route."

"They can sift us out of here without landing?" Reggie asked.

"Affirmative."

Nodding, she stared at Taleah and Mindy, who lay side by side up the slope. For a moment, she said nothing. Her gaze seemed oddly warm and thoughtful, as if an ancient fire had suddenly awoken from slumber somewhere in her heart.

More footprints stampeded up the hill toward them. Four more night-vision clad agents appeared with weapons ready. They invaded the arena like a swat team.

Agent Coles lowered his weapon and pressed the button on his radio. "ETA on the chopper, over."

"On the approach. We see the fire."

The blades of the helicopter churned the night into a cyclone of disorder. Agents scattered. Clark squinted and stared at Reggie. "I know you did the right thing," she said. "I was rooting for you since day one."

Reggie didn't know what to say. He nodded and tried not to look at her. Instead, she peered to Taleah. She must have been asleep. She had stirred when the Agents arrived, but now that hearing protection would have been advised, she was wide awake and somewhat disoriented.

The chopper settled to a stationary hover just above them. They lowered a stretcher. Two paramedics descended from a square of light. They landed on the ground, untethered, and tended to Reggie.

"Taleah."

"Don't worry, sir, we've got space for all four of you."

"And me," Agent Coles insisted.

The paramedic silently agreed. They hoisted Reggie onto the stretcher after a quick examination. Another person in the bay of the helicopter prepared another stretcher and waited for Reggie to ascend.

Twenty seconds later, he entered the light. A pair of agents began to inspect his wound and asked him questions. Somewhere below, they were loading Taleah onto the next stretcher. Reggie watched as a lone agent prepared a third stretcher.

"Headache," Reggie said in response to a question. "I think I need Vicodin."

"Concussion symptoms," one of the EMT's muttered.

"Also symptoms of bleeding," Reggie said.

"On a scale of one to ten, how do you rate the pain?"

Reggie winced. "Sev...Eight."

"Our ETA to Lewiston is twenty-five minutes," the pilot said. Reggie could swear he heard the voice of Richard Kerrin. He turned his head to look, but the paramedics advised him to stay still.

"Richard."

"Excuse me?" The agent he spoke with asked him to clarify, but Reggie remained silent. Taleah's stretcher lifted into the helicopter seconds later. The paramedics began preliminary treatment almost before they were finished with Reggie. The third stretcher lowered as they tended to Taleah.

Reggie didn't say anything. Taleah moaned when they touched her. Reaching for her, a wave of agony rolled across Reggie. In the light she looked much worse. Her hair was wet and muddy from the rain and the fight. Bruises and cuts marred her face and her clothing was torn, shredded as if Art—James Bullock had tortured her. Anger boiled within him, but it was misdirected.

He could never forgive him for this, though some degree of justice had been served. Did Bullock deserve to die? Reggie didn't want to think about it, but examining the dilemma caused him to entrust Taleah to the EMTs. Though his heart continued to ache, distracting his mind with other details entailed rubbing the pain out.

James Bullock's judgment was in God's hands now. While true that God's wrath certainly awaited, it seemed likely that God would exercise some mercy on him. Reggie didn't want mercy for a man who had kidnapped, tortured, and probably raped his only daughter. He wanted the shadow to burn in the furnace of hell. Only that seemed just.

The paramedics hoisted Mindy into the helicopter, followed by the agents. They waited until Coles and Willis were securely fastened to close the hatch and head off toward the hospital in Lewiston.

Reggie stared at Willis for a few moments without speaking. After a few moments a smile parted Willis's lips. "I did it."

"What?"

"I was talking to Agent Clark. I asked her to be my pen pal. She actually gave me her address." He shoved a small strip of paper into his face.

Reggie scanned it. "I think that's the federal prison."

"No way," Willis said. "She's a prison guard?"

Reggie rolled his eyes. Conversation with Willis felt meaningless. The only person he wanted to talk to right now lay at his right. He looked at her with the same terrified longing he'd displayed since the fight ended. He tried not to focus on her litany of injuries. Her medical case in some ways would be far more complicated than his. Though the pain was severe, nothing could match the emotional trauma that played out within him like the dreaded climax of some Shakespearean tragedy. A splotch of tears rolled down his cheeks.

"I'm here," he felt himself saying. The words seemed more intended for his comfort than hers but speaking seemed to help. "Taleah. I'm here and you're safe...."

"I'm here to help..." Reggie muttered this as if a third party spoke using his vocal cords. He noticed Willis staring at him but didn't care. The light seemed blinding and only served to intensify the headache. The torment that rocked him seemed as if it would never cease. The horror of the last week was almost more than he could fathom.

"Come to me."

"Always," Taleah whispered.

Willis listened to something Coles said, but let it pass through his mind before speaking. He stepped toward Reggie with a look of warm concern prowling his expression. His eyebrows shifted up on his forehead. A frown was perched on his face. He spoke in a gravelly voice, to imitate their boss, Ted Brickshaw. "They say everything happens for a reason. I think you just found the reason."

29
Cataclysm

Artificial light seemed to harpoon Reggie, spreading shock waves of pain throughout his body to places he didn't even know he could feel. The realization that he was in a hospital didn't immediately take hold until he'd been awake for more than twenty minutes. Before then, the world around him was constructed of hallucination founded upon a dream. During those twenty minutes, he wasn't certain of anything, not whether his memories had actually taken place, that Taleah had survived, nor whether Reggie was even alive. It was like being trapped in between reality and what some described simply as 'the other side.'

Remarkably, 'the other side' could have referred to numerous things and not just death. The phrase admitted the existence of a certain threshold. When viewing the past through a lens of memory, one could discern all its aspects, not only what he or she could see when the events unfolded around them.

Reggie looked around and studied every corner of the hospital room. He was alone for now but imagined that a number of people would want to see him soon. He'd been asleep.

The battle he'd engaged in, while both mentally and physically exhausting, didn't provide the numbness required for sleep. Instead, pain had kept him awake. He tried to remember everything that had happened. The best he could do was assume the doctors had given him some kind of anesthetic so that they could operate on his wounds. The pain of surgery didn't register as a memory. Now that the anesthetic wore off, a dose of painkillers didn't seem to be unreasonable. That, however, would have to wait.

The door opened, startling Reggie. He turned his head and shuffled his feet while blinking in the light.

Willis entered with a noticeable limp from whatever injury must have resulted from his fall. Reggie felt like an idiot. Not only had Willis managed to fall into one of Rassine's traps, but so had Reggie. Reggie was lucky his trap hadn't killed him.

"Not the face I'd expect from a victor, even considering the circumstances," Willis said.

"You look like a million yourself," Reggie scoffed.

Willis looked him over. A couple of times, Reggie noticed the makings of a cringe that Willis somehow managed to curtail. His face festered with open sores of concern, but he did his best to hide them.

"They really did a number on you. I don't suppose you're up for a round of skydiving."

Reggie shook his head and looked away.

"How about a monster truck rally?"

"Oh God," Reggie groaned.

Willis grinned, but it seemed forced. "I just saw him down the hall. He slapped me upside the head, but otherwise let me walk."

"Yet, you can't," Reggie said, referring to his limp.

"Old softball injury," Willis said, glancing to his feet. "They took x-rays, CAT scans, and one of those ink blot tests...what do you call them?"

"Rorschach."

"Just to make sure I didn't break anything besides the laws of physics. A little bit of a sprain, but nothing they didn't tell me to walk off. Just what Taleah's coach told me when the ball hit me."

"You've got your sense of humor back," Reggie said.

"Somebody's got to have one around here. They don't exactly have world-class entertainment in this facility."

"What are you talking about?"

Willis's expression drooped.

"What do you think I'm looking at right now?"

"I'll give you that," Willis said. He pulled a chair closer to the bed, sat down, and stared out the window.

Reggie hoped the conversation hadn't flattened out. Willis proved an invaluable confidant, but Reggie owed him something. Instead of speaking, he allowed the silence to loom like a storm cloud that somehow never accomplished more than a threat. Hospitals were meant to be cold and sterile, but Willis was anything but. For what seemed like ten minutes, he studied the expression perched on Willis's face. The lines around his eyes narrated stories of despair, hopelessness, and trauma. The stories were baggage that Willis would have to carry around for the rest of his life.

"Is Taleah safe?" Reggie asked.

"Just got done talking to her. I'm not going to lie, because what would that accomplish? It doesn't look good."

Reggie almost didn't want to hear it, but curiosity dragged him onward.

"She has a broken ankle, a fractured pelvis, an ugly infection from another injury she sustained before the fight. And they administered a rape kit, which they claimed is standard procedure. Other than that, she's as good as new."

"I want to talk to her now," Reggie said, attempting to get out of the bed.

"No."

"Then wheel her in here. Tell the doctors to put us together. You don't know what it's like."

Reggie didn't have to describe it. The true sensation was something like a thousand needles sewing poisoned threads across his skin while a mallet continuously rapped at his skull. He bit his lip, swallowed, and quivered. Defeat always came with a price, but this fell short of torture's value. He didn't say anything for two full minutes and resigned to let Willis do the talking.

"Well, Mindy is a lot better. They put a cast on her and put her on drugs, but she's already starting to recover. In six weeks, they'll remove the cast. I just don't know why she came."

"To confront Art Rassine," Reggie said.

"Right. What was his real name again?"

"James Bullock. He was a clever beast," Reggie droned. "You know why he never used his real name? It's because the alias intends a sort of mystic air. You don't think you're dealing with a real person, which only mentally builds him into even more dominance. The mind can't get around it, and so begins to fill in the gaps with perceptions and ideas. It makes him more a legend. And why shouldn't he be enshrined in every prison in North America? I'm the only person that could bring him down. And I don't think it was luck.

"You remember Lance Harrison? Harrison planted the bloody chair eleven years ago to get the attention of the authorities, not a couple of surveyors from Boise. Whether he knew it or not, Harrison was harboring Bullock. They no doubt had conversations. Harrison told Bullock about us, but at least Harrison had some sort of moral compass. He was working both sides, but not because he wanted to. Then Bullock catches on and kills him for it. When he found out all that info about me, it marked me as his opponent. No matter what you do, you don't beat him and get away with it."

"We did."

"All four of us are in the hospital and we're only lucky none of us is dead. James Bullock is dead, but he destroyed us and you know it."

"Yeah, maybe, but there is still hope. All wounds heal, my friend."

"Says the person among the four of us that is least injured," Reggie said flatly.

His heart sunk when flashes of frustration bulged across Willis's face. He shuffled his feet on the floor and clasped his hands on his lap. "But you could say I'm injured in a different way. I'm the one who fired the shot. And what does that get me other than an ill-placed pat on the back?"

"You don't think you deserve it?"

"I don't care if it's war, famine, disease, peace, or a softball game. Killing isn't heroic. I don't want my name made into a memorial on every street sign. I probably deserve some jail time. The FBI let me off and told me the same thing you're thinking."

"You saved my life, and probably Taleah's and Mindy's too. You don't think that merits some recognition?"

"I haven't decided," Willis lied.

Reggie could see that his argument was sinking in at least, which was all he'd hoped for. Sometimes, the idea only needed to burrow itself into a person's brain to blossom into action and a solid decision.

"What do you get out of it if you do go to prison? Such institutions are not there to bludgeon people with a conscience. Prison won't make you a better citizen. In your case, I think it will do more harm than good."

"No motorcycle tattoos or drugs for me," Willis said, thinking fast.

Unfair generalization or not, Willis had a good point, which proved that what Reggie was telling him was catching on.

"I'd assume that some prayer is in order," Reggie said, sinking his gaze deeper into Willis's eyes.

"Yeah."

Reggie let the conversation sag before changing the subject. "Are you going to write to her?"

"Who?"

"Agent Clark. You said she gave you her address."

"Mabye. I think she'd be too good for me like when you add oxygen to a fire that's burning down your house. I'm sure some sparks would fly."

"Well, sparks can be more than beneficial if you put them to use."

"Indeed." Willis looked around the room and then focused on the IV bag hanging from the stand near the bed. "We're really a good team. You think the FBI would want us? It seems we help them solve a lot of cases."

"We're too reckless," Reggie said, rolling his head back on the pillow.

"You know, recklessness denotes safe driving."

A faint smile flourished on Reggie's lips before disappearing into the void. "Not with you behind the wheel."

Willis sported a more honest grin, even if it was somewhat indulgent.

The door opened again. A nurse strode in and started making small talk. She checked on Reggie, refilled his water bottle, and then departed. As she left, she held the door open.

Two women entered.

Anna stared at Reggie as if to devour him with understated thanks. Her eyes were swollen but must have been on the mend. Reggie nodded at her without thinking. It could have been joy that caressed her face, but only bitterness resided there, dancing on the wings of victory. It could have been relief, but instead, agony paced across her face like a shadowy sentinel. This suggested that she'd already seen Taleah. Reggie didn't hold that against her.

She cautiously approached and then exchanged glances between him and Willis.

Rebekah's entrance was brighter, even if somewhat stereotypical. She darted past Anna, leaned over the bed and carefully flung her arms around Reggie's neck. One or two kisses didn't do it justice. Instead of allowing the moment to pass, Reggie wrapped one arm around her back and kissed her deeper. Tears rolled down his face as the passion mounted a streak of furious emotion that threatened to get the better of him.

After the greeting, conversation between the four of them lasted almost an hour. Sometime after Anna and Rebekah entered, Willis flushed out of the room, allowing a moment to rest his gaze on Anna.

He returned a few moments later. The doors opened wide enough for a gurney to be wheeled into the room. A pair of nurses pushed Taleah in with the IV tower in tow.

She looked better than Reggie had imagined, but only just. Pools of tears poured from his eyes and shone on his face.

"Daddy," she said. "I love you." Her face flashed a sullen hint of blue, like the dying moonlight on a clear morning. A shiver split Reggie's spine with a numbness Reggie couldn't recall ever feeling. Her image seemed to float like the memory of a dream in his subconscious mind. "I knew you would come for me."

"I always was."

A tear appeared next to her eye, but she let it dry. "I wouldn't be anywhere without you. And Mindy."

"The ace up our sleeve," Reggie said.

Rebekah glanced to her feet and pretended not to communicate discomfort.

"Seeing her got to Bullock. It made him alter his plans. Her presence alone saved my life."

"It was luck—or destiny," Taleah said. Her voice cracked just enough to reveal the strength she always believed herself to be constructed of. "Or maybe it was faith."

Willis stepped closer to the bed as a certain realization dawned on him. "You know what, Reg?" I've been doing some thinking. I'm going to join your church now."

Reggie laughed but could barely force a smile.

"He's coming around," Taleah said. "We all will, someday. That's what life is all about."

Her wisdom gleamed profound. A sense of pride coursed through Reggie's veins. He grasped her hand and this time vowed never to let go. She lived, and in this bliss, time did not exist.

He closed his eyes and visions of a pine forest, drenched in dew and imbibing the lust of sunrise, floated into his mind. Somewhere there in the trees lurked a shadow, but night was beginning to part. Rays of glistening sunshine pierced through the trees and emitted a glowing promise that light would always come around. That was all Reggie could ask for.

Acknowledgements

When I originally set out to write 'Era Sinistra' after the outlining phase, I didn't envision a sequel, as is probably the case with many sequels. I'm also not the type of person to write a sequel and then keep shoving the same characters through the same trials. There may be a second sequel to complete a trilogy, but I'm not one to make promises I may or may not be able to keep.

That isn't to say that the pipeline is empty. I've been working on an intriguing new project for a while now and, while I can't say much about it, I do anticipate releasing it in 2016 if all goes according to plan.

This book is the first I have chosen to self-release. Many factors went into the decision to do it this way. I can cite displeasure with the way business was handled previously. I'm not about to publicly disparage any firm here, but I also do not plan on using said firms again.

I feel that this book cannot be complete without acknowledging some great assistance I have received throughout the process. I began writing 'The Shadow' back in 2013, made it halfway through, and then shelved it for more than a year. Although against popular author advice, this allowed me to gain a different perspective on writing and publishing in general. I knew I had to do things differently, but I didn't exactly know where to start. What spurred me to finish the project in 2015 turned out to be you, the fans. Thank you for asking for more and waiting patiently. This project would not have been possible without your support.

I also wish to thank Stephanie and Martin Sabin for their helpful suggestions about character development and other general advice. When you are a writer, you can't hope to see everything even after multiple reads, so a second set of eyes go a long way. Stephanie is a great up-and-coming horror writer.

Also, I'd like to give a shout out to Jeanine Henning. Thank you for the unbelievable cover art. I'm still awestruck every time I look at it. I believe you are better at design than any publisher I've worked with.

As with any project, a novel can rarely get off the ground successfully without a first-rate editing job. Though I take pride in making everything the best it can be before I send it to an editor, I do miss things and not just grammatical and punctuation errors. Amanda Fitzpatrick helped to identify problem areas and did a thorough and timely job of making her remarks. Thanks for the professional service.

Before I leave you, I would like to express my deepest thanks to my wife Kristy for standing with me and supporting this process. While it would have been more financially beneficial to go about this project in slightly less professional manner, I feel that everything I put into the book would have been unfulfilled without the extra attention to detail. Also, thank you for giving me the time to work. It can be difficult to do with a toddler running around the house, but without your help I'd still be writing.

I hope you have all enjoyed reading 'Era Sinistra-The Shadow' as much as I enjoyed writing and producing it. Stay tuned in 2016...

-bm

About the Author

Brad Mathews bends genre rules by creating dynamic, unorthodox characters thrust into criminal investigations.

He is known to use abstract imagery to construct striking realities that build into suspenseful mystery tales.

Mathews is Certified in Plumbing design, and his extensive Building Information Modeling experience gives him a unique ability to detail mechanical and industrial settings in his novels.

Mathews resides in Boise, Idaho with his family.

Also By Brad Mathews